Praise for Ka

Blindsia

"A jaded television reporter and a gui bond in Walsh's delightful contempo romance is a nuanced exploration of ......, ..., and negotiating boundaries, without a hint of schmaltz or pity. The sex scenes are sizzling hot, but it's the slow burn that really allows Walsh to shine."—*Publishers Weekly*

"Karis Walsh always comes up with charming Traditional Romances with interesting characters who have slightly unusual quirks." —*Curve Magazine*

Sea Glass Inn

"Karis Walsh's third book, excellently written and paced as always, takes us on a gentle but determined journey through two womens' awakening…The story is well paced, with just enough tension to keep you turning the pages but without an overdramatic melodrama."—*Lesbian Reading Room*

Improvisation

"Walsh tells this story in achingly beautiful words, phrases and paragraphs, building a tension that is bittersweet. The main characters are skillfully drawn, as is Jan's dad, the distinctly loveable and wise Glen Carroll. As the two women interact, there is always an undercurrent of sensuality buzzing around the edges of the pages, even while they exchange sometimes snappy, sometimes comic dialogue. Improvisation is a true romantic tale, Walsh's fourth book, and she's evolving into a master romantic storyteller." —*Lambda Literary*

Wingspan

"As with All Karis Walsh's wonderful books the characters are the story. Multifaceted, layered and beautifully drawn, Ken and Bailey hold our attention from the start…The pace is gentle, the writing is beautifully crafted and the story a wonderful exploration of how childhood events can shape our lives. The challenge is to outgrow the childhood fears and find the freedom to start living." —*Lesbian Reading Room*

By the Author

Harmony

Worth the Risk

Sea Glass Inn

Improvisation

Mounting Danger

Wingspan

Blindsided

Mounting Evidence

Tales from Sea Glass Inn

Love on Tap

Amounting to Nothing

You Make Me Tremble

Visit us at www.boldstrokesbooks.com

SET THE STAGE

by

Karis Walsh

2017

SET THE STAGE

ISBN 13: 978-1-63555-087-0

This Trade Paperback Original Is Published By
Bold Strokes Books, Inc.
P.O. Box 249
Valley Falls, NY 12185

First Edition: November 2017

CREDITS
Editor: Ruth Sternglantz
Production Design: Stacia Seaman
Cover Design by Sheri (graphicartist2020@hotmail.com)

SET THE STAGE

CHAPTER ONE

Emilie Danvers stripped the damp orange kerchief off her head and tried to restore some order to her tangled, greasy curls, but eight hours of close proximity to industrial-sized deep fat fryers had done more damage than her weary fingers could undo. She gave up the attempt to make herself presentable—only a lengthy scalding shower and half a bottle of shampoo would do the trick—and pulled the polyester-blend tunic over her head. She kneaded the tight knots on her right shoulder and let her head fall back in a gentle stretch. The image of a massage table, complete with the soothing scents of eucalyptus oil and patchouli candles, flickered through her thoughts. A heated blanket, expert fingers to unravel the tension in her back and neck...

She sighed and returned to the reality of the cramped and cluttered break room. She tugged on a yellow T-shirt that had an image of galloping giraffes on it and reached for her jeans. She struggled for several moments, sucking in her stomach and holding her breath, before she was able to button them. Her curves had filled out after four months on a strict diet of fast-food hamburgers and fried bits of chicken, but she hadn't been able to turn down the free meals at work. She patted her hip pocket. Her wallet was the only lean thing on her person.

Would you like fries with that? Only two more weeks of asking that classic question, and then Emilie hoped she never had to cook, serve, or eat another french fry. She wouldn't complain, though. Because of this job, she had managed to pay her rent and utilities this fall, and she had certainly paid her dues for being a fool. Now she had another chance at the career she was born for, and she'd be damned if she'd ever allow herself to get back to the state of destitution she'd been in for the past months. She'd been in purgatory here, atoning for past transgressions as she slapped microwaved patties on buns and squirted them with ketchup, and the time had been good for her. After two years of doing next to nothing for herself and everything for someone else, she had been thrilled to have a job and paycheck of her own. This had been a time to regroup, and soon she'd be out of limbo and back to life, but she had to give her notice first.

She peered around the manager's half-open door and saw Ted Carver sitting at his cluttered gray Formica desk, his black-rimmed glasses resting on the tip of his nose. She'd jokingly thought of him as her prison guard while she did her time at the restaurant, but he'd been a benevolent one. Kindly and gentle, with a bad comb-over and pasty complexion, he'd seemed more like an indulgent uncle than a boss. His soft-seeming exterior hid a sharp sense of humor that Emilie would miss. As much as she disliked some of the parts of her job, she didn't like to disappoint him by quitting. It was time to move on, though. In the past, she'd stayed too long in the wrong place out of a sense of obligation—or a fear of moving forward?—and she'd learned her lesson. No more. She knocked on the door with resolution.

"Come in...Oh, hello, Millie. I have your paycheck right here."

"Thanks, Mr. Carver." She waited while he rooted through the stacks of papers and invoices on his desk and smiled when he handed her a slim envelope. During her orientation, he had tried to pronounce her name with a French accent—emphasizing a different syllable each time—until she had given up asking him to simply say it like he would the Americanized *Emily* and had suggested he call her Millie instead. She'd never used the nickname before, but she decided it fit the persona she'd adopted to keep her sanity while on the job. In the weeks that followed, she'd amused herself by developing an entire character bio for Millie and playing the role whenever she put on her orange and brown uniform. Like Ted, Millie lived for her role in the food service industry. Unlike Emilie, Millie didn't want to burst into tears at the end of one of those frustrating days filled with demanding customers, constant heat from ovens and fryers, and the relentless smell of near-rancid oil.

"I need to talk to you, sir," Emilie said when Ted seemed about to return to his endless paperwork.

"Of course, Millie. Is everything all right? How can we help you?" The corporate *we*. Even though he probably made little more than the minimum wage Emilie earned, he took his managerial role seriously. She had seen the way he took care of his employees, always willing to give them time off to study for high school finals or to take sick children to the doctor, even if it meant he had to step in and cover shifts. Millie never asked for time off and she never said no to overtime.

Ted pushed his paperwork aside and gestured for her to sit in the chair opposite him. He laced his fingers together on top of his desk and gave her the feeling of having his full attention. Emilie sat on the edge of the chair. The waistband of her jeans pressed into her belly, and she used the discomfort to keep her focused on finishing the unpleasant task of quitting.

"Everything's been fine." Not really a lie. The job sucked at times, but Ted and some of her coworkers had kept it from being too bad. There had been more laughter and camaraderie behind the scenes than she would ever have expected. "But I need to give my two weeks' notice. I'm going to be acting in the Oregon Shakespeare Festival, and rehearsals start in the beginning of January."

"You're going to be..." He paused and stared at her. Emilie could read the obvious doubt on his face. She must have played the part of Millie—part fast-food aficionado and part Dickensian waif—better than she'd thought. She must not have been allowing Emilie the professional actress to shine through at all.

Ted put his index fingers together and tapped them against his lips. "We respect the work you've done for our restaurant, Millie, and we want to do what it takes to keep you here. Although you haven't reached your six-month mark yet, we can make an exception—just this once—and give you your raise ahead of schedule."

"I appreciate the offer, but it's not the money." Emilie hated to think how much the extra dollar an hour he was offering would help her in her present circumstances. She should have threatened to quit a month ago. "I've signed a contract with the company and I start rehearsals soon."

"Of course you do," he said with an indulgent smile. He dropped the royal plural and leaned closer. "Look, I can't make any promises, but let me talk to my supervisor about moving you into an assistant manager position. The benefits are excellent."

Emilie felt a brief pang of guilt, but she shook it off. Since she'd worked at the restaurant, employees had come and gone with startling frequency. She'd signed on as temporary, seasonal help—never promising her life and soul to the fast-food chain. When she'd first taken the job, she hadn't known whether she'd be cast with the company or not, but she'd stayed close to Ashland, Oregon, because she needed to cling to the hope of reviving her near-dead career. She didn't blame Ted for doubting her claim to be headed for Ashland, because she sometimes suspected that she had only dreamed the phone call with the assistant director of the company, telling her she had the job. She had signed contracts and had her parts, but maybe those experiences had been grease-fume-caused fantasies. She wouldn't truly believe she was back in the business until she got her scripts. Or maybe, until she stepped onstage for her first rehearsal. Or for the first performance...*Then* she'd believe it was true. Until she was 100 percent sure, she'd go on faith. She stood up.

"I'm sorry, but no. You've been a great boss, and I've

appreciated getting to work with you, but acting is my career. My passion."

Ted stood, also, and shook her hand. "Very well. But if this acting thing doesn't work out, you have a place here with us."

"Thank you," Emilie said, but inside she cringed with superstitious anxiety. He had spoken her great fear out loud. She had left the business after making a successful debut off-off-Broadway, before she'd either proved or disproved her ability to live up to the potential some critics saw in her. She had spent the past two years answering the question *What if I had stayed?* in a variety of ways, sometimes with regret because she might have been a success and sometimes with relief because it was better to have quit than to have tried and failed. The latter response had been more comfortable to face than the first one, but she could never make herself fully believe it. Deep inside she knew she regretted not trying, whether she would have failed or not. But lately, as her time to go to Ashland loomed closer, her old doubts had resurfaced with a vengeance.

"I'll miss you, Millie. Be sure to let me know when your play is on, and maybe my wife and I will come watch you perform."

He didn't look like he believed she'd be acting, any more than he'd believe it if she'd come to tell him she had been elected to the Senate and was heading to Washington, DC. "I'll do that," Emilie said. She walked out of the room and felt the emotions connected with quitting slough off. She was moving forward. One step closer to becoming herself again.

Emilie shivered when she stepped out of the restaurant and onto the rain-soaked sidewalk. The night was artificially lit along this row of chain restaurants and strip malls, and the raindrops glistened green, red, and yellow in the glow of neon signs. Many of the businesses were open twenty-four hours a day, the constant flow of people and traffic making the neighborhood merely loud and undesirable rather than downright unsafe, and Emilie felt comfortable on the streets no matter what the hour. She was never alone out here—luckily, since she often volunteered for shifts at the odd hours when most other people didn't want to work, even with the late-shift premium. She dodged puddles and cracked cement as she walked the three blocks from work to her apartment, wrapping her arms and thin gray hoodie tightly around herself and trying to pull as much warmth from the cotton fabric as she could.

She let herself in a gate leading to a small courtyard and then climbed the steps to her second-floor studio apartment. She had only had three requirements when she started looking for a place to live: short-term, short commute, and low price. She got what she paid for, but it was home. Her home.

She turned on both overhead lights as she traveled the few steps from her door to her air mattress bed. She was living like a college student with only a few pieces of makeshift furniture and without any decorations on the walls or on shelves. Since she was a child, she had loved making her room her sanctuary, with personal touches and favorite colors spread everywhere, but she hadn't had a place of her own for too long. Once she was settled in Ashland, she'd get something sturdier than milk crates and particleboard. A real bed, maybe a desk, a few bookcases. Photos and prints on the walls. Even the basics seemed luxurious after a few months of feeling temporary.

Emilie shed her wet clothes and took a long shower, sudsing away the residual odor of the restaurant from her skin and hair. She combed the worst tangles out of her blond curls and braided her hair to keep it out of her face, not wanting to fuss with her hairstyle any more than necessary. She put on a pair of warm sweats and a thick wool sweater before going into the kitchen— or the corner of her apartment where the tiny appliances lived— and she sliced a Granny Smith apple and layered it on bread with crunchy peanut butter and a sprinkle of cinnamon. She craved texture in her food since at least two of her meals each day were soft and greasy fast-food burgers. She took her dinner over to a folding chair she had placed near the window and perched there with a book and her sandwich, unable to see much beyond the rain splatting against the windowpane. She preferred it this way, because the view was less attractive than the weather, and it consisted mainly of the back side of a Taco Bell.

She looked around her room as she chewed a huge bite of her sandwich, letting the juicy tang of the apple wash away the stale, oily flavor of the day. For all the shortcomings of her life here in Medford, with her less than ideal apartment and job, she had been happier here than she had been during the past few years as she had traveled across Europe with her ex-girlfriend. The accommodations and food had been pleasant there, but she hadn't been able to work much because they moved frequently with touring plays. Emilie had felt lost and directionless, but she hadn't realized how truly miserable she had been until she got here, with a place of her own and work to do. She had spent far too long trying to salvage her relationship, desperate to prove that she hadn't made such a huge mistake in agreeing to follow Leah on tour. Once she accepted that she had made a monumentally bad decision, the choice to move back to the States—after spending most of her savings and allowing her contacts with the American acting world to wither and fade—had been a surprisingly simple one.

She had been lucky to get the job with the OSF, and fortunate to have found a job in the meantime with a kind boss and plenty of hours. Her weariness at the end of the day blended with the peace of living alone and not in a hotel room full of the tension of unmet expectations and unspoken arguments, and she had slept soundly and deeply here for the first time in years.

She finished her sandwich and licked peanut butter off her fingers. She was thrilled to have the opportunity to act again, especially with a prestigious and interesting company, but she was almost equally grateful for these past few months of labor and solitude.

She was finally starting to forgive herself for giving up on her dreams, and to heal from the negativity of her failed relationship. Still, the upcoming months would set the course for the rest of her life, and those weeks of blissful sleep had come to an abrupt end about a week ago, when she had looked at the calendar and had seen less than a month between the day she was x-ing out with a red pen and her first day of rehearsals. Soon she would either discover that she really did have a talent for this career, or she'd be back here, begging Ted to give her the assistant manager job.

Chapter Two

Arden Philips pulled her red Kawasaki Mule off the paved trail and onto the gravel shoulder, even though there were too few visitors in the park at this time of year to worry about blocking some pedestrian's way. She parked and grabbed a rake and a bucket of pruning shears off the back shelf of the utility vehicle before heading toward the torii gate that marked the entrance to the Japanese garden. The wooden archway was dark from soaking up the steady supply of southern Oregon rain, and she laid her hand on one of the posts, scratching gently with her short fingernail. The moisture hadn't penetrated too deeply. As soon as they had a dry spell—*if* they had one before summer— she'd scrape away the buildup of mildew and treat the wood again.

She continued under the arch and into the small Japanese garden, pausing for a moment before she walked any farther along the path.

"Hey, Gramps," she whispered. This had been his favorite section of the entire ninety-three-acre Lithia Park. He had been a groundskeeper here, and she had been his shadow since she was a toddler, following him as he worked and eventually getting her own job in the park. She felt closest to him here, partly because his influence was everywhere in the plants and landscape elements of this garden, but mostly because she had scattered his ashes at the foot of his beloved gingko tree. Her actions had been strictly in violation of the municipal park's rules, but nearly the entire staff had been present at her impromptu service. Everyone who knew Delaney Philips knew he belonged here in life or death.

Arden walked along the path of spaced pavers. In the summer, the gaps between stones would be filled with ground-covering herbs and moss, but in January there was only slimy, slick mud. She paused now and again to wipe mucky leaves off identifying plaques. They were everywhere in the park, naming trees and plants in gold lettering on brass. She cleaned off the ones marking a photinia and one of the park's saucer magnolias. They didn't look like much right now, but soon they'd be covered in contrasting flowers, one with tiny, cascading showers of them and the other with large, impressive blooms. She turned away from them and continued on to a stand of Japanese maples, where she set down her bucket. She pulled out a pair of shears and started snipping off the tips of its bare branches.

She loved this time of year, when her work required more imagination than skill. The maples were beautiful now, with branches in a variety of reddish hues, but they would be even more stunning in the spring. Then their delicate and lacy leaves would start to unfurl against a backdrop of larger trees full of pink and white cherry blossoms. And in autumn, toward the end of the festival season, this whole garden would be a chaos of color, rivaling any state's fall foliage. She was pruning now, not to get the maple to a desired shape, but to get it to grow into the shape she wanted.

Arden trimmed the end of another branch and shook her head. She always got a little sentimental in this garden. She wasn't Michelangelo, releasing a sculpture from a block of clay. There wasn't any magic involved in what she was doing—just decades of experience from watching her grandfather and doing the work herself. She knew where to cut because she had been observing the way these trees grew since some of them were first planted.

She finished shaping the maples and raked the area underneath them and around a stone memorial bench, brushing twigs and debris off its surface even though no one would likely be sitting there for a few more weeks. She enjoyed the privacy of these days, separate from the bustle and crowds that came with the festival, but she couldn't stop the feeling of anticipation from catching in her throat. Everything she and the other groundskeepers did from mid-November to mid-February was in preparation for the tourist season. And everything they did during the other months was designed to keep the visitors happy and help them enjoy the park. Her work life revolved around the theater schedule.

She knelt on a paving stone and used a trowel to dig up some weeds near a bamboo and stone fountain. The park was silent, except for a few birds singing in the trees, an occasional car driving down Granite Street, and the distant sound of some local children in the playground near the park's entrance. She wanted to be fully present here in the quiet, to stop thinking ahead to the shouts and laughter and intercom announcements that came with the theater crowd, but she could no more stop hearing those future sounds than she could stop seeing the way the maples would grow.

Arden tossed the weeds into her bucket and stood. Like it or not, she owed her livelihood to the festival. She smiled to herself. Actually, she owed her life to this small town's annual celebration of Shakespeare and his plays. Her dad had been a director here for years, until the lovely Rose Canton, otherwise known as Mom, had come to play Ophelia. He fell in love, and for a few years, according to Arden's grandparents, they had been happy here, producing many acclaimed plays and one small daughter. Until bigger and better roles called, and they left her and the festival with barely a backward glance. They still kept in touch in their offbeat, unpredictable way, but Arden knew more about their lives from reading reviews of their plays in magazines than by talking to them.

She stopped next to one of her grandfather's best

contributions to the park, a series of narrow, primitive wooden troughs that were filled with white stones of varying sizes. The fountain was gorgeous in its simplicity, and the sound of water running through gaps between stones and dropping from trough to trough was musical. During the season, they offered Tai Chi classes here, and plenty of people came to sit on the surrounding benches and meditate to the sounds he had created.

Did she regret living here with her grandparents? Never. She had been happy with them, and she felt their loss deeply. She had considered them to be her true parents, and her birth parents were more like flaky older siblings. Would she have preferred that her parents had chosen to either stay here or take her with them? She didn't want to answer that question. She couldn't imagine what her life would have been like if they had stayed here.

She rested her fingers on the rough timber of the highest trough and yelped when a sudden gush of water sprayed over her hand. She turned at the sound of laughter coming from a maintenance shed hidden behind some dense rhododendrons.

"Way to ruin a contemplative moment, Jacob," she called. Her supervisor came out of the shed, where he had turned on the fountain, looking anything but sorry for scaring her.

"I owed you, Little Philips," he said, shaking his finger at her. He and her grandfather had been close in age and had worked together for most of their adult lives. Jacob was nearly a head shorter than Arden, with thick gray hair that made him look like Einstein. He had become her self-appointed guardian when Delaney had died four years ago, even though she was thirty-two at the time. He freely gave her advice about her love life and her career choices, whether she wanted it or not.

"Consider this step one in my evil plan to get back at you for the viburnum incident," he continued, shaking his head at the memory.

Arden couldn't keep from laughing. He had started this series of pranks months ago with a fake spider in her lunchbox, but he still hadn't found a way to get back at her for last year's elaborate hoax. He had brought a delicate viburnum to the park and planted it with as much care as if it had been his child. Arden promptly dug it up and replaced it with a dead plant she had salvaged from the local nursery's dumpster. He had tried four more of the shrubs in succession with the same result, determined to prove her wrong when she kept saying, *I told you that spot is too shady.* She wasn't sure how long they would have continued the game if he hadn't stumbled across the thriving patch of his plants that she had placed alongside the road. Her garden had been a gorgeous mass of cranberry and pink flowers in the fall, while the last one Jacob had planted in his original spot—threatening her job if she dug it up—had never grown as well as its transplanted cousins.

"Well, you sure startled me today, so I guess we're even now," she said.

"Hardly. I've repaid you for one single shrub. I'll work on the rest over the season."

Arden grinned. "Well, good luck. You're gonna need it."

Jacob picked out a few stray leaves that had been dislodged when the water flowed over the pristine white stones. Both fountains in the garden had been drained and shut down over the winter season. "Were you talking to your gramps just now?"

"I was just thinking about him and my parents," Arden admitted. "But sometimes I come here and talk things out with him."

"Me, too." Jacob gave the wood trough a pat. "I see signs of him everywhere in the park, but nowhere more than here. Sometimes I talk to him about you, and he gives me advice to pass along."

Arden rolled her eyes. Great, here it came. What was today's lecture? Probably the *find a nice woman and settle down* one. She heard it every year before the festival started. She didn't have trouble finding women during the season, but finding a settling-down type was another story. She had a weakness for passionate divas, even though they were destined to leave just like Rose and her dad had. She had tried to focus on locals, or even tourist theatergoers, but she couldn't seem to resist the actors with all the accompanying drama and high emotions they brought into her life. Maybe because opposites really did attract, and Arden didn't consider herself to be the passionate type. The only thing she was sure of was the need to keep her heart carefully under control during these relationships. They were fun while they lasted, but they didn't last long.

"Your grandfather made some big changes in this park, Arden. We both know every plant and every stone he placed here."

Ah, the career lecture, not the romance one. Jacob must be serious this time if he was calling her by her first name instead of the Little Philips nickname only he was allowed to use with her. "Gramps was a gifted visual designer," she agreed. He could have been an artist, but he had chosen flowers and mulch over oils and watercolors. Her dad had the same kind of vision, but he used his talent in the theater.

"You've inherited those same gifts," Jacob said, as if reading her thoughts. More likely it was because they had had this same conversation a hundred times before, and they each knew the other's views and arguments. "But I don't see *you* anywhere in this park."

"Well, I'll go to the nursery and pick up some geraniums," Arden said. "I can plant them so they spell my name in orange letters, and you'll think of me whenever you look at them."

Jacob laughed—in spite of himself, apparently, because he quickly erased his smile. "The park is a living being, Arden. We create it anew every year, and we each put our stamp on it. It's time you did your part."

"The park is a living being? Seriously?"

Jacob shook his head. "Come up with something of your own to add to the park. It doesn't have to be a centerpiece fountain or a new themed garden. Just a patch of ground that is different because you were here."

"Are you okay?" Arden asked, suddenly worried. She had

been feeling her usual exasperation at the lecture, but was he getting serious because he was sick? "Have you been to a doctor?" He patted her arm. "I'm fine. Just passing along a message from my dearest friend to his beloved granddaughter. Now think of something before the season is over, or I'll fire you."

She laughed with him, somewhat satisfied that he wasn't sick and trying to get her life in order while he still could. "Sure thing, boss. I'll come up with something to make you proud."

He nodded toward her and toward the trough fountain, as if assuring her grandfather that he was doing his part to whip Arden into shape. She sighed as he left, and picked up her bucket and rake again. She liked tulips and daffodils—maybe she'd plant a line of bulbs near one of the ponds and get Jacob off her back at least until next year.

She loaded her equipment on the Mule and got in the driver's seat, but didn't start the engine right away. She wasn't sure why she fought Jacob's attempts to get her more involved in the evolution of the park, but every time he brought up this subject she felt tension twist inside her stomach like the coil of stripes on a candy cane. She had been happy to create designs of her own while she was getting her degree, but she couldn't feel the same flow of imagination and vision when she was here at the park. Right after her grandfather died and Jacob had started on this particular mission to get her more involved, she had tried to convince herself that she didn't want to make changes to the park because so many of her memories of Gramps were tied to this place. But that wasn't a good enough excuse because the park was practically unrecognizable from the one she had known as a child. It changed all the time.

She just wasn't like the rest of her family. Visionary and ambitious and always looking for new horizons. Her grandfather had managed to balance stability with creativity, but Arden's parents had chosen one over the other. Over her. The women she'd dated from the acting company had been the same.

But she loved Jacob. He was her family now, and she'd

do whatever it took to make him happy. She had planted some herb gardens in her own backyard. They had a pleasing mix of scents and textures, and they were small. She could buy some seedlings and tuck a similar one in a corner somewhere in the park. Problem solved.

Arden started the engine and drove to her next pruning job.

CHAPTER THREE

Emilie drove her used Subaru from Medford to Ashland. The small, boxy car might have been a nice shade of forest green when it was first painted, but now it looked a bit sickly. At least the shade seemed appropriate given the odd groans and noises the car made while pulling the tiny U-Haul with all her worldly belongings in it, as if it had the flu and would rather be lying in bed than speeding along I-5.

The trip only took twenty minutes, but the two cities were worlds apart in style. Medford had an industrial, sometimes seedy look, and little imagination had been put forth in the design of its blocky buildings. Ashland was all small-town charm, with unique shops and restaurants in quaint converted houses and an abundance of Tudor-style facades. The town was filled with shrubs and trees, making it seem like an extension of the beautiful park Emilie had discovered on her initial visit here.

Another thing she had learned on that trip was how much her cost of living was about to increase. Cheap and easy meals were a staple in Medford, but not here. The nearly year-round season of the festival brought a healthy tourist trade to Ashland, and the prices and styles of the restaurants here were an indication of their taste and disposable income level. At least Emilie would be likely to lose some weight without even trying, once her burger and fries diet came to an end and she was reduced to eating ramen noodles in her apartment.

She drove down the main street, past the site of the festival and the touristy stores around it and toward the campus of Southern Oregon University. Emilie had found this quiet area when she was here to audition—because she had gotten lost, not because she was feeling adventurous. When she had started looking for an apartment to rent, she had decided to avoid the main part of town and focus her search near SOU. The relative peace would give her a chance to get completely away from the festival and recharge when she wasn't onstage or rehearsing. She had also decided to room with a group of graduate students instead of choosing one of the places where several company members were looking for an additional roommate. She didn't want to listen to other actors reading lines through thin walls, more because she didn't want to compare herself to them than because the noise would bother her.

Emilie's confidence had run the gamut from hopefully optimistic at auditions to ecstatically positive when she was hired to waveringly inconsistent after that initial elation. It had settled somewhere near nonexistent over the past week as she had packed up her meager belongings and prepared for the move. She hoped today's welcome meeting with the company director would help her feel more settled here, like she really belonged.

She followed the directions to her new home and parked in front of the two-story blue-and-gray Craftsman. The yard was small but neat, and the neighborhood seemed quiet and pleasant. Of course, being this close to the university might mean it turned into Party Row on the weekends, but she didn't mind. It couldn't be much louder than her place in Medford had been.

She had to spend five minutes ringing the doorbell and knocking with increasing firmness before someone finally answered the door. The woman held the door open a few inches, and Emilie could only see one of her blue eyes, a partial halo of short, mousy brown curls, and the ragged ends of an old red sweater with a rolled neckline.

"Hi, I'm Emilie," she said. Apparently the name wasn't enough to gain admission to the house. "I'm your new roommate," she added.

"Oh. The actress. I'm Olivia." She opened the door fully, then, but still blocked Emilie's way.

Emilie shook her hand. "It's nice to meet you. And I prefer actor to actress."

Olivia nodded. "Gotcha. No diminutives. Come in."

Emilie came into the dark, narrow foyer, feeling as if she had just passed some sort of test. They walked into a living room filled with mismatched chairs and sofa and a small TV.

"This is the common room. If you're obsessed with a particular show, you'll need to reserve the channel. Otherwise, the first one to get the remote gets to choose." Olivia gestured toward an end table that had a remote on it and a clipboard with a pencil tied to it with a piece of orange yarn.

Emilie hadn't bothered with cable during her short stay in Medford, so she doubted she'd be fighting over television rights. She followed Olivia through a small dining room with someone's textbooks and notebooks strewn across one quarter of it, and a partially finished jigsaw puzzle covering the rest. The picture was nothing but hundreds of candy corns, and Emilie was tempted to sit down and finish the border.

"Here's the kitchen," Olivia said, continuing the tour without a puzzle break. "You can use anything in the cabinets, but we each buy our own food. This is your cupboard, and you get the bottom shelf of the fridge."

The kitchen was sorely in need of an update and probably hadn't been renovated since the seventies. Everything was clean, though, from the laminated yellow countertops to the cream-colored cabinet doors. Olivia opened one of them, and then the fridge, and Emilie saw her name clearly printed on labels, marking her grocery territory.

"Everyone's responsible for cleaning up after themselves.

No dirty dishes in the sink, and no stealing food. Seriously. If Steph finds so much as a tub of yogurt missing, she'll turn psychotic. That's how we lost our last roommate."

Lost her. Emilie wasn't sure if Olivia meant she had moved out, or if this Steph person had psychotically killed her. Was she buried in the backyard, with nothing but an empty container of blueberry yogurt marking her grave?

"Your room is on the first floor. The bathroom down here is for guests, too, but mostly you'll have it for yourself. You're right in here."

Emilie paused as they passed the back door and got a peek at an overgrown yard with spindly, climbing plants covering the faded wood fence. A few chairs were scattered around a small brick patio, and the area looked pleasant and private enough. She continued on and joined Olivia at the door to her room.

She walked inside and set down her overnight bag. It was a square room with nothing more than a bed in it, but it was big enough for the bits of furniture she had bought in Medford. It would do.

"This will be nice," she said to Olivia.

Olivia shrugged. "It's a good place to live. We're all busy with classes, and Mary is working on her thesis, so we're usually quiet. Steph throws an occasional party on the weekend, and you've got a standing invite, but other than that we focus on school." She paused, as if appraising Emilie. "We weren't sure about having an actor join us," she said, drawing out the word *actor* with a haughty accent and a smile to let Emilie know she was teasing. "But I convinced the others to give you a shot."

Emilie grinned. "Well, thank you. I won't let you down."

"I'm sure you won't. And maybe you can repay the favor someday."

"Of course."

"Good," Olivia said with a smug expression, and Emilie wondered what trap she had just walked into. "I'm working on my master's in psychology. Maybe you can let me interview you for a project I'm working on for one of my courses."

Emilie gestured around the bare room. "Is this where you usually keep your lab rats?"

"Only the ones who don't steal yogurt. The thieves have to live in cages in the lab."

"I'll keep that in mind when I'm scampering through the house looking for a midnight snack. What's the topic?"

"I'm doing a study on people who pursue acting careers as a way to compensate for low self-esteem and a lack of security in childhood."

Emilie had to laugh. "That should make you popular here in Ashland, home of the Oregon Shakespeare Festival."

Olivia just smiled. "Your key is on the kitchen counter. Do you need help moving your stuff?"

Emilie shook her head. "No, I have to get to a meeting, so I'll do it later. Besides, if you do me another favor, you might expect the chance to dissect my brain as repayment."

"We'll start with the interview and worry about dissection later. Nice to meet you, Emilie."

"You, too."

As soon as Olivia left the room, Emilie shut the door and changed into a green shirt and a pair of black pants, with a thick black jacket over the top. She was tempted to flop on the bed and let her mind process all the changes and newness she was facing, but she didn't have time. She couldn't be late for her appointment. She grabbed her new key, checked herself in the mirror as she walked past the small bathroom, and left the house. She could easily walk the short distance from home to the theaters, but not today, when a light rain was starting to dot the sidewalk and she didn't dare make a bad first impression by being late. She got in her car and drove instead.

For all its grandeur and its prominence in Ashland, the main theater space wasn't immediately visible from the main street.

It was tucked on a side street, bordering the park, and gave the feeling of being somehow separate from the rest of the world. A brick courtyard and a high, dark brown fence surrounded the huge, open-air Allen Elizabethan Theatre, and the gift shop, administrative offices, and Angus Bowmer Theatre were clustered around this area that was aptly called the Bricks. Across the street was the smaller Thomas Theatre, where Emilie had auditioned last September, reciting her monologues amid the set pieces of ship and palm trees for the evening's performance of *The Tempest*. She managed to find enough room to parallel park her Subaru-plus-U-Haul along the street, but she knew this would be an impossibility once the season started.

She went into Carpenter Hall, where the sales office was already a hive of activity, and asked how to get to the artistic director's office. She was sent down a long corridor, the thick maroon carpet giving this part of the hall a hushed feeling, especially compared to the loud and active tiled sales space. Jay Winder's door was open, and he was sitting at his desk surrounded by head shots, stacks of scripts, and an overflowing box of fabric samples. She stood in the doorway and knocked.

"Come in, come in," he said, gesturing her forward without looking up from whatever he was furiously writing in a thick notebook. He held his hand out, palm toward her, and she assumed he meant he'd be with her as soon as he was done spilling his thoughts onto the paper. She sat in an ornately carved chair upholstered in a heavy brocade and waited for him to finish.

She had met him when she auditioned, and had liked him immediately. He had a palpable sense of energy about him, and an infectious enthusiasm for the festival and the plays they produced. She had auditioned for several roles in plays across the country, but only here for a place in a multi-play company, and she had received a few offers for her efforts. After meeting Jay—and comparing him to the somewhat blasé directors in the other theaters—she had quickly made her choice.

She knew he was in his late sixties, but his fashionably styled and highlighted hair as well as his mobile and active demeanor made him seem ageless. He was wearing a long-sleeved powder-blue polo shirt and faded jeans, and after every few words he wrote, he paused and tapped his fingers restlessly on the desk. Finally he turned his attention to her with a suddenness that made her startle.

"Emilie Danvers. Great to see you again. Have you settled in? See Bennie in the sales office if you need a place to stay. He can get you a room somewhere. You've got your scripts? Good. Rehearsals start next week for the openers, and not until March for the summer plays. Let's see, I just had your packets here a minute ago..."

Emilie had barely lowered her handful of scripts—which she had held up in answer to his question about them—before he was tossing stuffed manila envelopes at her while he rattled off her parts.

"Titania, *A Midsummer Night's Dream,* February to November. Understudy Cassella, *Skywriting,* February to July. Have you read the book? Sidman did the script, too, but you should read the words he originally wrote." He paused and rooted around on his desk until he found a three-inch-thick trade paperback of the bestselling book *Skywriting.* She caught it when he lobbed it in her direction, but the two envelopes she already had in her lap slid to the floor.

"Anne Page, *The Merry Wives of Windsor,* February to November. Lady Anne, *Richard III,* April to October." He laughed. "Two Annes! Try not to forget which one you're playing. What a disaster to get them mixed up."

Jesus. For all the potential catastrophes Emilie's too-active imagination had been concocting, that particular one had escaped her. Until now. Surely she'd remember whether she was playing a virginal teenager or a widow who was being courted by her husband's killer, wouldn't she? She shoved the new fear out of her mind and caught the next envelope.

"Martha, *Toxic,* July to August. Those are the main parts, but it's not uncommon for others to come up midseason. You'll have your rehearsal and performance schedules in the folders, as well as an updated script for each play. Any changes made from the earlier ones will be marked in red. You also have appointments for costume and wig measurements this week, and those departments will let you know when to come back for fittings. Needless to say, get these on your calendar and don't miss any of them."

"Of course. I mean, I won't," Emilie said, but he had already moved on to another topic.

"All members of the company do a minimum number of tours throughout the season, but if you want extra ones, let me know, and I'll add your name to the on-call list. It's a great way to make more money, and to feel like you're part of the festival. We don't want actors who say their lines and go home. We want company members who become part of the OSF family."

Emilie nodded, not so much at his last statement as at the making money part. The rare times when she had been in one place long enough to work in Europe, she had found jobs as a tour guide. She enjoyed doing them, with the set scripts, the chance to embellish with personal anecdotes, and the absence of the debilitating stage fright she felt when acting. Tours offered the joy of performing without the anxiety of being responsible for bringing someone's words and ideas to life.

She decided not to share all of this with Olivia. She wasn't prepared to have her mind and motives studied right now.

"I'm happy to be involved any way I can," she said.

"Good. You were stellar in your auditions, and you have a wide range of parts to cover this season. Show us what you're made of, Emilie."

Yeah, no pressure there. Emilie stood when he did, and shook the hand he offered. She resisted the urge to shake some feeling back into her fingers when he let go.

"The keyword here is communication. Schedules, fittings, performance notes. We communicate our expectations, and you communicate if you have any questions, concerns, or personal issues that might get in the way of your ability to perform at your peak. I'll be dropping by rehearsals over the next few weeks, so I'll see you soon."

Emilie thanked him and bent down to pick up the material he had given her. When she left with her armload of scripts and schedules clutched to her chest, he was already back at his desk, writing again.

She walked to her car and stowed what would be her life for the next eleven months in the trunk. He had talked about communication but hadn't given her long enough to take a breath and ask a question. He probably wouldn't have liked any of the ones coming to her mind. *What the hell am I doing here? Why did I agree to play four characters and understudy a fifth instead of taking a nice, easy bit part in a civic playhouse somewhere farther out of the spotlight? How exactly do I get out of this contract without needing to repay the advance that I already spent?*

Emilie got in her car and sat behind the wheel for a few minutes. She could go back to her new house and work on the puzzle. Go shopping so she wouldn't need to steal anyone else's dairy products. Instead, she got out of the car again and locked it before crossing the Bricks and going past the Elizabethan theater. She hadn't even seen inside the theater, except in pictures, and it would be the site of her very first performance here. Would she be a success or a failure? Or, possibly even more horrifying, just okay? She walked down a flight of brick steps and toward the park. Maybe a walk through the bone-chilling rain would clear her head and get her ready for what lay ahead.

Chapter Four

Arden leaned her elbows on the stone railing of the Atkinson Bridge and watched Ashland Creek rushing beneath her. The small river was swift and deep, already swelling from runoff from the melting snow in the nearby mountains. She wasn't sure what she was hoping to find while staring at the water, but some inspiration would be welcome.

She had spent two weeks avoiding Jacob because she still didn't have any idea what he expected from her. She took good care of the plants and trees in her park, and she loved her job for its simplicity and the satisfaction she felt when everything was healthy and in full bloom. Why did he need her to do more than she did?

Luckily, they had a few inches of snow a week ago, and the entire crew had been kept busy clearing paths, breaking ice off branches and limbs, and making sure the more delicate shrubs and bushes were still heavily mulched. Basic care took precedence over innovation.

But now the weather had warmed a few degrees. Heavy rains had melted the snow practically overnight, and the sun had even made a rare appearance this morning. For all of five minutes. Arden had gotten jumpy again, expecting Jacob to appear at any moment and demand some sort of signature showpiece from her.

Arden sighed and pushed herself upright, crossing to the

theater side of the park and climbing a hill that led to a little-used jogging and bike trail. She remembered when those labyrinth circles were popular. Did people still walk around them and pretend they were meditating? She wasn't sure where they would be able to fit one, but the flat surface of the tennis courts came to mind. She could suggest they spray paint one there. Or maybe Jacob would prefer a gnome garden near the first duck pond? They could dress the small statues in period costumes and pretend they were performing one of Shakespeare's plays. *Macbeth*, starring gnomes. Or maybe they could plant a corn maze and charge admission for tourists to try to find their way out again.

Arden counted chain link panels in the fence until she came to the fifth one from the trailhead. She reached behind the metal post and made sure the tiny magnetic box was still in place. The park was full of geocaches, and even though it wasn't part of her job, she checked them regularly. During the season, she'd often see plenty of people wandering through the park, staring at their phones not because they were texting or searching online, but because they were following GPS coordinates and trying to find the hidden caches.

She was about to head back to the main trail when she heard a woman's voice coming from somewhere ahead of her. The sound was too faint for her to pick out any words, and she walked quietly toward the source. Probably a couple of teens making out behind some bushes and needing to be shooed out of the park.

She recognized the lines from a play as soon as she was able to hear a complete sentence. She wasn't hearing amorous high-schoolers, but a fairy queen. Titania, from *A Midsummer Night's Dream*. The play was one of her favorites, probably because it was the first one her grandparents took her to see. She had only been six at the time, but they had talked to her about the language and story for several weeks before the play opened, so by the time she saw the performance she was able to understand most of what she was watching. Even if her theater-loving family hadn't prepped her, though, she would have been carried away to a magical forest that night.

She paused for a moment, uncertain whether she should continue eavesdropping or walk away and let the actor practice in peace. She closed her eyes and let the words move through her. The woman's voice was soft, but powerful. Haughty, yet playful. She was speaking quietly, but her voice carried with a resonance that made Arden assume she was a professional, one of the company members most likely.

Arden couldn't make herself leave but instead was pulled toward the woman. She crept to the edge of the path and peered around a heavy oak tree trunk and into a small clearing where the speaker was standing on a tree trunk stage, about two feet across and a foot high. She was facing away at an angle, and Arden stared at her profile. *Here we go again*, she thought. The woman had an elegance about her, a queenly grace befitting the role she was practicing, even though she was dressed in modern, businesslike clothes. Her look was softened by gorgeous blue-green eyes and by the thick blond curls that had pulled loose from her braid and were now framing her face and matching the curve of her cheekbones. She was beautiful, and Arden felt herself falling, heading toward a new infatuation and the inevitable end-of-the-season crash.

Normally, Arden would be ready to step out of hiding right now. Turn on the charm, ask her out, rush into the relationship—such as it would be—as quickly as possible. Before common sense had a chance to make a case against another ill-advised tryst with an actor. This time, though, she wasn't in a hurry to break the spell the woman was casting around her tiny stage.

Once Arden stopped her own internal monologue about the *should I or shouldn't I ask her out* debate, she stopped feeling like an observer and had the sensation of being drawn out of the park and into a different place altogether. She rested her hand on the rough bark of the trunk and just listened. When Titania called for her attendants to come forward, Arden took a step before she could stop herself.

A twig snapped under her foot, and the woman whirled to face her.

"Hey. Sorry. I'm Arden. I work here…in the park, I mean. I was walking by and heard you…" Arden sighed. Smooth. She cleared her throat and started again. "I didn't mean to interrupt, but you're amazing. You transported me."

She was rewarded with a smile that made her breath hitch in her throat. "Thank you for the compliment, but I haven't really worked on the part yet." The woman walked closer and held out her hand. "I'm Emilie."

Arden shook her hand, her attention focused on the texture of Emilie's skin against hers. She needed to get her imagination under control and to stop imagining Emilie's hand moving over the rest of her body. Either get control or ask her out and make her daydream come true. "Are you playing Titania here in Ashland?"

Emilie frowned. "Yes. Among others." She stepped away from Arden and sat down on the stump.

"Who else?" Arden leaned against the tree she had been hiding behind only moments before. She usually avoided all talk of the festival when she was with one of the company women she wanted to date, but she was fascinated by the expressions shifting across Emilie's features, and she wanted to learn more about her. She seemed in control of her emotions when playing a part, but adorably transparent when she was being herself.

"I'm an understudy for the lead in *Skywriting* and the alcoholic older sister in *Toxic*. In the Shakespeare plays I'm Anne Page and Lady Anne. And please don't make any jokes about getting the two Annes mixed up when I'm onstage."

Arden laughed. "I wasn't going to say a word. This is your first year at Ashland, isn't it? I would definitely remember you if you'd been here last year."

"Yes, it's my first season here. Did my impromptu rehearsal in the woods tip you off?"

"No. You'll see almost everyone from the company in the park at one time or another. They're usually wandering around with faraway looks on their faces while they mumble lines from their scripts. You can't miss them. Unless, of course, you're doing the same thing. Then you might run right into them."

"That'll be a good incentive to memorize my parts quickly. So I can watch where I'm walking while I rehearse."

"Well, you already know Titania, so you're twenty percent there."

Emilie stood, and Arden felt a sense of panic at the thought of watching her walk away. Foolish, since the town was small and they'd likely run into each other fairly often, but she didn't want an opportunity to see Emilie again pass her by.

"If you're looking for more advice about surviving in Ashland, I'd be happy to act as tour guide. I can show you all the hidden spots, take you to my favorite restaurants..." Arden's voice trailed off when she saw the expression on Emilie's face. She wasn't sure what words Emilie would use to say no, but Arden could hear the word loud and clear in the silence.

"I'm sorry. I appreciate the offer, but I don't think I'll have time," Emilie said, avoiding Arden's gaze and frowning. "I just got a huge stack of scripts and schedules, and I don't know when I'll have time to breathe, let alone start dating."

"Date? I didn't mean to ask you on a date," Arden lied. "I was only offering to show you around. Introduce you to some other locals. That sort of thing."

"Oh, of course. I shouldn't have assumed you meant..."

Arden watched a blush creep up Emilie's neck and swore softly. She closed the distance between them and gently touched Emilie's arm, quickly pulling back when she felt the temptation to linger. "I really was asking you out. I was just trying to save face when you turned me down. Don't worry about it, okay? You're going to be incredibly busy this season."

Emilie put her hand over the spot Arden had touched, not like she wanted to rub it clean, but as if she wanted to hold something close.

"I wish I could say yes, Arden. You're very..." Emilie paused and shook her head, changing the direction of her explanation. "I left acting a few years ago. My girlfriend at the time was offered a part with a touring company, so I went with her to Europe. It was awful. We fought all the time, and I felt I had lost everything that was mine, that made me who I am. I'm finally getting a little of it back. Acting has to be my priority right now."

Arden nodded. If anyone had the right to use the *I need time to take care of myself* argument, it was Emilie. "That's why I hate dating actors," she said. "Their dreams usually eclipse your own."

Emilie laughed. "Should I feel insulted, or happy that you understand me?"

"Just happy, I hope," Arden said. They were silent for a moment, and she felt a sense of companionship take the place of the awkwardness she had been feeling moments before. It took a moment before she could identify what she was feeling as relief. She wouldn't have to lose Emilie at the end of the season if she never had her in the first place. "You're the one who turned me down, so you have to finish your sentence. I'm very...what?"

Emilie paused. "Adequate looking."

"Sweet talker," Arden said with a burst of laughter.

"I am, aren't I? I was going to say nonrepulsive, but I thought I'd put a more positive spin on it."

Arden took a small spiral-bound notebook out of her pocket and turned to a blank page. She wrote her name and number on it and gave it to Emilie.

"In case you need a friend," she said, surprised by how much she hoped Emilie would contact her, even though the romantic relationship wasn't going to happen.

"Thank you," Emilie said, folding the paper and slipping it in her pocket. "I just might."

CHAPTER FIVE

Emilie gripped the hand rests of her chair while the company's wig maker, Velda, raked her hands through Emilie's hair and muttered comments to her assistant, who wrote down everything she said in a notebook. Even with the pain in her scalp to distract her, Emilie's thoughts wandered back to Arden and the secluded area of the park where they had met. Arden's hand on her arm had been soft and comforting, and Emilie imagined how gentle it would be as it sifted through her curls. Not like this demon woman, who seemed determined to make Emilie bleed before her appointment was over.

"Your hair. It curls very much." Velda spoke with a heavy accent that Emilie guessed was Eastern European, but she couldn't place it specifically. Probably because of her increasing headache. "And is thick."

Emilie would usually consider those phrases to be compliments, but Velda's voice seemed to convey her opinion that Emilie had grown her hair like this on purpose, just to spite her.

"It *was* thick," she said. "But I think you've pulled half of it out."

Velda poked her on the shoulder. "You. *Sh.*"

She continued to describe every last cowlick and slightly uneven portion of Emilie's hairline to her assistant. Then she turned Emilie toward the mirror again. "We make you wigs that move like your real hair. You will forget is wig while acting. Now I show you how to braid for putting under bald cap."

"Thank y—ouch!" Emilie gasped as Velda started separating strands and weaving them into a tight braid. She scrunched her eyes closed and held her breath until the worst of it was over, then she forced herself to look in the mirror. She'd need to be able to copy what Velda was doing if she wanted her wigs to fit properly. "I look like I just had a face-lift," she said, gingerly touching her stretched forehead.

"I know. You're welcome." Velda coiled her hair and fixed it with at least a hundred bobby pins. She handed Emilie a mirror and turned her chair around. "You do exactly like this every performance."

Emilie used the smaller mirror to peer at the back of her head, where her hair was pinned into an intricate pattern to keep it as flat against her head as possible. At least she didn't see any blood dripping down her neck. "Can you draw a diagram for me?"

"You remember and do it right. Now the bald cap, and we measure." She stretched a flesh-colored cap over Emilie's head and used an adhesive to blend the edges onto Emilie's skin.

She grimaced at her reflection. She had worn stock wigs in plays before, but had never had one made specifically for her. She should appreciate the hours Velda and her staff would devote to each wig. She would, as soon as the pain eased a little.

When Emilie had seen *wig fitting* filling a three-hour block on her schedule, she had figured she would probably be waiting during most of the time. She hadn't realized she would be in this chair for all three hours, enduring the various torture devices Velda had tucked in her smock. Who knew a flimsy little tape measure could hurt so much? If Emilie had any secrets to tell, she'd be spilling them right now. If she'd known she was going to die during her wig fitting, she wouldn't have turned down the chance to go on a date with Arden.

She put her palm over her stomach as Velda spun her chair

around. Emilie had been feeling queasy all week, since her meeting with Jay. She was overwhelmed and exhausted. Her last play had been at a well-respected theater, but the atmosphere had been much more casual than what she was experiencing in Ashland. Rehearsals for two plays had already started, and the third would begin the day after tomorrow. She'd be required to have all three parts memorized by next week, including the blocking and stage directions she'd been given already.

As usual this week, whenever she felt ready to hyperventilate, she mentally retreated to the place in Lithia Park where she had stood on a tree stump and spoken Titania's words. Arden had told her that she felt transported, and Emilie had experienced the same thing. Not because of her impromptu performance, but because of meeting Arden. She had been funny and honest and real. Not to mention beautiful. Tall and athletic, with a graceful way of moving around the trees and close to Emilie. She had seemed at home in the woods, with her thick chamois shirt and those jeans with the muddy knees and the sexy way of hugging her thighs. She seemed confident enough to fit in anywhere, though. Emilie's daydreams had put her in a dark bar where soft dance music played and the two of them swayed together, and on a red carpet with Emilie on her arm and a black tux outlining her curves and muscles. Or naked, in—

Emilie grabbed at her stomach again as Velda spun her in the opposite direction. She wasn't going to complain this time, though, since she had needed to have her mind spun back to sanity. Arden was tempting, but Emilie couldn't give in to temptation right now. That's what had gotten her in trouble before, although Emilie wasn't sure if it had really been Leah who had tempted her away, or if it had been a sneaking sense of relief because she was scared to try to be a professional actor and fail...

She pushed aside her thoughts of Arden and her past and let her throbbing scalp keep her centered here in the present. They needed five stiff foam molds of her head for her plays, plus an extra one, "just in case," as Velda had said. In case what, Emilie wasn't sure. Whenever Velda turned her attention to the molds and away from wielding the tape measure, Emilie watched the procedure with fascination. Exact replicas of her bald-cap-covered scalp were created and marked, and every measurement was precisely replicated on her and the wig head. Where Anne Page's bob should cross her jawline, how long the first wave of Titania's hair should be, how high Lady Anne's bun should be placed. Even the hairstyles from the modern plays were carefully marked on the wig heads before a single strand of hair would be sewn into a wig.

Finally Emilie was released from the chair of horrors, and she tried to unpin her braid as she walked to her next appointment. She had half of her hair released—and probably reduced to a frizzy mess—by the time she walked into the costume fitting area.

"Oh, my," a booming voice said from behind her, "looks like you just had a visit with Velda."

Emilie turned and faced the tall man who was lounging just inside the costume room. He looked as if he had been carefully posed there by a fashion photographer, with his hands in his pockets and one ankle crossed over the other. He was wearing a pink-striped shirt under a navy V-neck sweater and dark denim jeans.

"How could you tell?" Emilie asked, looking at her handful of bobby pins as if they couldn't possibly have given her away.

He gestured toward her hair. "Well, *that* gave you away. Good luck getting a comb through it ever again."

"I feel like every strand was strip-searched," Emilie said, pulling at more pins and trying to dislodge the heavy braid.

"At least you're not crying. I was in tears after our first session last year. Here, let me do that."

He put his hands on Emilie's shoulders and turned her around. She felt a tiny bit of pressure release with every pin he removed.

"You're Emilie, aren't you? I'm Geoffrey. I'll be your Richard III in one play, and your druggie cousin in *Toxic.*"

Geoffrey Cranston. Emilie had heard of him, of course, but she'd never seen him act. Now she'd be sharing a stage with him. She hated the part of herself that didn't believe she belonged there.

She shoved the remaining bobby pins in the pocket of her jeans and faced him again. "Thank you. And nice to meet you."

"You, too." He waved when one of the costume makers called his name. "Must go. But I'll see you at rehearsal on Friday. And Jay wants me to teach you newbies how to lead tours. We'll meet Saturday at noon, in the courtyard in front of Carpenter Hall. 'Bye."

"'Bye," Emilie said weakly. The tours had sounded like fun before she had realized how stuffed her schedule and her brain were going to be. She wasn't sure where she'd fit all the new lines she needed to learn.

She was called soon after Geoffrey, and she stood on a short pedestal for over an hour in her underwear, while every single inch of her body was measured and analyzed. If she hadn't been so relieved to have costume fitters who didn't share Velda's masochistic tendencies, she would have been mortified by the experience. As it was, she turned and moved and raised her arms like a doll when told to, while her mind tried to process everything she needed to do.

She shouldn't add more to the list, but she needed something *other.* Something outside the theater and the festival. She thought of Arden's phone number, sitting on her bedside table where she had placed it last week. Had she really meant it when she offered friendship? Would Emilie be able to resist the attraction she felt—especially when she was weakened by self-doubt and the obsessive desire to run away from all of this?

Maybe, maybe not. All Emilie knew was that she wanted to see Arden again. For a few brief minutes with her, Emilie had felt relaxed and complete. Not lacking or frazzled. She deliberately kept her eyes away from the mirror, while her fast-food-padded waist and hips were measured, and let her mind wander back to the sanctuary of the park.

❖

After her seemingly interminable appointments were over, Emilie tied her hair in a loose braid—Geoffrey had been correct, and Velda had somehow rendered it impervious to a comb—and walked to the park. She decided to let fate decide if she should see Arden again instead of calling her, but since she worked at the park, Emilie was giving fate a fighting chance.

She only had to walk the winding circuit of the park twice before she found Arden bent over the bench of a picnic table, as if she was looking for something underneath it. Emilie tried to look anywhere besides Arden's shapely rear end, and she cleared her suddenly dry throat to get Arden's attention and make her sit up. When that failed, she reached over and tapped her on the shoulder.

Arden yelped and hopped off the bench, making Emilie leap away in response.

"Shit, Emilie. You scared me."

"Me, too," Emilie said. She sat down at the table while she waited for her heart rate to return to normal. "Are you always this jumpy?"

"Not usually," Arden said, sitting next to her. "I thought you were someone else. Someone who tried to put a spider down my shirt today." She waved her hand in a dismissive gesture. "Long story about a viburnum. Luckily, he was scared of the spider and dropped it before he got too close to me, but I have a feeling he's going to try again. So, what's up?"

"I came here to ask you if the offer to be my local guide still stands, although now I'm wondering if it might be dangerous to stand too close to you if there are insects involved." Emilie's doubts about whether she should have sought Arden's company rather than avoiding her disappeared in an instant. Arden was playful and had a life outside the festival with friends—albeit rather suspect ones if they were in the habit of flinging spiders at her.

Arden grinned. "I doubt any of them will be venomous, so you'll be fine. And I'd be glad to show you around."

"Great," Emilie said. She hesitated, then decided to speak her mind. Arden seemed to be the type who would appreciate clarity up front. "But I still mean what I said last week about not getting involved with anyone right now. Especially now, since I know how crazy this season will be. I really could use a friend, though, if you're willing."

"I am." Arden fidgeted with the silver wolf-shaped zipper pull of her vest. "It'll be good for me, too. I sort of have a habit of getting involved with actors and, obviously, it never ends well. You can be my buffer. If other company members see us together, they'll assume I'm off-limits, and I'll be saved from myself."

Emilie wondered why Arden's relationships *obviously* failed. She had mentioned the pitfalls of dating actors when they first met—in a joking way, but with a hint of unhealed pain behind her statement. "It's a deal, then. No…kissing. Just friends."

She had been about to say *no sex*, but that only made her think of Arden naked and tangled in the sheets with her. Emilie felt the warmth of a blush spread across her cheeks.

"No kissing," Arden said, holding up her hand with an expression of deep seriousness, like she was making a vow. She flashed an impish grin that immediately called an image of Puck from *A Midsummer Night's Dream* to Emilie's mind. "Unless, of course, you need to run lines. I'd kiss you if it was in the script. For art."

"For art?" Emilie shrugged and studied Arden with her head tilted to one side. "Yes, that might work. You'd make a believable hunchbacked murderous king, so I'd be able to get into the character of Lady Anne."

Arden laughed and shook her head. "Again with the compliments. You need to stop or I'll be too conceited to handle."

Emilie smiled. "I'll try. Now, any chance you'd want to get dinner tonight? I've been eating nothing but soup at home this week."

"Do you feel like meeting some of my friends? We were going to meet at a pub just a few blocks from here." Arden stood and held out her hand to Emilie.

"It depends." Emilie pretended to hesitate, even though an evening of laughter, good food, and beer sounded too unbearably wonderful to miss. "Is this place called the Bard's Pub?"

"Ah, you've noticed a trend in business names, have you? Don't worry, it's called the Dog and Crow."

"What a relief." Emilie let Arden pull her to her feet, but she quickly dropped the contact between them. She had to keep her distance, and even such a simple touch made her crave more. Arden started walking toward a nearby maintenance shack, and Emilie went with her. "The *B* section of the Ashland phone book must be three times as thick as any other letter."

"The worst one was the Bard's Sushi Palace," Arden said. "Needless to say, it didn't last long."

Chapter Six

Arden took a quick shower in the miniscule staff room and then changed into a black shirt and a clean pair of worn jeans. Every time she walked back and forth to her locker, she could see Emilie sitting on the little covered patio. She was chewing on a piece of hair that had broken free from her braid and studying a script. Emilie had seemed a little on edge when they'd first met—first-day jitters were to be expected—but Arden was surprised by the change she saw in her after only a week. She was still funny and easy to talk to, but there was a deeper tension in her than what Arden had seen before.

She guessed it was because this season meant so much to Emilie. Arden had seen how much Emilie cared about this job in her expression and had heard it in her voice when she talked about giving up her acting career to follow her ex. Now she saw it in Emilie's tense jaw and in the shadows under her eyes. She seemed to think this summer at the festival would be her turning point—either back to her beloved acting or away from it for good. Arden had been around actors enough to know she couldn't convince Emilie that there would be other chances if this one didn't go well. Things were more black and white for passionate people like Emilie.

Arden was doubly surprised, then, that Emilie had agreed to go out with her. She hadn't expected Emilie to allow anything to stand in her way this year, and Arden's obvious interest in dating her should have been something Emilie tried to avoid. Her need to get away from the stress of the company must have overridden her need to concentrate fully on her part in it. Or had she been unable to resist Arden's charisma and charm?

She laughed to herself as she combed her straight hair and tucked it, still damp, behind her ears. Unlikely. But Arden was happy to have a chance to be around Emilie some more. She was good company, and Arden hadn't been lying when she said she needed to be saved from herself and her ridiculous weakness for actors. When the season ended, and Emilie moved on to bigger roles and greater fame, Arden would be left unscathed, with only her memories of a nice friendship and not a heated love affair. She wouldn't care one bit when Emilie left. In fact, they'd be able to keep in touch, unlike the other women Arden had dated.

Yeah. They'd be pen pals. Arden didn't feel like laughing at the thought. Could she really be sure Emilie wouldn't break her heart at the end of the year, whether they slept together or not? She wasn't sure, but she was going to close her eyes, jump in, and see what happened.

"Ready to go?" she asked when she came outside. Emilie closed her script and blinked a few times in a way that seemed familiar to Arden. She was coming back from whatever world she had been in—maybe the tomb in Richard III's castle or Titania's magical forest.

"Sure," Emilie said, recovering quickly and smiling at Arden. She reached over and ran a tentative finger over Arden's hair, following it as it curved behind her ear. "Do you need to dry your hair first? It'll turn to ice out here."

Arden shivered, but her reaction had nothing to do with the weather and everything to do with Emilie's touch. She was in deep trouble here, but she felt helpless to stop. "We just have a short walk, and there'll be a fire in the pub. I'll survive."

Maybe. They started walking out of the park, and Arden gestured to the right. Everything in Ashland's business district was within walking distance from the theaters.

"How was your week?" she asked, focusing on the chill on her scalp—it really was too cold to be out here with wet hair— and letting the weather erase the heated trail Emilie's finger had scorched from her temple to her ear.

"Ugh. Crazy. The pace here is faster than I'm used to, and then multiply everything for three plays. I know that as soon as I feel like I'm getting used to them, rehearsals will start for the next two." Emilie reached up and rubbed her forehead. "As if the plays weren't bad enough, today I had to meet with an evil wig maker. She's probably collecting real scalps for her creations, so be careful if you're outside alone at night." She stopped and faced Arden. "Do you see any welts? Permanent scars?"

Arden saw only touchable skin. She poked Emilie gently between her eyebrows. "All I see are frown lines, and hopefully those aren't permanently etched in just yet."

"Great. Thanks." Emilie bumped Arden with her shoulder and continued walking.

"Tell me about the wig maker. I want to be able to recognize her if we meet on one of the secluded trails in the park."

"Well, she'll probably be holding a huge pair of recently sharpened shears. That'll be your first clue…"

Emilie went on to describe her appointment, and after a few minutes Arden was nearly doubled over with laughter. "Stop, my stomach hurts," she said, blinking back tears from laughing so hard. "It can't really have been this bad."

"It was worse," Emilie said. "I'm leaving out the parts where I sobbed and begged for mercy because I don't want to embarrass myself."

Arden shook her head and led them down a curved staircase and into the basement of a two-story brick building. A Thai restaurant was on the first floor, with a real estate agency above. The windowless pub was cozy and warm after being outside, and they stood in the entrance for a moment as their eyes adjusted to the dim light. As Arden had promised, a fire crackled noisily in the corner of the room, giving everything in it a moving glow.

Posters from past festival seasons and signed head shots filled the walls, and a red telephone box stood between the bar and the restrooms. Round wooden tables were grouped around the main floor of the pub, some regular height with padded leather chairs and others tall with stools.

Arden took Emilie over to the bar and leaned her elbow on the sticky granite countertop. "Hey, Lisa," she called.

Lisa flipped the towel she had been using to clean spilled beer off the counter over her shoulder and came to their end of the bar.

"Arden, good to see you. Marty and Rebecca already got your beer. Who's this, then?"

Arden hesitated for a brief moment. Lisa's short stylish white-blond hair and her killer body—evidenced by the bare space between her tank top and her low-rise jeans—combined with her British accent to make her irresistible to almost anyone who came into the bar. Maybe she shouldn't have brought Emilie here.

"This is Emilie. She's in the company. Em, this is Lisa. She owns the Dog and Crow."

Arden hoped the nickname might imply more intimacy between her and Emilie than was really there, but Lisa didn't seem to notice and held Emilie's hand a little longer than necessary. Arden was ready to grab one of the soda taps and hose her down.

"Great name for a pub," Emilie said, her voice carrying easily over the noise in the bar.

"Free pint if you can tell me the source," Lisa said with a wink. Arden rolled her eyes, ready to drag Emilie away and to her friends' table. Although Marty and Rebecca probably would be just as flirtatious…

Emilie frowned and looked into the distance as she probably ran through every line in every Shakespearean play. "It sounds familiar, so I think I've said the line before…" Her smile was sudden and bright, and Arden's arousal flared unexpectedly. She tried to turn her gasp into a more publicly acceptable sigh.

"*Much Ado About Nothing*. Beatrice would rather hear a dog barking at a crow than a man telling her...Oh, that's clever of you."

Lisa grinned and gestured toward the tap pulls. "What's your pleasure, my lady?"

Damn. Arden searched the room for her friends while Lisa poured an ale for Emilie. "C'mon, Em," she said. "We're over here."

She gave Emilie a little push toward the corner of the room and turned back to Lisa before following her. "Tone it down a little, okay?"

Lisa laughed and flicked her towel at Arden. "Can't take the competition?"

Arden shook her head. "We're just friends. I'm just trying to protect her from the local predators."

"But who will protect her from *you*?" Lisa called after her, hopefully not loud enough for Emilie to hear.

Arden caught up with Emilie and pointed out the table where her two friends were sitting. And arguing, from the looks of it. The three of them had grown up together, and Arden always took on the role of mediator between the other two.

"Hey. Marty, Rebecca, this is Emilie. She's new in town."

"New in town, in January," Marty said, pretending to be deep in thought. "Hmm, let me guess. You're a dry cleaner."

"Please," Rebecca scoffed, waving her hand. "Look at her. She's obviously here to sell shoes."

Emilie shook her head. "You're both wrong. I'm starting a new business in Ashland. The Bard's Doggy Daycare."

"I suppose you'll dress them in costumes and have them bark lines from the plays," Rebecca said with a laugh.

"Like *Antony and Cleopawtra*?" Emilie asked. "What a great idea!"

Marty handed Arden her beer and raised her own mug in a mock toast to Emilie. "Well, enjoy your last weeks of anonymity. Once the festival starts, you'll be a celebrity around here and won't be able to go out without people stopping you on the street and talking about the plays."

"Just like Hollywood," Arden said, taking a drink of beer. "Except this crowd takes their beloved Shakespeare seriously. Your fans are as likely to critique your performance as to ask for an autograph."

Everyone laughed except Emilie. "Seriously?"

Arden gave her shoulder a reassuring squeeze. At least she hoped it was reassuring for Emilie, because all it did for her was make the nerve endings in her hand flutter. "Don't worry. You'll be amazing, and they'll only have wonderful things to say about you. But in case anyone tries to give you acting notes, remember this line: Thank you for the advice, and I'll take it under consideration."

"And if they're too far out of line, say *unsolicited advice* instead," Rebecca said.

"With a pointed emphasis on the word *unsolicited*. And a glare," Marty added.

"So you've actually seen this happen to the actors in the festival?" All three nodded. "And do any of you take part in this informal criticism?"

"No, of course not," Marty said. "I mean, I'm sure you wouldn't possibly mess with the meter of the lines. That'd be the only reason I'd publicly humiliate you."

"And as long as your comedic timing is spot-on, which I'm sure it will be, then I won't say a peep," Rebecca said.

"Don't look at me." Arden raised her hands in a gesture of surrender when they all turned to look at her. "I've already seen Emilie perform on a stage of sorts. She was phenomenal, and I wouldn't dream of saying anything negative about her." She leaned toward Emilie and spoke in an exaggerated whisper. "As long as you work on your accent, of course."

Emilie laughed weakly and took a gulp of ale. "I guess as long as you don't heckle me from the audience, I can live with the rest. Oh, shit."

Her attention was caught by a group of people coming through the door. She waved when they spotted her.

"I'm going to go say hello before they come over," she said. "I've met them in rehearsals, but I only remember two of their names—I think—and I don't want to seem rude by not introducing them to you. I'll be right back."

"Really?" Marty said. "You can't remember five names, but you expect to memorize how many lines?"

"I have to revise my earlier statement," Rebecca said. "Put *forgetting her lines* in place of the comedic timing part."

"I'm going to gently set this beer on the table and not throw it at any of you," Emilie said, putting her mug down with deliberation. She got up, brushing against Arden's leg as she rose from the table, and walked toward the door. Arden watched her go, and then turned back to the table to see her friends staring at her with those annoying knowing looks they had perfected over the years.

"When we came over, you two seemed to be going at it. What's the argument this time?"

"The movie we saw last weekend," Rebecca said, her voice rising as she seemed ready to pounce back into the argument. "Remember the scene when the robot—"

"Don't let her distract you," Marty said with a shake of her head. "She's just trying to get us off the subject of Emilie and how she'll destroy Arden when the season is over and she goes away. Leaving us to pick up the broken pieces of our friend and to try to jigsaw them back together."

"We're just friends," Arden said, spinning her half-empty mug on the table. "She needs a break from the stress of the festival, and I volunteered."

"Uh-huh." Marty shook her head.

"Seriously. Just friends."

"Honey, we believe that part," Rebecca said, patting her knee. "Otherwise you wouldn't have brought her here to meet us."

Arden stared at her. "You've met women I've dated before."

"Yes, if we happened to run in to the two of you somewhere. But never like this." Marty gestured around the room. "Socially. Just for fun."

"Then why did you sound suspicious when I said we were friends?"

"Because it doesn't matter what the two of you are doing together in bed or out of it. What matters is how you feel about her."

Arden knew her friends would see right through her lie, but she felt compelled to protest anyway. "Nonsense. I don't feel anything different for her than I do for either of you."

"So you wouldn't mind if I asked her out?"

Arden glared at Rebecca. "Go right ahead. You won't survive until date night, though. Stop laughing, Marty. I'm just protecting Emilie."

Luckily, Emilie returned to the table then and ended that part of the conversation. At least Arden hoped her friends would drop it, although she couldn't be 100 percent sure.

"In case you forgot, I'm Arden." Marty pointed at herself, then Arden and Rebecca. "And this is Rebecca and Marty."

"Wait, let me write that down before I forget." Emilie rummaged in her bag and brought out a pencil and notebook. She pointed at Marty, then around the table, mimicking Marty's gesture perfectly. "Left to right, Smart Ass, Slightly Less Smart Ass, and Why Is She Friends With These Two?"

Arden laughed and clinked mugs with Emilie, ignoring the eloquent look her friends gave each other.

Chapter Seven

A rden came out of the maintenance shed with her lunch bag, looking for a quiet spot where she could eat, when she saw Emilie sitting outside waiting for her. She looked up and smiled broadly when she saw Arden, and Arden felt an answering grin start inside her and flow onto her face.

"Lunchtime?" Emilie asked with a hopeful tone in her voice.

"Yes, but I can't tell if you want my company or my food." Arden sat next to her on the bench.

"Mainly the first, although I wouldn't say no to the second." Emilie jostled Arden with her shoulder. "I'm between appointments and thought I'd see if you have a little time to spend with me. And I haven't eaten for hours."

She put a tragic emphasis on the last word, and Arden had to laugh as she pulled out a peanut butter and jelly sandwich and handed half to Emilie. Em took a huge bite while she watched Arden take cookies, a bag of chips, and an apple out of the bag and set them on a paper napkin.

"What, are you twelve?" Emilie asked, her voice thick with sticky peanut butter. She finished her half sandwich and took one of the cookies. Arden ate some of her own sandwich to occupy her mouth and keep herself from tasting Emilie.

Arden laughed. "It's easy to make. Tease all you want, you won't be able to come up with anything I haven't heard before from Jacob and the rest of them. I'm immune."

She took a bite of the apple and handed it to Emilie to share.

"So, are you adjusting to life in Ashland?" she asked, distracting herself from the sight of Emilie using her index finger to wipe juice from the apple off her chin.

Emilie shrugged. "The people in town seem very friendly," she said, obviously avoiding the topic of her company work. Arden didn't fight the direction of the conversation.

"It's a good place. Most everyone loves the festival because they appreciate the money it brings here every season." Arden crunched on a salty chip and amended what she had just said. "It's more than money, though. Ashland hosted Chautauqua lectures right here for over twenty years, so this town has a history of supporting education and culture, and we're proud of what happens here every year. It's like we've all had a hand in it."

Emilie nodded. "The plays are great, but you're right. Without the restaurants and the park and everything else there is to do here, Ashland wouldn't have nearly the same appeal to tourists." She looked around them, and Arden did the same, noticing the beautiful stone bridge and the ferns overhanging Ashland Creek. "This place is so peaceful and natural—it's the perfect backdrop to the plays."

Arden had always felt the same way, and she liked how Emilie had noticed it, too. "When did you eat last?" she asked as Emilie finished the last of the chips.

"This morning. My roommate likes the festival all right, but she has a rather unflattering view of actors in general. Today's breakfast conversation was all about the way narcissistic personality disorder runs rampant through the acting community."

Arden laughed and choked on a piece of apple. She swallowed and took a drink of water. "What did you say to her?"

"I said I couldn't talk about that because I was too busy planning my day and deciding what to wear, and did she think my hair looked better in a ponytail or hanging down, and did she want the privilege of hearing me run lines? At least she got my joke, and she said she'd stick to less hot-button topics in the future, like religion and politics. She's great, but I sometimes feel like a specimen in her lab more than a roommate."

Arden laughed, enjoying Emilie's wit. She let her mind wander to a fictional place where they could share wisecracks and serious conversation over breakfast with each other every morning. She only let the fantasy linger for seconds before stowing it away.

"Come here, and I'll show you the beginning of the festival," she said, packing up the waste from their lunch and stuffing it in the paper bag.

She led Emilie a few yards down the trail, and turned her so she was facing the Angus Bowmer Theatre and the Elizabethan Stage, both barely visible through the park's heavy foliage. She had her hands on Emilie's shoulders, but the feel of her was too nice, too tempting, and she let go. She stayed close behind her, though, speaking quietly in her ear.

"Angus Bowmer was an English professor at the college here. One day, he was standing close to this spot when he looked at what was left of the old Chautauqua dome and thought it resembled the curved walls of the Globe Theatre. He came up with the idea to stage some of Shakespeare's plays there, and Ashland gave him a chance to try. The festival lasted three days every year at first, and it grew into what you're taking part in today, with world premieres and almost ten months full of plays every season. You've seen the ivy-covered walls around the Elizabethan? Well, those are the old cement walls from the dome."

Emilie managed—somehow—to understand what Arden was saying to her and not to fixate on her nearness and the soft exhales that brushed against her skin. She had been focused on her own role in the company—she knew what Olivia would have to say about that—but Arden's description of the origin of the festival made her feel connected to a greater whole. Of course, that meant even more pressure on her to do well. Great.

Emilie watched Arden while she talked. Her words made the

claim that there was a strong connection between the townspeople and the festival, but her expression convinced Emilie of the truth. Neither the city nor the festival could be removed from this place without irreparably changing the other, and together they seemed to possess something resembling the notion of true love that Emilie had always believed in. Like family or lovers, they might have occasional squabbles and disagreements, but the underlying bond was unbreakable. Arden was part of the history of this place, relying on its revenue for her livelihood, its plays for entertainment, and its stars as her personal dating pool. She might have personal issues with actors who had a propensity to follow a nomadic lifestyle, but she saw the festival itself as something stable and deeply rooted in the community.

Arden cleared her throat and Emilie suddenly realized that Arden had been silent for a few minutes while Emilie stared at her and had disconcertingly envious thoughts about the type of relationship forged between the city and the festival, and—especially—between Arden and the beautiful actors she must have met along the way.

"So…" Emilie searched frantically for a question to ask that would redirect Arden's attention away from her heated face and onto some new topic. She looked around and saw the sign with its old-fashioned font advertising Ashland's water. "Why is it called Lithia Park? Is there really lithium in the drinking water? I haven't had anything but bottled water since I got here."

"Not here exactly," Arden said. She gestured for Emilie to come with her as she walked to the park's entrance. "Some people tried to turn Ashland into a health resort in the early 1900s to get back the tourist trade they'd lost after the Chautauqua ended, with mineral spas and delightfully lithium-rich water for sale. The town voted to tax itself and pipe water in from a spring that's a few miles away. The plan never came to much, but you can still try the water."

She stopped in front of a large rectangular concrete block, with stairs leading up to the white marble fountains. The contrast between the plain cement and the ornate drinking fountains was strange, and Emilie had avoided the monstrosity.

"It looks like a mausoleum," she said warily, not moving beyond the bottom of the steps. "That doesn't back up the whole healthy-water claim."

Arden looked at the fountain and shrugged. "Yeah, it's ugly as sin. But you can't truly be a part of Ashland until you've tasted the water."

Emilie sighed and walked up the two steps. "This feels like peer pressure," she said, poking a questioning finger into the stream of frothy water that was spewing out of a bronze ball-shaped spigot.

"Think of it as an initiation into an exclusive club," Arden suggested.

Emilie bent forward and merely let the fountain wet her lips, without taking an actual sip. She coughed and backed down the steps. "Ew, that's gross. It can't possibly be good for you."

"It's full of minerals, and you didn't even take a real drink," Arden said, laughing while Emilie wiped her mouth with her sleeve. She handed her a bottle of water. "Besides, the city removed the *Do not drink* signs a few weeks ago."

Emilie looked for signs that Arden was joking, but she looked serious. "What was wrong with it?"

Arden waved off her concern. "A little extra barium in the mix. But it's been tested and it's perfectly safe now." Arden stopped laughing and looked at her with a serious face. "I wouldn't have had you drink any if it was dangerous. I watch the city inspector do the tests every week. Think about it. You just tasted part of the history of Ashland, and that's pretty awesome."

"It is," Emilie conceded. "Disgusting, but slightly awesome."

Emilie still wanted a little payback, so when they skirted around the water fountain she quickly hopped up the two steps and caught a handful of water, flinging it at Arden. Arden shrieked in surprise and jumped aside before running to the far side of the fountain and splashing water toward Emilie in return. They jumped around, landing nothing more than droplets of water on each other, until Emilie remembered that she had Arden's water bottle in one hand still.

"Oh, no you don't!" Arden exclaimed, laughing and grabbing Emilie around the waist from behind and trying to grab the bottle.

Emilie was laughing too hard to be able to hold the bottle steady enough to fill. She held up her hands. "Truce?"

Arden had gotten hold of the top of the bottle while Emilie kept her grip on the bottom. "Truce," she agreed.

They both let go at the same time and the plastic bottle fell to the ground. Arden bent down to pick it up. When she stood again, she looked as composed as ever, although the corner of her mouth quirked as if she was holding back more laughter. "Shall we continue with our tour?" she asked formally.

"By all means," Emilie said with a little bow. She bumped Arden's shoulder as they walked. She hadn't laughed that hard since...well, she couldn't even remember. "What's our next stop?"

"Have you been to the old Black Swan Theatre yet? You'll probably be rehearsing there." Arden pointed in the general direction of the city, and they walked off the park grounds.

"I've seen it on my schedule, but I haven't been there yet." The out-of-shape laughter muscles in Emilie's face relaxed, and she had to fight the urge to lean against Arden as they walked. She brought out everything Emilie had thought was in hiding, too deep inside her to be found again. Emilie was happy to see the recurrence of joy and playfulness, but she kept a tight hold on the blossoming desire that threatened to break free along with them.

"I think I was going to audition there, but it was closed for repairs. Poisonous gas leaks, perhaps? Or a plague of bedbugs in the upholstery? This town seems fraught with danger."

Arden beat her chest with her fist. "A little barium now and then keeps you strong," she said with a laugh. "And the theater was closed last year because they were renovating the basement, but they're finished now. It's used for storage and offices, besides the rehearsals."

They stopped in front of the large picture window with the building's name printed in elegant black letters on the glass. Arden cupped her hands and peered inside. "The Swan was a black-box theater. Tiny and intimate as hell—the audience was practically part of the cast. You could see the actors spit when they enunciated, my gramps used to say."

Emilie looked inside with interest, but all she could see was a foyer decorated in pale blues and stark whites, a sharp contrast to the type of theater it had once held. She had never performed on that sort of stage before. "Did you ever see a play here?"

"Yes," Arden said, with excitement clearly expressed in her voice. "The Thomas Theatre replaced it in 2002, but I saw a few productions here, including an amazing version of *Macbeth*. My grandfather and I made a diorama of it together for my English class at school. How nerdy does that sound?"

"Perfectly nerdy," Emilie said with a grin, picturing a younger Arden and her grandfather working together on the stage. She had some good memories from her own childhood, but none like that. None that had shaped her in such a positive way as Arden's grandparents had seemed to have done. "Do you still have it? I want to see."

Arden started walking again, covering the short distance back to the park with her long steps, her arms gesturing as she talked. "I think it's in the attic, but I'm not sure where. The set was simple, with only a few pieces of rough-hewn rock, but the way the lighting was arranged made the shadows fill in the empty places, giving the illusion of walls and towers, or of battle encampments. It was brilliant. Someday I'll take you to see some photos they have in the festival's archives."

They stopped near the water fountain. "Well, my lunch hour, and therefore our tour, has come to an end."

Emilie smiled and softly touched Arden's arm, barely moving

the fabric of her shirt. "Thank you for showing me around. And for making me drink the Kool-Aid…I mean, the water."

"You're one of us now," Arden intoned in a deep voice. "You will await our instructions."

"I will obey," Emilie said, with equal somberness. She was kidding. Really, she was. Sort of.

Arden winked at Emilie and turned away, walking farther into the park while Emilie turned toward the steps leading to the festival. Back to their normal lives. Emilie turned once and looked back, catching Arden just as she glanced over her shoulder and toward Emilie. Emilie jogged up the steps, but she knew she'd be back. She couldn't resist the way she felt when she was around Arden. She'd visit her again, looking for companionship and a break from the hectic theater life. And nothing more.

CHAPTER EIGHT

Emilie hugged a pillow over her head, trying to squeeze in a few more minutes of sleep before she had to face the day. Her schedule was skewed toward evening, with some of her rehearsals lasting late into the night, but her roommates only seemed to have a four-hour window of sleep most nights. They were up late studying or hanging out with friends, then up early for class.

Other than the noise associated with her ground-floor room, Emilie was content with her living arrangements. She had a little oasis here, far from the world of the festival. Her housemates were friendly enough, and Steph had finally stopped examining every item Emilie pulled out of the fridge to make sure it wasn't something of hers. Mary was quiet to the extreme, and she and Emilie had once sat at the dining room table and worked on a puzzle together without saying a word for 126 minutes. Emilie had kept track. She could have broken the silence herself, but after a half hour of not speaking, it had seemed weird to suddenly ask about Mary's day or comment on the weather. She had come to find Mary's company soothing, since absolutely nothing was expected of her when they were together.

Olivia continued to ask probing, personal questions. Emilie answered when she could, and took the Mary approach and remained silent when she wasn't comfortable with a line of inquiry. Olivia had no qualms about delving into every aspect of Emilie's childhood in her attempt to discover the deep psychological reasons behind Emilie's desire to become an actor. If she'd only listen, Emilie could tell her exactly why, but the reality didn't make as exciting a thesis as Olivia was apparently seeking. The truth was, Emilie's childhood had been fine. Boringly, blandly fine. Emilie's first role in a play—as Peter Pan in a disastrous grade-school production—had given her a taste of the other possible worlds and emotions.

The back door slammed shut, and Emilie tossed her pillow to the side. She stretched her arms over her head, arching her back and easing the stiffness out of her muscles. Long days and lots of sitting cross-legged on the stage were taking their toll on her lower back. She sighed and rolled off the bed. She was due at the theater in a little over an hour. Time to start the day.

Emilie took a quick shower, and then filled her travel mug with coffee. As different as she and her roommates were, their trajectories all converged at the coffeepot. Emilie had a feeling she would be forgiven for not paying her rent on time, but if she forgot to contribute to the caffeine fund, she'd be on the curb with all her belongings before anyone could say, *We're out of cream*. The pot was huge, and always full of fresh coffee. Emilie peeked inside to make sure she didn't need to start more brewing before she left, but it was over half full. She carefully twisted on the lid to her mug and walked out the door.

She stood on the front porch for a moment to get her bearings. The shift from being safely tucked inside her house and becoming her outside, public self was always jarring. She had thought her trepidation about returning to acting would ease once she had been to a few rehearsals, but it was only getting worse. And once she had to go onstage…well, she was familiar enough with her stage fright to know what to expect then. She'd have a brief respite while she was in front of an audience, but then she'd be sick and shaking again before the next performance. Sadly, all of her time with the company in Ashland seemed to be an extended version of her pre-performance anxiety.

This house was her only place of solace. Well, the house and Lithia Park. She forced herself to walk off the porch and toward the main part of town, and the only thing keeping one foot moving after the other was the thought that she'd have a break between rehearsals today. She'd have a chance to get to the park, surround herself with growing things, and clear her head. Something about being around trees and plants was very soothing.

Of course, it had nothing to do with Arden.

Emilie walked a little faster along the sidewalk. She had been visiting Arden almost daily for over a week now. They hadn't been out again, but she would trail after Arden while she tended her plants and listen to her talk about them. They managed to keep the conversation away from most topics that were more personal than a preference for flower colors—Emilie liked purple ones, and Arden preferred a soft, peachy kind of orange. Arden occasionally talked about her grandfather, though, and Emilie realized it was because she saw him in every inch of the park. Arden couldn't talk about it without bringing him up.

Emilie wanted to ask more. About Arden's mysterious parents and her personal hopes and dreams, but then she'd be opening a door she wouldn't have the strength to shut again. Plus, she'd be expected to respond in turn to questions about herself and her concerns about her career, and she wasn't ready for that either. Arden always asked about her rehearsals, and Emilie always answered with some version of the word *fine*. And changed the subject by asking about aphids or slugs or some other impersonal, nonromantic subject.

Their casual conversations didn't keep Emilie's mind from wandering off-topic, though, and onto the way Arden's delicate hands gently cradled flower buds when she talked about them, or the way her shirt would slide up and reveal her slender waist and incredibly sexy abs when she reached up to trim a high branch... Emilie was just managing to keep her thoughts and hands to herself during those tempting moments, and she'd clear her throat and ask about some plant that happened to be nearby.

Emilie pushed through the glass door of the Thomas Theatre, where her first rehearsal of the day would be held. If she were feeling more secure in the company, she'd most likely toss aside her determination to remain unattached and take a chance with Arden. But she was on shaky footing here. Her moments playing Titania weren't disastrous, but they also were fairly bland. She knew the director expected more from her, and she felt the same way. She hadn't been able to recapture the transfixed feeling she'd had when Arden had caught her playing the role alone in the woods.

Emilie joined the rest of the cast onstage. The mostly black interior of the space, combined with the arrangement of the seats, made the theater seem very intimate. She looked around, imagining an audience of three hundred or so people filling the teal and wood seats. They would be very close. Emilie closed her eyes, trying to get back to the present, but her mind continued to spin. Right now, they were rehearsing while the stage crews erected the sets for *King Lear*. The stage was set in the three-quarter thrust configuration, with audience members on three sides, but for her play, *Skywriting*, the theater would be changed to an arena. The stage would be in the center, completely surrounded by the public. All entrances and exits, as well as some scenes, would take place on the aisles. Close enough for people to touch her. Or easily hit their intended target with a rotten tomato.

"Okay, people. Act two, scene one. Emilie, let's start with you."

Emilie put aside her concerns about being pelted with decaying fruit and concentrated instead on the more immediate worry about playing Cassella. She didn't seem to have a good grasp of this complex character, even after reading the book and studying the script until her head ached. She had been an understudy before, in high school, but then the job had consisted of watching the others rehearse and being ready with her lines in case she had to step in. Here, she was onstage during rehearsals nearly as often as the lead actor, Gemini. And the director had no qualms about reminding her almost daily that being an understudy didn't necessarily mean she had the part if Gemini—no last name, she was that big a star—couldn't do it. She'd go on if Gem was ill, but if she needed to be replaced entirely, it might not be with Emilie. Personally, Emilie would have been happy to have another actor take over, since she couldn't connect with the character. But professionally, being kept in the understudy role while another actor was hired to play the part would be damaging to her future.

She walked over to her first mark and took a deep breath, mentally reviewing the scene and the notes she had been given by Jay and the director the last time she had spoken these lines. Her best hope was that Gemini would play the part as scheduled, and Emilie would be a dutifully prepared, but never needed, understudy.

She launched into her first lines, already sensing the awkwardness of her portrayal of Cassella, and tried to silence her jeering internal critic. She'd be more relaxed if Geoffrey hadn't shared the rampant rumor that Gem had been offered some other role, in some unspecified South American country, and that her agent and a posse of lawyers were trying to break her out of this contract. It all sounded too dramatic and strange to be true, but too often, those unbelievable stories turned out to be fact.

Emilie managed to get through her rehearsal without calling too much attention to herself. She knew her lines and understood the emotions the director wanted from her in every scene. But it wasn't enough to be invisible and okay. She needed to stand out—in a good way—or she wouldn't be acting after this season.

She felt deflated by her mediocrity as she walked down the brick staircase and into the park. The large Elizabethan theater loomed above her, and she found its presence somewhat comforting. Inside those brown-beamed and whitewashed walls, she would be playing Titania on a more familiar type of stage, with the audience a decent distance away. She had been doing well in those rehearsals. Good enough, at least. She'd be fine. Really…

Emilie crossed one of the stone bridges and saw Jacob farther down the path. He gestured toward the Japanese garden, and Emilie waved her thanks. She was already breathing a bit easier here, with the damp and bracing wind blowing through the trees and washing away the day. She passed beneath the torii gate and saw Arden crouched on the ground near the maples.

"Hello, Mr. Philips," Emilie said quietly, greeting Arden's grandfather the way she had overheard Arden do one day when she didn't realize Emilie was nearby. She walked down the path and knelt by Arden. "Hi."

"Hey, Em. I wasn't sure if I'd see you today." Arden smiled at her, and Emilie felt the weight of the day lift as suddenly as if Arden had shoved it off her shoulders.

"I have an hour between rehearsals. Do you need help pulling those weeds?"

Arden laughed. "I'm putting them in, not pulling them out. But thanks, anyway."

"Ah. On-purpose plants. I still don't know how you can tell the difference. They're all green with leaves."

Arden looked ready to begin a plants-versus-weeds lecture, until she seemed to notice Emilie's smile. She shook her head. "Funny. We lost some of the ground cover in this section, so I'm replacing it with woolly thyme."

She handed Emilie a tiny plant and she ran her fingers over the soft leaves. "Well named," she said, popping the plant out of its fiber pot and sticking it in one of the holes Arden had already made. She pressed the soft dirt around it, covering its roots and anchoring it in the ground. She had never thought of herself as an outdoorsy person until coming here, but now she understood why people were drawn to gardening as a hobby. The feel of soil under her fingernails and the coolness of the earth were grounding, and she loved the idea of watching the plants grow over the coming months. Her life was ephemeral and hard to grasp right now, with elusive roles and subjective performance standards. But being here with Arden centered her. Everything was physical, from the texture of the shrubs and flowers to the feeling she got deep in her belly when she saw Arden smile or laugh.

"How have rehearsals been going?" Arden asked.

Emilie frowned. This was usually where she said something vague and changed the subject, but today she couldn't do it. "They suck. I suck," she said instead.

Arden started to laugh, but then she looked at Emilie's face and stopped. She sat back on her heels. "I thought everything was fine. What happened today?"

Emilie shook her head. "Today and every day. I'm not really measuring up."

"You've only been in rehearsal for two weeks, Em. You're learning the parts and figuring out what the directors want. You can't expect to be perfect this early in the process, and no one else should expect it of you."

Emilie bit her lip. Part of her knew Arden was right, and that she was new to the company and rusty after years away from acting. And nervous because her future depended on her performance at the festival. But part of her was angry, too. Not at Arden—even though Emilie felt the ridiculous urge to lash out at her for being so practical and *right*. No, she was angry at herself because she could feel her desire to run away. Give up. Latch on to Arden or anyone who would be kind to her and give her a way out.

Arden was watching her with one of her inscrutable expressions. "What?" Emilie asked, with a sharpness to her voice. "Sorry. I'm frustrated."

"I can tell." Arden nodded. She looked around the garden and then pointed toward her grandfather's fountain. "Stand over there, right at the bend of the first trough."

Emilie sighed but had to roll her eyes at how melodramatic she sounded. "All right. But why? Are you just trying to distract me so I stop whining?"

"A little. But I need help with something, and it'll give you a chance to practice some lines. I'll be brutally honest and tell you if you really do suck."

"How sweet." Emilie walked over to the place where Arden wanted her. Somehow, her irritation was seeping away. "Okay, I'm here. Now what?"

Arden tilted her head to one side. "Move to the right about a foot. That's better. Now, be Lady Anne."

Emilie looked around. The peace of the Japanese garden was directly opposed to the turmoil in Anne's life, but somehow it captured the character's strength and grace. She closed her eyes and took a deep breath before speaking Anne's opening lines. When she finished with the monologue, it took her a few seconds to return to her own body.

"Um, that was..." Arden visibly swallowed, and turned away. "That was great, Em," she said over her shoulder. "Now come over here."

Emilie followed her down the path and to one of the duck ponds. She was dazed from the sensation of allowing another personality to inhabit her body, and almost gasping with relief that she was still capable of acting as deeply as she just had. She hadn't been anywhere near this feeling since she had started rehearsals.

"Right here. Near those stones." Arden gestured toward a flat place near the pond. Ducks waddled out of the way and dropped into the pond with small splashes when Emilie invaded their space. "Good. Now be Titania."

The setting wasn't the same as the hidden forest lair she had found before, but Emilie pretended the ducks and the family walking along the path were her fairy entourage, and she moved as easily into this part as she had with Lady Anne. She should have felt more self-conscious since Arden was watching her with such an intense gaze, but instead she felt as if she was slipping on a bodysuit and becoming someone else.

When she finished the monologue she had chosen, she barely registered the applause of the family that had apparently stopped to listen to her. All she could see was Arden's beautiful smile. She nodded her thanks at the couple and their little girl, and turned back to Arden as they walked away.

"You're amazing, Em," Arden said. "Even if you really are having trouble in rehearsals right now, once you're onstage you are going to be spectacular."

Emilie tried to read the emotions she saw on Arden's face, but they shifted too quickly for her to identify them. Arden meant what she was saying, and she honestly seemed happy for Emilie, but there was something else there, too. Something sad, or lonely. Similar to the way Arden looked on the rare occasions when she talked about her grandfather and her parents.

Emilie gave up. Arden was in control again, and watching her with an unruffled expression, so Emilie was left with her own conflicting emotions. She was elated because she had enjoyed acting again for a brief time, but uncertain whether she could replicate the experience when it mattered. Something about this park, about Arden, put her at ease. Even though she worried about the temptation Arden represented and the threat to her focus—especially when she was weakened by self-doubt—Arden somehow helped her become more herself. Emilie seemed to need Arden as much as she needed to protect herself against Arden's allure.

"I'd like to do more of this, whatever we're doing, but I need to get to my next rehearsal."

Arden gave Emilie's hand a quick squeeze, then dropped the contact. "I think I got what I needed. I hope you did, too."

Emilie smiled with what she hoped looked like breezy confidence. "I guess I'll find out in a few minutes," she said before she walked out of the park and back to the theater.

Arden watched Emilie until she disappeared behind a Sitka

spruce whose branches were reaching across the path leading from the pond to the brick staircase. She took her pruning shears and trimmed a few of the evergreen's offending limbs, releasing a bitter scent with each cut. The young cones were still smooth, but would soon grow dry and rough with seeds. Arden was in the habit of collecting cones and leaves and other items to have on hand when she led tours for schoolchildren through the park, and she plucked a few of them off the branches and put them in her pocket while she reenacted Emilie's performances in her mind.

Arden carried her armload of branches back to the maintenance shed and tossed them on the mulch pile. She had asked Emilie to play some scenes because she had wanted to help her regain the air of spontaneity that had shimmered around her when she had played Titania in the grove. Arden had thought the game would make Emilie smile and have fun with her acting, because she didn't seem to be enjoying her rehearsals so far. Plus, Arden had wanted to see someone acting in the natural environment of the park to determine how engaging the experience would be. The family watching Emilie had certainly seemed fascinated by her performance, and Arden—well, she had been mesmerized.

And torn. Emilie was beautiful to watch when she let herself get lost in a part. Arden would never allow herself to wish anything less for Emilie than the success she deserved, but she had witnessed talent from the outside for as long as she had been alive, from her mother to the company women she had dated. She knew what happened next.

Arden pushed the thought out of her mind as she went into the shed and used a heavily citrus-scented cleanser to wash the pitch off her shears. Even though Arden couldn't fully ignore the likely course of Emilie's career and the places where it would take her—away from Ashland and Arden—she still felt a thrill when Emilie became her characters. Arden had almost forgotten her original intent for the experiment, but not quite. She rinsed her hands and sat at the table, pulling out her sketchbook and using the movement of her pencil on the rough paper to refocus her mind onto the lines of her drawings and off the now-familiar curves of Emilie's body. The way she moved into an acting role with the grace and fluidity of someone passing through a membrane and into another world. The way her hands expressed meaning with a surety that Arden could almost feel against her skin...

The pencil lead snapped, and Arden pulled out her utility knife with a sigh and whittled it to a sharp point again. She erased the dark flecks from the paper and determined to capture her ideas on paper while she still had at least a little control over her wandering thoughts.

Chapter Nine

Arden sat on a bench next to the park's main path and flipped nervously through her notebook. She had finally brought her sketches to show Jacob, but even now she was hesitant to reveal them.

She wasn't worried about his reaction to her idea of incorporating small stage settings in the park. She knew it was a good one, and that tourists and locals would love the miniature tableaux. This was exactly the type of novel inspiration Jacob had been asking for—as opposed to the gnome theater she had jokingly proposed to him the week before, complete with drawings. He hadn't been amused.

Arden set the notebook on the bench next to her and then picked it up again and thumbed through it. She wasn't sure why she was so reluctant to share her plans. Maybe because she had never considered herself to be either ambitious or particularly passionate about her work. Ambition left town and passion broke hearts. Arden knew that all too well. Whatever the reason, Arden hadn't even told Emilie what she was working on these days, and Em had been the one to provide the original seed for Arden's vision. First as Titania, alone in the woods, and then when she had followed Arden's directions and brought several characters to life among the park's plants and water features. Arden had been partially convinced of the validity of her idea when she saw the family stop to watch Emilie perform, but mostly she had been sold on it by Emilie herself.

Arden sighed audibly when she remembered how Emilie had looked that day. Slipping in and out of different personae with ease, blending art and nature in an organic way. Looking so alive and beautiful that Arden had been forced to pick up a pencil and occupy her hands with sketches because they were almost aching with a need to touch. She had let her fingers trace the curves and planes that formed Emilie, but only through the media of lead and paper.

As if conjured by her thoughts, Emilie was walking down the trail toward her. Arden put the notebook down again and rose to meet her. Emilie's face still showed signs of garish stage makeup, and her thick blond hair was loose and heavily curled. Arden's heart jumped at the sight of Emilie's welcoming smile, but she had to remind herself that Emilie liked being around her because she was a safe place, a refuge from the stressful theater world. Still, Arden felt her muscles stretch into an involuntary grin in response.

"Hey, Em," Arden said. Once Emilie was close enough, she reached out and twisted a lock of Emilie's hair around her finger. When she pulled back, the curl bounced like a released spring. "You look pretty wild for a young maiden."

"I know," Emilie said, with the wide eyes and naïve look that Arden had come to associate with her portrayal of Anne Page. "Mama and Daddy would be shocked if they could see me. I'd be locked in the tower for *days*." She flipped back to her normal Emilie expression. "I might have to submerge my head in the duck pond so I can get it under control again. Those braids are so tight, my hair practically explodes when I take them out."

"How was the dress rehearsal? Did you ever figure out the artistic reasons behind the whole flapper, gangster setting?"

Emilie shook her head and ran her fingers through her hair, unsnarling some of the tangles. "No. The director tried to explain his vision, but it didn't make much sense. I think he likes to imagine himself as a mobster from the Twenties, and he's forcing Shakespeare's play into his fantasy world. He even takes on an accent when he's giving us directions. "You go stage left, see, and meet Legs by the fountain."

Arden laughed at Emilie's exaggerated gangster voice. "I take it you're Legs?"

Emilie smiled and sat on the bench. "Hardly. He calls me Dollface sometimes, but the guy who plays Fenton is Legs. He has decent ones, I guess," she added with a shrug. "And the rehearsal went well enough. I don't get the reason behind this time period, but the costumes are fabulous and I think the audience will like it. I hardly have any lines, so I spend most of my time thinking young and virginal thoughts."

"Huh. I don't have any of those." Arden sat next to Emilie and casually moved the notebook to her other side.

Emilie propped her elbow on the back of the bench and grinned at Arden. "Maybe someday you can tell me about the old, nonvirginal thoughts you're having. But for now, I'll settle for hearing about the notebook you're trying to hide from me."

Arden hesitated, but finally handed it to Emilie. She suffered from self-doubt and stage fright. If anyone understood Arden's uncertainty, it would be Emilie.

"It's an idea I wanted to show Jacob. You know he's been after me to contribute to the park in some way, and I came up with this after watching you rehearse out here."

"The gnomes were a no-go?" Emilie asked, not looking up from Arden's drawings.

"He accused me of being facetious. Can you imagine? I tried to convince him I was deadly serious—I don't joke when it comes to garden statuettes."

Emilie met her gaze and smiled. "Did he really use the word *facetious*? I can't picture him saying that."

"Well, I think the exact phrase was *smart-ass*. But you get the point."

Emilie gave her back the notebook. "This is brilliant. Why haven't you shown him yet?"

"I don't know," Arden said, avoiding eye contact with Emilie. She still hadn't figured out her reasons in her own mind, so they were hard to explain to someone else. Hopefully, Emilie would get what she was trying to say. "It's really not my thing. I take care of plants and pull weeds. I don't need to do more."

"That doesn't make any sense." Emilie poked her thigh. "You're all dressed up, and you have a great idea."

Arden squirmed. "I'm not dressed up," she protested, even though she had spent more than her usual thirty seconds choosing what to wear this morning.

"Yes, you are. Nothing you're wearing has holes in it, and I can't see—" Emilie paused and cleared her throat. "Usually I can see skin. So what are you afraid of? You know Jacob will be all over this idea."

"Yeah, but…"

"What's the worst that will happen? This will be a big hit in the park, and you'll have more opportunities to use your landscape design degree?"

"I thought you'd be more compassionate." Arden leaned forward and rested her elbows on her knees. How had she misread Emilie like this? "Like I try to be when you say rehearsals aren't going well."

Emilie crossed her arms over her chest. "I'd be compassionate if I thought that was what you needed. And when I whine about rehearsals, you never tell me to give up. You listen, and then you get me to read lines for you. Or you make jokes that lighten my mood." Arden wasn't sure if she heard frustration or anger in Emilie's voice, but she settled on anger when Emilie kicked her foot sideways and caught Arden in the calf. Not really hard, but…

"Ouch."

Emilie continued as if she hadn't heard her. "And if I told you I was quitting, you'd talk me out of it because you know how much it means to me to have a second chance with my acting."

Arden tried to come up with a reply, but Emilie was right. Still, their circumstances were different. Emilie was following a dream. Arden was doing a job.

Emilie poked her in the ribs. "There he is. You go talk to him, and I'll hide."

"Ouch," Arden said again, rubbing her side, but Emilie had already moved to the other side of the path and was standing behind a huge Douglas fir. She got up and walked over to the maintenance shack, where Jacob was standing next to his Mule.

"Hello, Arden," he said. He raised his voice slightly and added, "Hi, Emilie."

Emilie's arm appeared from behind the trunk and waved in their general direction before it disappeared again, leaving only a few inches of her red sweatshirt showing. Arden rolled her eyes. Apparently Em hadn't played much hide-and-seek as a child.

"What's up, Little Philips?"

"I have something to show you," Arden said, gesturing with the notebook. He looked about to protest, so she hurried to continue. "Not a joke this time. A serious idea."

"Let's see what you've got, then." He took the notebook and set it on the driver's seat of the small utility vehicle, opening to the first drawing.

"I was thinking we could make small stages and put them around the park. See, this one is Tudor inspired, but we could also make some that represent different settings, like a garden or the inside of a house. We could ask some of the company members to show up and do impromptu rehearsals every once in a while, but anyone could have a chance to be onstage."

Arden flipped to another page, losing herself in the concept. She could almost feel the excitement of park goers who might stumble across a spontaneous performance, and tourists who were inspired by watching a play and who wanted to take part in the festival in their own way.

"We'd make weatherproof boxes and fill them with scripts. Short monologues and scenes that fit the settings. Everyone who walks through the park will have a chance to playact if they want to."

Jacob was nodding while she spoke. "I'll bet some local high school and college drama students would be happy to stop by as well. You'll turn the entire park into a living theater." He looked up from the drawing of a minimalist stage in the corner of the Japanese garden. "Your grandfather would be proud, Arden. These drawings are beautiful, and each stage you've designed honors the part of the park you've chosen for it. See? I knew you had serious talent you were hiding in there."

He poked a finger against her breastbone, and Arden frowned. Why was everyone jabbing at her today? "Well, I'm glad you like it."

"I love it." He held up the notebook. "I'll get permission from the board, but you go ahead and start getting the materials you need. Start with the six you have in here, and be thinking of more."

Arden nodded and stepped back as he got in the Mule and drove down the path, waving at Emilie again as he went past her. She came out from behind the tree and walked over to Arden.

"That went well! I couldn't hear what he said, but he looked impressed. We'll have to play a scene together to christen the first stage you make. When do you start?"

"Right away, I guess," Arden said. She felt confused. She was excited about the project, and knew it would be a perfect fit for the town, the park, and the festival. But she felt kind of sick at the same time.

"Walk with me," Emilie said, linking her arm through Arden's and heading deeper into the park.

"You're demanding today," Arden said, but she laughed and leaned toward Emilie. Her nearness was calming, and eased some of Arden's conflicting feelings.

"You needed it. But now that I forced you to talk to Jacob, I can be the compassionate listener you wanted me to be. You have the same nauseated look I always see on my face in the mirror after I've been onstage. Hyped up, but strangely let down at the same time. Why was this so hard for you to do?"

Arden sighed. Was she glad Emilie had pushed her, or would she have been happier going on as she always had? Maybe a little of both.

"I told you my grandparents raised me, but I never really told you why. Have you heard of Rose Canton?"

Emilie made a scoffing laugh. "Of course. Who hasn't? I saw her in New York once, and it was amazing. She was acting in…Oh. She's your mom?"

"She played the part for a brief period. Then she moved on to bigger roles."

Emilie came to a halt, pulling Arden around until they were facing each other. Standing so close. Arden clenched her fists to keep from closing the short distance between them and stroking Emilie's concerned-looking face.

"And your father? Don't tell me. Harrison Ford?"

Arden had to smile. "No. He's a director, not an actor. He was with the company here when they met. Brent Philips."

"Almost as much of a legend," Emilie said with a shake of her head. She still had her arm entwined with Arden's, and she rested her other hand on Arden's shoulder. "When did they leave?"

Arden stopped the nearly involuntary shrug she always used when talking about her parents—as if to prove that their departure meant nothing to her—because she didn't want to make Emilie move her hand away. "I was four. According to my grandparents, they were going to take me with them, but Gramps convinced them to let me stay where I'd have a real home and could go to school." Arden looked over Emilie's shoulder, focusing on a dogwood behind her that needed pruning. "Of course, I've never been certain if that was true or just something they told me to make it seem like my parents still wanted me. However it happened, leaving me here was probably the most unselfish selfish thing they could have done."

Emilie stared at her with a sad expression, and Arden marveled again that even though it was easy for Em to become another character, when she was being herself she was somehow completely without artifice.

"I thought when you talked about actors leaving, you just meant women you'd dated. And you seemed so relieved when we decided to just be friends. I didn't realize…"

"I didn't tell you." Arden finished her sentence. "How would you have known? The other women are reminders, I guess, especially since I seem compelled to reprise my parents' departure scene every few years or so. You and I are just friends, so this time I won't get hurt when the season ends."

Lie. Arden decided she might have some of her mom's acting talent stashed away in a gene somewhere because Emilie didn't call her on the obvious falsehood.

"But you still seem to love the festival, even though it must be a reminder, too."

Arden started walking again, tugging Emilie with her. "My grandparents loved the theater. They shared their passion with me and taught me to appreciate the plays we saw together, and I feel close to them every time I attend a performance. Besides, I owe my existence to the festival. I can't really hate the thing that brought my parents together."

"But you can hate the profession that took them away from you. *My* profession."

Arden bent over to pick up a fallen branch without releasing Emilie's arm. "Hate is too strong a word. Mistrust might be better. Or maybe I just understand all too well what kind of sacrifices someone might make for an acting career."

"And so you don't want to make the same choices in your own career and make ambition a priority."

"Exactly," Arden said with satisfaction. She was relieved that Emilie finally understood.

"But I don't see how it's the same thing at all. You're just—"

Arden stiffened. "Just a gardener? Nothing to compare with an actor?" The words were as chilling as a dip in Ashland Creek.

"That is not what I meant," Emilie said sternly, shaking Arden's arm as if she wanted to jostle the tension out of her. "I meant, you're just *you*. Single, without kids. You can decide to take a job designing gardens at the White House, and you wouldn't be leaving anyone behind. Arden, most people who move because of their jobs don't leave their children behind. You would never do that—you'd take your family with you."

Arden didn't even have to pause and think. Emilie was right—she'd sacrifice any career aspirations for a child or a partner. She even did so for the child she used to be, even though it wasn't logical at all.

"No. I'd stay in one place with my family. It wouldn't be fair to make anyone move because of me." She saw that Emilie was about to protest, but she continued. "You know better than I do, Em, how hard it is to give up your life to feed someone else's dreams."

Emilie closed her mouth. "Touché," she said after a few moments of silence. "I guess we can agree that it's a bad idea to date an actor, but it's okay to be one."

"Or a landscape designer with her sights set on turning the White House lawn into a mock representation of the Senate. With gnomes."

Emilie laughed. "Well, we're lucky we didn't get involved with each other, aren't we?"

Arden gave in to temptation and brushed her thumb over Emilie's lips, still reddened from stage lipstick. "Lucky. Yeah, that's exactly the word I was thinking."

They sighed in unison, and Arden smiled. At least she wasn't the only one who was wanting more, even though *more* would only cause them pain. She started moving again, with Emilie at her side. She'd take the companionship Em willingly offered, and keep her heart safe.

CHAPTER TEN

Emilie squeezed through a crowd of actors when her name was called and sat in a reclining black leather chair in front of a brightly lit makeup mirror. The seat was narrow, and she was hemmed in on either side by various company members. Fairies and royalty from her play intermingled with Roman guards and senators from *Julius Caesar*, which was being performed simultaneously in the Angus Bowmer Theatre. Emilie wouldn't perform there until *Richard III*. Tonight she'd be on the open Elizabethan stage, and she hoped the rain wouldn't wash off all the makeup they were about to put on her. She tucked her backpack between her knees and leaned back when directed to.

She had survived two of her three February premieres so far. She had spent most of the time before *Merry Wives* lurking near the bathroom in case she had to throw up, but she had managed to get through the night without any major problems. Her performance surely hadn't inspired critical acclaim, but she had few lines to say and not much stage time. She wasn't expecting that play to be her ticket to stardom, and she was happy to have the lower-stress show as a counterbalance to the others. Titania and Lady Anne were her most promising roles. They were solid tests of her acting skills, and good performances in both plays should lead to meatier roles in the future. Cassella would have given her a chance to make a huge splash, but she would also have had a chance to be an enormous flop.

She closed her eyes while Betsy, one of the makeup artists, stretched the bald cap over her tightly bound hair and then applied the foam latex prosthetic that emphasized her cheekbones and sharpened her features to an elf-like delicacy. Contrary to the rumor mill, Gemini hadn't deserted the company, and Emilie had hovered backstage as understudy while Gem and the cast performed *Skywriting* to perfection. The reviews had been dazzling, and Emilie wasn't sure whether she felt more relief because she hadn't been pushed into the challenging role or more sadness because she hadn't had the chance to shine. She wanted to believe that she would have been just as good or better in the role, but she couldn't quite convince herself of the fact. Especially given the feedback she had received during rehearsals.

Arden had been to both performances, and she would be here tonight as well. Emilie fought to keep her face still while Betsy put on her makeup, but the memory of Arden's reactions to her performances made her want to smile. She had been effusive in her praise of each word Emilie had spoken as Anne Page and had shrugged off the performance of *Skywriting* as if it had been nothing more exciting than a grade-school play. Emilie had identified that trait in Arden—she was fiercely loyal to the people and places closest to her. The memory of her grandparents, Lithia Park, her close friends. Emilie was surprised to see evidence of her inclusion on Arden's roster of important things, and she attributed the warm glow she felt inside to her long hiatus without support and true companionship. And gratitude because Arden hadn't rejected her offer of friendship and never pushed for anything more.

Although Emilie had to admit she wouldn't mind if Arden pushed a little. There were plenty of times these days when Emilie would be willing to say yes.

She tried to keep her attention on the sensations she was feeling now and not the imagined ones that Arden would surely evoke in her. She stayed in the present and felt her skin being pushed and pulled in different directions as the soft pinkish base coat was smeared over her face and neck, blending the prosthetic until it became part of her. When she opened her eyes and looked in the mirror, she saw herself transformed from mere mortal into a fairy queen. Glittery, pale makeup highlighted the planes of her cheeks and forehead, while tones of blue and purple were expertly added to the shadows on her face.

"Look up," ordered Betsy. Emilie did, trying not to blink while one-inch long, bright blue false eyelashes were glued to her lids. As soon as Betsy was finished with her, she was scooted along the assembly line where a cast of her own head sat on a shelf, wearing a disturbingly serene expression, especially considering how claustrophobic she had felt while making the mold.

She turned away from her doppelganger while one of the wig makers lifted the mass of curls off her decapitated self and stretched it over her scalp. It was surprisingly light and easy to wear, even though the wig was thick with intricately woven hair, pearls, and flowers. The edges were glued down and covered with foundation, and she was ready for wardrobe.

A thin film of gauzy lilac fabric flowing over a green catsuit was the extent of Emilie's clothing. She had costume changes, but each was a variation on this outfit. She looked around the room at the rest of the cast. Arden had told Emilie about her first experience with this play, and Emilie was sure this evening was going to be bittersweet for her. The costumes and set were as magical and glittery as the ones Arden had described from her childhood, and the play was going to bring back memories of being at the theater when her grandparents were alive. Emilie was torn between feeling grateful that she would help recreate that night for Arden onstage and wishing she was going to be sitting in the audience with her instead, supporting her through whatever emotions arose.

The actors who would be first to go onstage were slowly filing out of the green room, opening up more space in the cramped room. She knew some of the other actors felt confined in the underground tunnels, with their cinder block walls and low ceilings, but Emilie was comforted by the crush of people and the enclosed space. Upstairs on the open stage—that's where she would experience the painful jitter of nerves.

She swallowed with a gulp, pushing down the nausea that came when she realized she had forgotten all her lines. As always. And, as always, they would all come flowing back to her once she stepped on the stage. The words were embedded in muscle memory, not in her mind. But even though this same drama played out in her mind and stomach before each performance, her logical side had no chance of convincing her panicky, frightened self that everything would be okay.

Emilie flicked her gauze skirt, waving cool air over her suddenly overheated skin. She rested her hip and shoulder against the concrete wall and sent her mind somewhere safe and happy. Out into the park where she knew Arden would be right now.

❖

Arden clapped along with the crowd as the troupe of jugglers finished their performance. The Green Show took place on a stage in the park, entertaining visitors with period music, acrobats, and dancers in a constantly changing performance. Arden usually stayed after work to watch even if she wasn't attending a play, but tonight she hurried toward the Bricks as soon as the last flaming torch had been tossed.

She had mixed feelings about seeing this play, but she had felt the comforting presence of her memories of her grandparents all day, along with the thrill of anticipation because she'd be watching Emilie speaking the words that had originally drawn Arden to her. She hurried up the steps and handed her ticket to an usher, following the throng of playgoers into the theater.

She loved this space, but tonight she barely registered the whitewashed walls and dark beams of the Tudor-style theater because she was intent on finding her seat and distracted by thoughts of Emilie. Until she glanced up and saw the set. She stopped abruptly, and the couple behind her bumped into her.

"Sorry," all three of them spoke at once. Arden smiled over her shoulder at them and moved forward again. As soon as she was in her seat, with a wool blanket wrapped around her legs and her heavy coat buttoned against the chill night air, she let herself soak in the scenery. The stylized trees and distant castle added color and fantasy to the stark theater, and the floor of the stage had been transformed with a layer of bright green moss and scattered flowers. The contrast between this set and the strangely twentieth century setting of *Merry Wives* was startling.

When she was able to drag her gaze away from the stage, Arden saw that the children in the audience—and many of the adults, too—were as mesmerized as she was. She was hopefully going to be able to elicit similar responses with her small stages in the park, but the thought of creating a fantasy world on a grand scale like this made her feel a coil of excitement building inside. She had never been able to project herself into the theater world before, and she had only been an observer as her parents and the few company people she met had left Ashland, driven to pursue their dreams.

Now, though, she could almost see the attraction of actively living a theater life, not just passively sitting in the audience. All because of Emilie. She had inspired Arden that day in the park, when she had played Titania among the trees, and the stages Arden was planning were the result. Would it end there? Arden had always known she would follow in her grandparents' footsteps. They had lived a settled life here in Ashland, giving Arden the stability she had needed as a child. Arden had subconsciously been doing the same thing, although—as Emilie had pointed out—she didn't have anyone relying on her to provide a stable home. She suddenly had a feeling she could do anything, and go anywhere. But she had hoped she would be able to find someone local someday, someone who would stay here with her and build a life with her. Someone who would be as appealing as the actors she found so damned attractive, but without any of the excessive drive or drama they tended to bring into relationships with them.

She shifted uncomfortably on the hard seat, pulling her blanket more snugly around her. Emilie was everything Arden found desirable—she was passionate and ambitious and fiery. But she was also grounded, somehow, and Arden had never felt as centered and sure of herself as she felt when Em was around.

She was relieved when the lights dimmed and the play began because it forced her to stop thinking about Emilie and how she made Arden feel capable of living out her wildest dreams—ideas as fantastical as the play she was about to see—and made her concentrate instead on the show unfolding in front of her.

Luckily, the production was enough to wholly capture Arden's mind. Even the air particles she was breathing felt changed somehow, and Arden was caught in the past—in her childhood memories of the play—and in the present, so she was able to escape thoughts of the future, for the most part. She had a brief lapse when Emilie first appeared onstage, looking ethereal and powerful all at once, but Arden let go of anything resembling hope or possibility and instead paid attention only to what was happening in front of her.

Emilie was magical onstage. Not as effortless and transporting as she had been when she thought she was alone in the woods, but still, she lit up the stage whenever she was standing on it. She had a charismatic vibrancy that Arden had glimpsed in *Merry Wives* and had seen full force the day they had first met. Even if Emilie was never able to reveal all her talent in front of an audience, she still was destined to be a star.

Arden stayed in her seat during intermission, curled under her blanket and trying not to let the real world intrude on her thoughts. She wasn't completely successful. She had thought she could escape the pain of Emilie's eventual departure from Ashland by embracing her friendship and not pushing for a romantic relationship, but her heart had somehow gotten snared anyway. She would never wish for Emilie to fail, and she would be thrilled if Em ever managed to show her true potential and break down the barriers between giving a good performance and really becoming the character she was playing. But Arden was going to hurt when she left, no matter whether they had slept together or not. She had been foolish to think that refraining from sex would make a difference in her connection to Emilie.

Maybe she needed to look more fully into her own dreams. Arden unfolded her legs and leaned forward again, noticing the small details of the set. The way certain sections of the stage were framed to highlight the scenes that took place within them. The way colors and shadows gave depth and interest without detracting from the prominence of the actors. The stages she was going to make in the park could do the same thing, not just on a smaller scale, but on a more intensified one. She'd be showcasing an actor's monologue or a brief scene, and her sets would each have a story to tell, helping to flesh out the scenes played upon them. She checked all her pockets, but she had left her pencils in her work jeans. She'd have to remember the ideas flowing through her mind.

The distraction helped, and the intermission seemed to speed by. Maybe she could avoid the pain of eventually being left behind by igniting her own ambition, and not watching the ambitions of others from the sidelines, waving good-bye as they left her alone.

Maybe. Right now, though, she would watch Emilie's dreams sparking to life in front of her. The lights dimmed again, and Arden smiled as the actors returned to the stage. She ignored the easy flow from thoughts of her future to thoughts of Emilie's, as if they could possibly be intertwined in some way, and let herself get lost in Shakespeare's words.

❖

Emilie hurried to get changed into her street clothes after the performance. The mood in the tunnels and the green room was high as the entire cast celebrated a successful show, and Emilie could see the same flow of emotions she was feeling in the expressions of the rest of the actors. The thrill of being onstage was waning already, but it surged now and again and overcame the mix of weariness, satisfaction, and a strange sadness that surfaced after the adrenaline had drained out of her. Before the show, she was nothing but nerves, and after it, she was pummeled by the ups and downs of conflicting emotions. But during the play, she had been calm and soft. Happy to be acting again, to be part of the world she created with the other actors and the rapt audience. Happy to know Arden was in the audience, sharing the experience with her in some way.

She used a spare few inches of mirror space as she cleaned off most of her stage makeup and carefully avoided noticing her chaotic after-show hairdo. She had resigned herself to the fact that she was going to spend the season looking like a family of birds had taken up residence in her curls, and right now she cared more about getting out of the theater and finding Arden than her appearance.

Weaving quickly through the crowds—and getting stopped every few feet to either congratulate a cast member on a great performance or thank someone who was telling her the same thing—she eventually made it through the back exit and hovered at the edge of the Bricks. She stayed in the shadows, unnoticed by the horde of theatergoers, and searched for Arden.

She finally spotted Arden where she was standing near the gift shop and scribbling something in a book. Emilie exhaled and felt her body relax for the first time all day, but the sensation made her stiffen again. She shouldn't let someone else ground her like Arden did. She should let her own confidence carry her through the performance, and the awareness of a job well done soothe her back to normal after the show. She needed to be careful not to rely on Arden too much, but at the same time, she couldn't keep herself from wanting to celebrate with her tonight because she knew she had been good as Titania—not spectacular, but certainly not disastrous, either. For the first time since she had come to Ashland, she felt like she might survive the season and hold her own in the company, and Arden would understand what that meant to Emilie. Plus, Arden would need someone to talk to, as well, about what her grandparents would have thought of the production.

So tonight she would ignore her concerns about her growing feelings for Arden and would just enjoy spending time with her. She stepped out of the shadows and walked across the Bricks, smiling at the people who recognized her from the cast and even signing a few programs along the way. Arden seemed to sense her approach, because she looked up from her writing and directly at her. Everyone else seemed to fade into the background when Arden grinned at her, but Emilie wasn't going to worry about that either. Just for tonight.

Arden met her halfway across the Bricks and pulled her into a tight hug.

"You were great tonight," she whispered in Emilie's ear, giving her a quick kiss on the cheek before stepping out of the embrace.

"Thanks," Emilie said, relieved she could get at least that one word out while her mind was reeling from Arden's closeness, the sweet nectar-like scent of her—did she wash her hair with honey?—and the tingling feeling where Arden's breath had grazed her ear. Emilie cleared her throat and pulled herself together. "The show seemed to go well."

Arden playfully punched her in the arm. "*Seemed to go well?* I think the standing ovation you got proves you have a gift for understatement."

Emilie smiled. The standing ovation had been for the entire cast, but someday—maybe—she would get one of her own. Still, the applause for her had seemed to swell a little, and the people who had talked to her out here had been warm with praise. "I feel like celebrating," she said.

Arden tilted her head to one side. "Champagne or ice cream?"

"Ice cream," Emilie said without hesitating. Her defenses were already weakened after the emotion-filled premiere day. She didn't need to add alcohol to the equation.

"I know the perfect place." Arden linked her arm with Emilie's and started walking. They blended into the dispersing crowds of people who were heading away from the theaters and back to hotels or out to Ashland's bars and restaurants.

"You really were amazing as Titania." Arden gave her a nudge. "And you look different somehow. More sure of yourself, I guess. Does it help to have three opening nights out of the way?"

Emilie sighed. "Absolutely. I guess I spent the last month feeling like an imposter here, but now I fit in as part of the company. It's a relief."

Although she should want more than to merely fit in. She should want to be outstanding and memorable, and not feel so damned relieved just to have gotten through a performance without toppling over or forgetting her lines. She shook her head. She had been here a little over a month, and she was already feeling more confident. She'd let herself be satisfied with the small steps she'd taken tonight.

"How many *Midsummer Night's Dreams* have you seen over the years?" she asked. "It seems to be part of the standard repertoire here."

"I've probably seen this play more than any of the others, except maybe *Hamlet*." Arden waved her playbill. "I should count these and find out. But this was honestly one of the better productions I've seen. Very magical and ornate. You could play Lady Godiva with all the hair they had on you."

"I practically am, since I'm only wearing some little bits of gauze and a bodysuit. I'm grateful for every strand in that wig."

Arden steered her down a side street and into a small diner. "Hopefully, they have someone guarding it. I might be tempted to break into the wig department and snip some of it off."

Emilie felt her cheeks flush, and she pretended it was because they had come out of the cold night and into the heated restaurant. She looked at the menu board with flavors written in different colored chalks and willed the blushing to subside.

"What do you recommend?" she asked.

"Well, first of all, I'd get rid of the bodysuit entirely...Oh, wait. Are you talking about the ice cream or your costume?"

"The ice cream," Emilie said with a mock stern look at Arden. But was she, really? Maybe it wouldn't hurt to entertain the idea of something more with Arden. Something more physical. More than the friendship she was trying so carefully to maintain. She had gotten through her first performances, and they should set the tone for the rest of her season. Her roles were safe, but they would give her a cautious reentry into the acting world, while still leaving room for her to have a life outside the company. A life that just might include Arden, for as long as Emilie remained in Ashland.

Arden sighed dramatically. "Fine. Ice cream it is. If you want local flavor, you should try the pear and hazelnut. It's my favorite."

The diner was crowded since two plays had finished close to the same time, but Emilie and Arden managed to find two stools together at the end of the counter. Emilie took a bite of the homemade ice cream, with chunks of sweet pear and crunchy hazelnuts, and closed her eyes.

"Mmm. You were right. This is heavenly."

"Of course I was right. Just like I was right about you taking Ashland by storm," Arden said in a smug tone as she licked apple pie ice cream off her spoon. Emilie watched her tongue capture the drips and decided she might be safer if she closed her eyes again. And kept them shut during the entire ice cream eating episode.

Emilie concentrated on the bowl in front of her. "I don't know if *by storm* is the right phrase. Maybe *with a small breeze* would fit better."

"Hey. Don't sell yourself short, especially not to me. You have an amazing talent, Em." Arden paused, then added in a softer tone, "It must be hard to return to acting after a few years away, but you've proven you belong on that stage with the rest of the cast."

"Thank you," Emilie said quietly. She hadn't told Arden much about her hiatus, and Arden had never pushed for more information, but Emilie felt open tonight. Willing to share more of herself with Arden. "It's not just returning to acting, but returning to myself. There were times in Europe when I couldn't even recognize who I was. Everything I loved and wanted was put on hold."

Arden hesitated, as if unsure whether she should ask her next question. "Surely you could have acted while you were there, couldn't you? Even if your schedule wasn't exactly the same as your ex's, you could have had your own life. I mean, she wasn't exactly holding you captive, was she?"

Emilie paused with her spoon halfway to her mouth. Arden's words hurt because they echoed her own self-criticism.

"I'm sorry," Arden said, swiftly filling in the silent moment. "It's just…you seem so strong and determined to succeed. It's hard to imagine you letting someone else control your life."

Emilie put her spoon down and covered Arden's hand with her own, enjoying the soft warmth of skin connecting with skin even though her mind wasn't comfortable with the conversation. "Don't be sorry. You're right. Again. I gave up control over my life while I was there, and I don't understand why. It started before we left, after I had gotten some great reviews for a play I was in. I got scared for some reason. I wasn't sure I could live up to the potential they saw in me, and I thought it would be easier to take a break. My fear combined with her jealousy, and it sort of spiraled downward from there until I lost myself."

Emilie paused. A more self-confident girlfriend wouldn't have encouraged her to give up her dreams so easily. Someone like Arden would have kept after her to keep trying, to see how far she could go. But no matter what anyone else had done, Emilie had been the one to acquiesce every step of the way, and sometimes she hated herself for it.

"She could have been more supportive, and we could have shared opportunities on tour, but she didn't like to have anyone else in the limelight with her." In Emilie's deepest heart, where she was free to be completely honest, she could see the truth— she had always been the more talented of the pair, with more glowing reviews and more job offers, and her girlfriend hadn't been happy about that. Perhaps Emilie had needed to experience firsthand what jealousy could do to a relationship. "Looking back, I guess it was good for me to have someone like her to force me to stand on my own. To follow my dreams without anyone else's help."

"Maybe," Arden said slowly, cautiously. "But maybe having someone who wasn't trying to keep you down in order to satisfy her own ego would have made you stronger, as well. Someone who cared about you and believed in you might have."

Emilie shrugged casually, but inside she knew Arden's words made sense. But her own interpretation—that she had learned the important lesson of not relying on anyone else—helped to soothe the guilt and pain those wasted years caused. She couldn't let go of her justifications yet. She wasn't sure how the lessons she had learned in Europe fit in with her growing desire to get closer to Arden, so she stopped trying to figure it out for the moment, and thought about Arden instead. Had she ever had someone encourage her to dream and grow, or had she always been around people who were happy to have her stay where she was? Girlfriends in the company who were focused on their own careers. Grandparents who loved her, but who perhaps were relieved when Arden seemed settled in Ashland because they had already had a son and daughter-in-law leave them to pursue their own goals. If Emilie selfishly gave in to her attraction to Arden, would she be any better than they were?

All Emilie knew for certain was that the day had finally taken its toll, and she was exhausted. Decisions, regrets, and serious contemplation would have to be put on hold for now. They finished their ice cream in silence.

Chapter Eleven

Three days later, Arden found herself in the courtyard outside the Thomas Theatre, waiting for Emilie. She was early, impatient to see Emilie again even though she thought it might be best to get some distance from her. Every time she made up her mind to push past the boundary of playful flirtation they had set when they first became friends, she learned something more about Emilie. Something that made her remember how important this season was for her, both as an actor and as an individual. She could read Emilie's signals well enough to recognize that the attraction between them wasn't one-sided, but she could also read Emilie's hesitation and her determination to regain control over her life.

Arden flipped to a new page in the unlined journal she had bought at the gift shop after watching Emilie's play. She had filled several pages with drawings for her stages, as well as sketched reproductions of the set for *A Midsummer Night's Dream*, while she had waited for Emilie on the Bricks that night. She carried it with her everywhere now and had more ideas for the park's impromptu stages than she would be able to use. Still, the process of imagining a concept and putting it on paper was enlightening—she was using her mind in new ways, but at the same time, it felt as if she was doing what she had been born to do. She felt connected to her plants and gardens in Lithia Park, but somehow the pencil lead and paper were more natural for her to wield.

Unfortunately, when she spent more of her time drawing Emilie as Titania—the Titania she had first met in the woods—she lost sight of her resolve to put more space between them. After their evening at the ice cream parlor, Arden had decided she needed to step back and protect both herself and Emilie from the connection growing between them. So when Emilie had called yesterday and asked her to come on the backstage tour with her, of course Arden had said yes immediately. And of course she had gotten here a half hour early, just to have extra time to sketch Emilie and think about Emilie and want Emilie...

She was relieved when Em actually walked across the courtyard toward her, wearing the smile she always seemed to have when she first spotted Arden and that made Arden's heart beat faster than a sprinter's during a race. Arden put away her journal and her fantasies about Emilie and stood. When Em got close, Arden thought she saw the same hesitation in her expression, the same question about how they should greet each other. Hug? Kiss on the cheek? Hearty handshake? They both settled on a hello accompanied by a goofy grin.

"I'm glad to see you," Arden admitted, laughing a little at the feeling of having a schoolgirl crush. "Thanks for inviting me."

Emilie bumped Arden with her shoulder as they walked toward the glass door entrance to the theater. "I thought you might say no. I'm sure you've been on this tour hundreds of times with all your old girlfriends."

"I've taken the backstage tour a few times, but I never went with anyone I was dating." Arden had usually avoided seeing her dates in the context of the festival. Once she had started seeing someone, she never went to see her perform unless specifically asked to—which was rare, since the women she had dated seemed happy to keep her separate from their work lives as well. When she had gone out with them, it was always to the most non-festival-related places she could find in this Shakespeare-mad town.

Emilie stopped with the door halfway open. "Why not?"

Arden shrugged, trying to appear unconcerned, although she was struggling with the same question. "I guess seeing one of them giving a tour or acting or anything connected to the festival would only make it more obvious that they were here short-term. I prefer to forget about the eventual ends of relationships while I'm in them."

"But you're here with me. Should I assume that means you don't care about me leaving?"

Arden raised her hand and cupped Emilie's chin, making sure they kept eye contact because she wanted Emilie to truly understand how seriously she meant what she was saying, even though she kept her tone light and had what she hoped was a playful smile on her face.

"Exactly the opposite, Em. You're going to break my heart when you go."

"I don't want to," Emilie said, her voice barely above a whisper.

"And I would never want to keep you from moving on." Arden shrugged. She pulled her hand back slowly, letting her fingers shiver along Emilie's jawline. "That's life in a theater town. Always changing."

Emilie finally opened the door all the way, and they walked into the elegant foyer where other members of the tour group were already milling around. A group of teens was being herded from photo to photo by an enthusiastic teacher, and several senior couples were clustered together and poring over a map of Ashland. A family with two small children stood on their own near the door.

Emilie and Arden wandered over to the wall of pictures while they waited for Geoffrey to come start the tour. Emilie was here as an observer, and she'd be starting tours of her own in a week or so. More stress to add to her life. She didn't need Arden acting moony over her right now, and Arden made a conscious effort to return to their normal lighthearted banter.

"Gemini," Arden commented as they paused by one of the stills from *Skywriting*. "That can't be her real name."

"Maybe she's actually a twin. One body, two egos." Emilie slapped her hand over her mouth. "Shh," she hissed from behind her fingers. "I shouldn't say anything bad about other company members."

Arden glanced over each shoulder as if she was checking for spies. "I don't think anyone overheard you," she whispered. "I'm guessing she's a bit of a diva?"

"Unfortunately, she earns the right to be a prima donna. She's very talented."

Arden had to agree. Gemini had been amazing in her performance as Cassella, and the play had been one of the most emotionally moving ones Arden had ever seen at the festival.

"Ugh, I can see it all over your face," Emilie said with a scowl. "You're thinking about how wonderful she was in that damned play."

Arden trotted after Emilie as she stalked over to the next photo. "I was thinking about how wonderful the damned play was. And how much better it would have been if only the understudy had been onstage."

Emilie crossed her arms over her chest and looked directly at Arden. "Tell me the truth. Do you really think I could play the part as well as she does? Complete honesty."

Those blue eyes demanded nothing less, and Arden couldn't lie to her. She chose her words carefully, though. "The part requires an actor who is willing to let go completely onstage. To be vulnerable and weak and without an ounce of self-consciousness. If you played the part like you played Titania the first day we met, then I believe you would be even better than Gemini was."

"And if I played Cassella as well as I played Titania at the premiere?" Emilie waved her hand. "No, don't say it. You already answered the question in a roundabout way. I agree, but I don't know if I'll ever be able to bring the same kind of performance to the stage as I do when we're alone in the park. Luckily, I don't have to worry about it this time."

Arden worried that Emilie would sink into the low place, where she seemed to wrestle with self-doubt, but she smiled brightly at Arden instead.

"Don't look so nervous, Arden. You're being honest, and you help me see things more objectively. Where I need to improve, and the level at which I'm capable of performing right now. C'mon, Geoffrey's about to start."

Arden breathed a sigh of relief when Emilie took her hand and pulled her over to the gathered tour group. She half listened to the introduction she had heard many times, in various versions, since she was a child. She was more focused on Emilie's hand in hers, the way it was calm and steady while Arden's was always flickering with movement. Ready to stroke the soft skin between Em's thumb and forefinger, or to link their fingers tightly together. Instead, she opted for a gentle squeeze before they both let go when Geoffrey started leading the group through the foyer.

They filed into the theater and sat a little ways apart from the main tour group sitting in a small cluster around Geoffrey, who perched on the edge of the stage. The teal upholstery on the seats was the only splash of color in the room, since almost everything else in the theater was painted black, and the set for *King Lear* was dark and spare. Arden hadn't been to see the tragedy yet, but she had a ticket for next week's performance. She couldn't recall a season when she hadn't seen every play *except* for the ones in which someone she was dating was performing in a starring role. Now she knew she'd be disappointed by any play that didn't have Emilie in it.

Arden listened to the tour spiel for a few minutes, while Geoffrey explained how the company functioned and told several funny stories about mishaps he'd experienced during his three-year run in Ashland. When he started asking people in the group where they were from and what had brought them to the festival, Arden leaned closer to Emilie and whispered her question.

"Is Geoffrey Irish? I don't remember him having an accent when you introduced us last week."

Emilie had her elbow on the armrest between them, and when Arden moved closer to her, their shoulders and knees touched. Arden barely registered Emilie's answer to her question.

"He's from Minneapolis. I've heard him give three tours now, and he changes his accent every time."

"Are you planning to do the same thing?"

"I might pretend to be a wee lassie from Scotland. Or maybe I can convince everyone I'm from Mexico, or France, or Germany."

Arden covered her mouth to hide a burst of laughter at Emilie's words. Her accents were spot-on, but she switched them around so they didn't match the country she was naming at the time. Arden knew she should return her attention to the tour, but she liked hearing Em's voice and feeling the exhale of breath against her skin when Emilie tilted her head toward her.

"What's it like to act on a stage like this?" she asked, searching for a topic to prolong their intimate conversation.

Emilie shrugged, creating an arousing sense of friction where their arms touched. "Actually, I never have. I've only rehearsed in here. It's…" She paused, as if searching for the right words to describe what she felt. "It's quieter, in a way. Like I'm talking to individuals and not projecting to an audience. And more mobile. We have to choreograph the scenes, not just set marks as guidelines, since we need to make sure we're not standing with our backs to a quarter of the audience for very long."

Arden looked at the stage again, with a new perspective. For *King Lear*, the back portion of the set was curtained off, but when she had been at the performance of *Skywriting*, there had been seats on all four sides. Comparing her memory of the other play with what she saw in front of her, she could see the way the set designer had cleared sightlines, not only making the actors visible for every spectator, but making the stage workable for the performers as well.

Arden was caught in the wonder of the way set, script, audience, and actors were interconnected, and she didn't realize the tour was leaving the theater until Emilie pulled on her sleeve. The weather had turned drizzly outside, and they hurried across the street and into the Bowmer Theatre. The Elizabethan stage was almost gaudy, with its beams and different levels, while the Thomas cleared away everything that might get between the play and the audience. The Bowmer was somewhere in between. Simple and elegant and traditional. They sat in comfortable gray seats in the middle of the theater, and Arden let Geoffrey's words fade into the background while she watched the stagehands who were working on the set for *Julius Caesar*.

She pulled out her notebook and quickly sketched the set in front of her, as well as the one she had just seen in the Thomas Theatre, wanting to get the details in place before they had to move on to their next tour stop. She'd think more about the dynamics of set creation later, when she had time to go over her drawings and try to interpret the intentions of the directors and set designers. She felt Emilie watching over her shoulder, but she didn't stop sketching until the group rose and followed Geoffrey. Arden was moving with them, but Emilie grabbed her forearm and tugged her down the stairs and toward the stage.

"Shouldn't we go with them?" Arden asked, gesturing toward the door that was closing behind the group.

"We'll catch up." Emilie raised her voice and called to one of the people on the stage. "Hi, Gwen. Mind if we come up?"

A woman in her early fifties waved them forward. She was wearing a long-sleeved black shirt and black jeans, as if conditioned to fade into the background onstage, and she had a short ponytail of graying hair and a pair of large red glasses. "Sure, Emilie. Just mind those planks."

Emilie climbed the short flight of steps, keeping hold of Arden's arm as if she might bolt, but Arden wasn't about to go anywhere but onto the stage. "Arden, this is Gwendolyn Bryson. She's the head set designer for the festival. Gwen, Arden works in Lithia Park. She's interested in set design, and she's been working on some stages for the park, where actors and tourists can do impromptu performances."

"Um…" Arden was at a loss for words, unable to get past Em's assertion that she was interested in set design. Was she? She had noticed sets before, of course, but had never dissected their form and function the way she was doing today. Emilie had sparked something in her, though, when she had brought her rendition of Titania into the woods. "Nice to meet you," she finally said, shaking Gwen's hand. "I'm not doing anything on this scale in the park. Just a few platforms, to make the festival accessible in a small way."

"*Pssht.* Not as small a scale as you think, Arden," Emilie said, nudging her arm. "Quite a few of the company members are already making plans to get involved as soon as the platforms are built. Geoffrey and I have already picked out a scene from *Much Ado About Nothing.*"

"What an interesting concept," Gwen said, tapping a finger against her mouth. "Will the stages only be open to actors?"

"No, I want the public to take part, too, and get a taste of what it would be like to be an actor. We'll have laminated scripts at each stage, with short scenes from Shakespeare's plays, and a box of simple props. So people can spontaneously take part if they feel inspired."

Emilie gave Arden a quick smile, as if she was thinking about her spontaneous performance, too. The performance that had brought them together.

Gwen nodded, giving Arden the impression that she was taking her project as seriously as if she was developing a concept for the staging of a major play. "I love it. I'll come by the park soon, to check out these stages of yours."

"She's there almost every day," Emilie said. "You have to see the plans she's made for them—they're going to be works of art. But we should catch up to the tour now. See you soon, Gwen."

Arden barely had time to say good-bye, let alone take the time to roll her eyes at Emilie's comment about her platforms being anything with artistic merit, before Emilie had grabbed her hand and was pulling her off the stage and out the door the tour group had taken. They jogged through the empty foyer and through a door leading backstage.

Arden had done the tour enough times to know which staircase led to the catacombs beneath the stages, but she let Emilie guide her along until they reached the cinder block tunnels. Green stenciled markings pointed the way to different areas of the two stages accessed by these underground routes, and Arden imagined Emilie down here, in full stage makeup and costume, as she prepared to perform.

Arden stopped suddenly. Emilie continued forward for several steps, without realizing Arden wasn't moving with her anymore, but bounced to a halt when she got to the end of Arden's reach. Arden gave a swift tug, and Emilie was in her arms.

She stood silently, giving herself the permission she often denied and studying every detail of Emilie's face. Those expressive blue eyes that were able to convey a range of emotions from innocence to sultriness when she was acting, and that now stared at Arden with a widening look of surprise and the slight darkening of what Arden hoped was arousal. Those beautiful lips, often curved either in a playful smile or in a frown of concern, and rarely set in a neutral expression.

Right now, Emilie's mouth was slightly open. She was a little out of breath from their run through the corridors. Arden raised her free hand and gently stroked Emilie's lips with her fingertips. Then the delicate curve of her cheekbone, then the arc of her eyebrow. She had a soft beauty about her, made irresistible because Arden understood the strength and determination she had inside.

"Thank you," she said, her voice nearly inaudible.

"For what?" Emilie asked in the same near-silent tone.

Arden shrugged. How could she explain how Emilie's belief in her—in her abilities and her potential—somehow made Arden believe things about herself she'd never dreamed of before. Or how she wanted to repay the favor and erase all Emilie's self-doubt and help her see how truly wonderful and talented she was. Arden didn't have the words to express what she was feeling, and she had no choice but to show Emilie what she meant.

Arden's relationships had always sparked high. Passion, in her experience, was laced with anger, or fear, or drama. Never with peace. But the moment her lips touched Emilie's, she felt a wave of emotions run through her that was nothing like she'd experienced before. A sense of connecting and communicating. Coming home. And wanting, more than she had thought possible.

The sensation of burying her fingers in Emilie's hair and the gentle roughness of Emilie's tongue moving across her lower lip overrode any concerns Arden had been feeling. Thoughts faded as Arden's nerve endings took over, pulsing in rhythm with her rapid heartbeat every place where Emilie's body met hers, from thigh to hip to breasts. Warmth and strength seeped into her from Emilie, making her feel invincible, able to handle what was happening between them now, and what would happen later.

Arden blindly reached for Emilie's hand where it rested on her hip and took it in her own, lacing their fingers together and gripping her tightly, anchoring them together. She would need to protect herself, eventually. Just because her feelings for Emilie were so different—so much deeper—than anything she had felt for past lovers didn't mean the end of their relationship would be any different. Emilie was still an actor, with dreams she'd follow wherever they took her. She'd still walk away from Ashland, leaving Arden alone in her park. The only real change would be the way Arden would feel. Broken, but changed for the better, too.

Arden pulled back slightly and rested her forehead against Emilie's. She put her free hand on Emilie's waist, keeping Emilie's hand firmly in her other one, and felt the rapid movement of her rib cage match the overheated rhythm of her own breathing. Emilie was going to rip out her heart and take it with her when she left, but she had managed to dislodge ideas and possibilities in Arden's mind, and they had a life of their own now. They weren't going to go away.

She tried to speak, but her voice caught. She cleared her throat and tried again. "We should catch up. The tour is probably over."

"Screw the tour," Emilie said, but she stepped away from Arden with a sad-looking smile. Her cheeks were flushed, and she dropped her gaze to Arden's lips before meeting her eyes once more. "But you're right. We should go."

Arden followed her through the maze of tunnels, holding on to the memory of their kiss and refusing to let herself wish for more.

❖

Emilie hurried through the catacombs, her fingers still woven together with Arden's. She couldn't look back yet, because if she saw Arden's face, her lips, she would have to shove her against the gray cement walls and kiss her again.

The route through the tunnels was familiar to her now, and the twists and turns had been learned as surely as Emilie's lines. She figured Geoffrey and the tour group were in the wings now, looking out on the Elizabethan stage, and she let muscle memory propel her forward while her heart and mind flew back in time and place to Arden's kiss.

Emilie had been aroused—she wouldn't have expected anything less from being held in Arden's embrace—but the kiss had surprised her, too. Arden always seemed strong, physically and mentally, but her lips had yielded to Emilie's with a softness that made Emilie ache inside. And when Arden had taken her hand…

Emilie tripped on the staircase, and Arden immediately was there to steady her. Even that practical touch carried a dimension of tenderness with it, bringing them to a level of intimacy Emilie had never experienced before. Arden's hand intertwined with hers had made her feel the same way, as if Arden was offering and asking for support and a different kind of closeness, even while their bodies were tangled in a kiss that was startlingly, absolutely driven by physical desire.

She came to an abrupt halt once they were close to the stage, needing a little time before they returned to the tour. The heavy velvet curtain brushed against her arm, shielding them from the group and muffling Geoffrey's resonant voice. Arden came close behind her, wrapping her arms around Emilie's rib cage and nestling their hips together. Emilie dropped her head back onto Arden's shoulder.

"Are you okay?" Arden asked, so softly that Emilie wasn't sure if she heard her, or if she just understood the pattern of Arden's breath against her neck.

Emilie nodded, rubbing her cheek against Arden's as she did so. She inhaled the mixture of Arden's sweet scent and the chalky, backstage smell of the theater. She was better than okay as long as Arden was close, but the feeling was fleeting. It had to be. The kiss, the connection—those were things that belonged in the shadows behind the scenes. Emilie's real life had to take place in front of the curtain.

She twisted her head a little until she was able to reach Arden's mouth with her own. The kiss this time was delicate, lingering. No clashing tongues or roaming hands, but even so, Emilie felt a reverberation shudder through her body. Her arms rested on top of Arden's, and she squeezed them closer in a brief hug before she broke free and walked onto the stage.

Chapter Twelve

Two mornings later, Emilie was awakened by the shrill chime of her phone. She considered ignoring it since she'd had both a performance and the first rehearsal for *Richard III* yesterday and was exhausted, but her half-awake mind thought it might be Arden calling her. She smacked her hand across the bedside table until she found her cell, and she pulled it under the covers with her. If she was going to talk to Arden, she couldn't think of a better place to do it than snuggled deep in her bed.

"Hello?" She had tried clearing her throat first, but her raspy voice left no doubt she'd been asleep only moments before.

"Emilie Danvers? This is Joanne at the OSF office. A ten a.m. call has been issued for *Skywriting*."

"Got it, thank you," Emilie mumbled before hanging up. She sighed. A double disappointment. First, it hadn't been Arden. And second, now she was too awake to burrow back for some much-needed sleep. She flipped onto her back and stared at the ceiling, wondering how much concern she should be feeling about her unconcealed hope that Arden had been on the other end of the line.

They hadn't mentioned the kiss, but it had somehow woven itself into Emilie's mind. In her dreams and daydreams, she was never as quick to move away and return to the tour as she had been in the tunnels. If Arden kissed her again—or if she kissed Arden, which was a distinct possibility—she doubted she'd be as determined to put distance between them. She was losing sight of the reasons why she needed to hold herself apart from Arden.

Was this a dangerous path, or was it safe? She was getting comfortable here. Excited to play Lady Anne, and settled in her routine performance as Titania. Maybe she could add a little romance to her life without jeopardizing her career goals...

She flung the covers back and rolled out of bed. She might be in the frame of mind to think it was okay to want more out of their relationship, but she couldn't just consider her own point of view. Arden had been very clear about her unwillingness to get too attached—no matter whether her actions betrayed her true desires—and she had confided in Emilie about the reasons why. Emilie felt a fierce need to protect her newly restarted career, but somewhere along the way she had developed an even more pronounced need to protect Arden's feelings.

She couldn't make the decision to either pursue Arden or to resist her attraction based on her needs alone. Arden's were as important—or more so—to her. Emilie wouldn't add her own name to the list of people who had left Arden behind, and she knew all too well how challenging it was to be brought along as a passenger on the quest for someone else's career goals.

Emilie tied a robe around her waist and stumbled into the bathroom for a reviving shower. She didn't have to worry about a relationship right now since she had another full day ahead, and she was relieved to focus on activities instead of emotions for a while. As soon as she was shocked awake by the cold water, she walked into town for a bagel and a latte before she headed to the theater. She had been booked to the gills already, with performances and rehearsals and fittings, but she hadn't realized how many unexpected appointments came up during the season. Costumes needed to be resized or changed, wigs needed to be ratcheted even more tightly onto her poor scalp, and new lighting or sound cues needed to be learned.

And even though the directors moved on after rehearsals ended and performances began, each show's stage manager was responsible for the continuing production. Emilie had already been called to a few of these last-minute rehearsals, like the one she had this morning. This one wasn't a surprise, given the high-profile new play and the complex staging in the small theater.

Emilie paused outside the door to the Thomas Theatre and drained the last drops of her coffee. She hitched the strap of her backpack, heavy with its stack of scripts and notes for each play, higher on her shoulder as she pushed through the glass door. A few of the cast members were already there, chatting in groups of two or three as they waited for the morning call to start. She walked up behind Elizabeth and Rick, ready to join in their conversation.

"What better way to sabotage the play? Wait until after the opening, so the comparison is—Oh, hey, Emilie. How are you?"

"Fine, thanks. And you?" Emilie hesitated just inside the door as Elizabeth stopped midsentence to greet her. Everyone else in the cast had turned in their direction. All of a sudden, Emilie didn't feel anywhere near fine.

"I'm good. Looks like we're about to get started. See you inside."

"Okay," Emilie said weakly, even though Elizabeth and Rick had already moved away. The others began to drift toward the doors leading to the stage, and Emilie hesitated, torn between following them and fleeing the building. She swallowed. She was just imagining the strange looks everyone had given her, wasn't she? She would walk onstage, and Gemini would be there, flipping her hair over her shoulder and looking smug right before she gave her usual flawless performance. Business as usual.

Emilie walked down the short aisle to the stage, where the cast—minus Gemini—was gathered. She dropped her backpack on one of the seats and joined the others, sitting a little apart from everyone. She felt a growing coil of tension forming in her stomach, and she wished she hadn't eaten an entire bagel with about a pound of cream cheese on it. Stage fright was usually reserved for performances, not for rehearsals.

Lendon Grey, the stage manager, finally arrived. He looked harried, with handfuls of notes and his shirt half untucked, but he always looked like he was mid-anxiety attack. Emilie squinted in his direction. Did he seem more nervous than usual today?

"I'm sure most of you are aware of this by now, but Gemini called this morning. She's unable to perform for the rest of *Skywriting*'s run because she was injured in an accident."

He spoke the words *injured* and *accident* with as much emphasis as if he had made frantic air quotes around them. Emilie was still processing the news, and coming to the conclusion that Gemini had managed to get herself out of her contract, when she realized what it meant for her.

"Emilie will play Cassella tonight." He finally looked in her direction. "We don't have time for a full rehearsal, but we'll run through a few key scenes. Emilie, you're comfortable with your lines and with the board?"

Emilie nodded. She knew her lines, of course, but her throat was too constricted for her to be able to speak. The board was the list of costume changes behind the scenes of each of the plays. They were color coded by time, and listed in order. As Titania, she had a few changes with plenty of time before she had to get back onstage. As Cassella, she had numerous changes, often with less than a minute to accomplish them. The tight schedule didn't allow for any running to the bathroom and being sick.

She managed to find her voice, but in it she could hear how uncomfortably she wore this character. Cassella was complex and uncertain, tortured by the loss of her child and tormented by an undisclosed mental illness. Emilie had been mesmerized by the challenging book when she had first read it. Cassella was the epitome of an unreliable narrator, and the reader was never quite sure what was real and what wasn't. The mystery of what really had happened to her son plagued Cassella as she struggled with the dysfunctional relationships in her life, with homelessness, with institutionalization.

Emilie didn't have any way of connecting with her, try as she had over the weeks since she had first learned she would understudy the role. And her relief when Gemini had seemed resigned to stay with the company and fulfill her contract had been immense.

But now Emilie had to find some way to redeem herself and bring this award-winning book to life on the stage. She had the part down cold—even if she forgot the lines before going onstage, she was sure they'd come back to her as soon as she moved into the first scene. But they were only words if there was no power and engagement behind them.

This role more than any other made her doubt her ability to act. She could find Anne Page's naïveté and stubbornness inside herself, not too deeply buried under her everyday personality. She could be a fairy queen, playing in the forest and having adventures. She could understand Lady Anne's grief and her survival instincts, and draw on her own inner sense of poise and grace—even if they weren't qualities she was convinced she exhibited on a daily basis. But acting was a hell of a lot more than isolating aspects of her own personality and wearing them publicly for an hour or two. And Cassella seemed determined to laugh at her efforts—with that eerily cackling giggle Gemini had perfected—and make her want to run away from the challenge.

Emilie stood in the space that represented the therapist's office at the institution and performed the scene in which Cassella flipped through imaginary pictures of her lost child, feigning with the therapist and dodging the truth about the boy's death. She moved to the right places, said the right lines, but that was about all she could say about her performance.

Too many *if onlys* got in her way. If only she was more talented. If only she could access some inner Cassella and channel her for just a few more months. If only Gemini had quit earlier, giving the festival management time to find a more suitable replacement...

Emilie stopped midstep as the last thought filtered through her mind, joining with the snippet of Elizabeth's conversation she had overheard. Gemini had quit at the perfect time to get vengeance on the company that had refused to let her out of her contract. She had been a huge hit on opening night and had left on short enough notice that the company had to let Emilie play the part. Everyone had seen how she performed during rehearsals, and they were all aware of what Emilie had hoped was a secret known only to her—that she was going to be a major disappointment. An embarrassment to the company. Gemini had used her, and Gemini's brilliance would shine even brighter, as Elizabeth had said, when her performance was compared with Emilie's.

She stumbled over her words for a few lines before she caught the thread again and continued. Lendon didn't even comment on her lapse of concentration. He just sat in the front row of seats with a resigned look on his face.

Somehow, she made it through the rest of the rushed rehearsal. All she wanted to do was run home again and climb under the blankets, back where she had been cozy and happy with fantasies of Arden to keep her warm. She wanted to find the real Arden, not her daydream version, and tell her what had happened, but she didn't have time. Maybe after the rehearsal for *Richard III*. Before tonight's performance of *Skywriting*. Emilie stopped on the Bricks, tempted to run down the stairs leading to the park.

Maybe Arden was planning a tour of Europe and would ask Emilie to leave with her. Tonight. Emilie laughed weakly at her own joke, glad she at least had a little of her sense of humor left. She wouldn't run away this time. She was humiliated and scared, yes. But she would stay and play Cassella. As long as the company would let her.

She turned away from the steps and went into the Bowmer Theatre instead. She hadn't gotten halfway to the stage before Geoffrey reached her and pulled her into a tight hug. Great. Any hope that no one outside the cast of *Skywriting* knew about the Gemini drama was dashed.

"You're going to be spectacular as Cassella," he said, gripping her upper arms and looking her in the eyes. "Don't let her theatrics spoil the theater."

Emilie shook her head. "Don't pretend I can play this part anywhere near as well as she did. I'm sure you've heard all the juicy rumors about how poorly I've done Cassella in rehearsals."

"I don't pay attention to rumors, darling. You have a great chance here. It's the part of the season, and any dirty gossip is the result of jealousy."

"I'm the first to admit that I suck in the role, and I'm not jealous of me."

"Stop," Geoffrey said, with a sharper edge to his voice than she had heard before. "Don't waste this opportunity because you feel sorry for your little self. You were given the understudy role because they believed you could play the part well, if you had to take over. So step up and do your job."

Emilie opened her mouth to speak, and then closed it again. When he put it that way, she could see how ridiculous she was being. She sighed, releasing some of the tension building inside her. "Ouch," she said. "Are you getting into character for today's rehearsal?"

He smiled. "Yes. Geoffrey would let you cry on his shoulder. Richard would call you out and not let you get away with any poor-little-old-me crap. I thought he'd be a better motivator."

"Right. I can see the business cards now. *Richard III, motivational speaker. If you can dream it and can kill enough people, you can achieve it.*"

"Bullet point one—think positive, or I'll throw you in the tower," Geoffrey said in a booming Richard voice.

"Okay," Emilie said. "On the positive side, expectations of me are so low, all I need to do is stand onstage in the correct costume, and everyone at the festival will celebrate my massive accomplishment. I'll be performer of the year."

"Bullet point number two—lose the sarcasm, or I'll have you beheaded." Geoffrey laughed as they walked down the stairs and joined the rest of the cast. His friendship and frank talk had helped pull Emilie out of a pit, and she rallied herself for the rehearsal. Lady Anne was a part she could play with confidence. She had been looking forward to this play, and since they were still blocking out the scenes, she didn't have to prove herself right now—as long as she paid attention and read her lines on cue, she'd get through today without any problems. She thought of Arden and the park, and imagined herself standing among the trees with only an audience of one. The one who really mattered to her. She lost herself a few times in the character, and the director seemed pleased with her performance. Maybe she'd be able to do the same thing tonight, with Cassella. A moment or two of truly feeling the part might lead to more moments in the future. Until she could get through the entire play.

Emilie stepped outside after the rehearsal and checked her watch. She still had over three hours before she had to check in at the Thomas Theatre and start getting into the matted hair and ragged clothes she'd wear in Cassella's first scene. The story was told in a series of flashbacks, and she would return to the first costume several times during the night, switching to less grimy outfits as the earlier parts of her history were shown. Cassella's character arc followed a downward trajectory, but the play didn't unfold in a linear way. She had played the part all the way through before, but never with the added stress of clothing changes to accompany the personality changes.

She shook herself mentally. Geoffrey was right. She had a dream opportunity that people with more years in the company would love to have. She couldn't let it slip away. This was what she had longed for when she was in Europe, and what she had worked for since her return. She'd damn well better not let it slip through her fingers.

Emilie started walking toward her apartment, then changed her mind and headed into the park. She didn't want to sit around and worry before the performance. She'd go see how Arden's stages were coming along, instead. Think about Arden and the passion she didn't seem to see within herself, although it was obvious to Emilie.

And think about that kiss…

Chapter Thirteen

Arden held a two-by-four in place and used a power drill to screw it tightly into a post. When she finished, she stood back and checked her progress. The framework was in place for this stage, and she imagined how it would look when it was painted to match the Elizabethan stage, but in miniature form. She had decided this platform would have a comedic focus, and she had already collected—with Emilie's help—some great scenes that included court jesters and buffoons from Shakespeare's works. The stage was the first one visitors to the park would see, placed near the main duck pond and practically in the shadow of its inspiration, the Allen Theatre.

This was the exact place where she had asked Em to stand and recite some dialogue when she had first been playing with the idea of building these stages, and she felt a shiver of satisfaction run through her. Her grandfather must have felt this same kind of pride when he saw the completed fountain he had created for the Japanese garden. She was contributing something special to her park. She had resisted Jacob's insistence on it from the start, but now she understood exactly what he had wanted from her. To become part of a legacy, along with Gramps.

Arden pushed against the frame, checking to make sure the stage was solid and sturdy. She was completing the task Jacob had set for her, but the platforms felt like a beginning instead of an end. She didn't want to stop with these small sets. She wasn't sure where she might go from here, but she was feeling an unaccustomed sense of excitement about the future.

Tempered with sadness. Emilie had helped set her on a new path, one that might possibly veer away from her anticipated one of staying in this park her whole life, like her grandfather had before her. But Emilie wouldn't be around to see where Arden went from here. Maybe they would try to remain friends, keep in touch and share triumphs and failures through email and online updates, but Arden didn't think she would be able to keep up the charade much longer. She had wanted Emilie from the start, and getting to know her had only made the attraction more profound and real. Em would eventually realize how talented she was, and then she would feel secure enough to let someone get close to her. There'd likely be a long list of candidates waiting for the chance, and Arden did *not* want to get that kind of update in her in-box. She'd rather never know.

She picked up her tools and loaded them in the back of the Mule. She drove them back to the maintenance shed and picked up cans of paint and some brushes. She was ahead of schedule, and she might as well continue to work while she had daylight on her side. She had been pushing herself at a faster pace than usual, avoiding breaks and meals, because every time she sat down to rest, she was catapulted back into the underground corridors, back to the place where she had kissed Em. She didn't need to keep returning to that place and time.

So she painted. And hammered, and sawed, and spent hours choosing fonts and typing dialogue. She had gotten through two days like this—her mind reeled to think of all she could accomplish if she had to spend a lifetime keeping busy so she didn't dwell on thoughts of Emilie.

She'd probably master an instrument, learn a few languages, and cure cancer. Right now, though, she had managed to get her first platform completed. The stage was a replica of the larger one, but she had changed the proportions so it was squatter, fitting with the scenes from comedies she hoped would be performed on it. Even with so many thoughts and emotions roiling through her, she had to smile when she looked at it. She could almost imagine the gnomes she had originally pitched to Jacob stepping on the stage and performing a funny play.

She heard laughter behind her, interrupting her thoughts, and she turned to see Gwen standing there. She was wearing black again, different clothes but the same color. Today's glasses were a shocking shade of purple.

"How charming," she said, walking around the small theater and chuckling. "I can picture Beatrice and Benedick bickering up there."

Arden grinned. "Thank you, Gwen. Can you really tell that this stage was designed for comedies?"

"Absolutely. You told me through the shapes you chose, and other people will recognize them as well. Do you have any others done yet?"

"Just one," Arden said, after hesitating briefly. She wasn't sure if she had expressed her concept as well with the other, but she had designed it with Emilie in mind after their tour the other day. It had taken shape in her mind surprisingly quickly, and she had finished building it in less than a day. Of course, she had worked on it like a woman possessed, since the memory of their kiss had been fresh in her mind, her nerve endings still raw after contact with Emilie.

Gwen was looking at her expectantly, so Arden picked up her painting supplies. "I can show you the stage if you don't mind taking a short walk. It's in the Japanese garden."

"Oh, I love it there," Gwen said, falling into step with Arden. "I've gone a few times when I've felt stuck on a design problem. I'm usually inspired by running water, and the sound of the trough fountain focuses my mind and helps me see solutions."

Arden wasn't surprised. She had heard similar comments from others, including Marty, who came to the garden to sketch ideas for her glassblowing creations when she was feeling blocked. Arden had probably seen Gwen in the garden before, but not from close enough to recognize her. She and the other maintenance staff usually avoided the garden when they saw someone quietly sitting in it or walking slowly along the paths, because they didn't want to interrupt their solitude or time of contemplation.

"My grandfather designed and built that fountain," Arden said.

Gwen nodded. "Ah. I see where you got your ability to communicate through form language."

Arden had a feeling her self-deprecating grandfather would have laughed at the comment, but he also would have appreciated his fountain's effect on Gwen. She kept silent as she took Gwen through the gate and over to the stage.

She fidgeted during the long moments of silence that stretched between them as Gwen studied the platform from every angle. Arden had created it because of the talk she and Em had had about the stage in the Thomas Theatre. Unlike her other designs, this one didn't have a backdrop but was open on all sides. The platform was broken up with low rectangles and squares made of plywood that could be shifted to form walls or seats or other props, and everything was painted in shades of brown, blending into the trees and ground around the set.

Arden wanted this to be a place where some of the most famous monologues would be spoken. The actor would be visible from all sides, standing in the center of the clearing like the deepest thoughts in the center of someone's mind. She wondered if Gwen would be able to read any of that from a few blocks of wood.

"Introspection," Gwen said, "with nowhere to hide."

Arden nodded, speechless.

"This is good work, Arden. Will you show me the other plans you've drawn?"

"Okay," Arden said. Luckily, she wasn't in charge of writing the scripts for her stages, since she apparently didn't have as much ability to communicate verbally as Gwen thought she did with forms. They went back to the maintenance shed, and Arden showed her the other sketches she had planned for the first phase of stages, plus the less developed ones she hoped to build if the initial attempts were popular with tourists.

Gwen left soon after, to get back to the theaters in time for the evening's performances, and Arden spent a few minutes sitting at a picnic table, erasing lines and incorporating some of the suggestions Gwen had made for her designs. She was busily at work when she felt a tap on her shoulder.

She knew it was Emilie before she turned around. She wasn't sure what she noticed first, the scent of jasmine or the way the air felt charged and more intense whenever Emilie came close to her.

Em gestured over her shoulder. "I can't believe you finished the Elizabethan stage already. I can't wait to try it out."

"We'll be posting the signs explaining all about them this weekend. You can give the inaugural performance. You'll be sure to win a Tony for it."

"I'd be honored." Emilie bowed with a flourish. "I'll mention you in my acceptance speech. If I have time, after naming all my gnome costars."

"How did you know I was planning to incorporate gnomes somehow?" Arden asked with a laugh.

Emilie grinned. "I figured you'd get gnomes in there somewhere, if only to make Jacob crazy. How are the rest of the stages coming along?"

Arden handed her the notebook, and she sat down on the bench and flipped through the pages.

"Oh, Arden, I love this one," she said, her voice serious as she looked at one of the more ornate designs Arden had planned. The backdrop was a trellis, and living plants would mingle with the painted vines and flowers to make a garden setting. "It reminds me of the clearing where we met. Titania would be happy to live here."

Arden scooted closer and rested her chin on Emilie's shoulder. "I was thinking of you when I came up with this idea.

I wanted to recapture that day." She reached over and traced her finger over the floor of the stage. "There's a tree stump near the rose garden, and I'm going to build the stage around it."

Emilie leaned her head against Arden's for a moment before turning to the next page. "Oh. This is a new one, isn't it?"

"Yes, but it's built already, in the Japanese garden. Gwen just stopped by, and I showed it to her, and she seemed to like it."

"It's like the Thomas Theatre. Minimalist and exposed. No barriers."

"Exactly. Maybe you can do a scene from *Skywriting* there, since it's sort of modeled after the play's set."

Arden felt Emilie stiffen before she finished her sentence. She sat up straight, putting her fingers under Emilie's chin and turning her head. "What's wrong? You played Cassella the other day, when I asked you to read lines in different places around the park. I was being honest when I told you I believed you'd be worlds better than Gemini if you really gave yourself over to the part."

"She's gone," Emilie said, her voice barely above a whisper.

"Who's gone? Cassella?"

Emilie shook her head. "Gemini. She had some sort of accident, or at least she's claiming she did. She left the company this morning."

Arden sighed with relief. Em was only feeling the stage fright she said she experienced before every performance. "That's great. You'll be playing the part, won't you? I wonder if I can get a ticket on such short notice..."

"I don't want you there," Emilie said sharply. Arden felt as if she'd been slapped in the face, but Emilie reached for her, putting her hands on Arden's shoulders and keeping her from getting up and leaving. "I'm sorry, I didn't mean it the way you think. I just don't want you to see me screw up the part. You'll feel bad for me, and you'll try to lie about how well I did, and I'll see right through it because you're so honest, and—"

"Whoa, Emilie." Arden held up her hand to stop Emilie's

rambling descent into a pessimistic version of the night ahead. "You won't screw it up. You'll be a star, and I'll sing your praises after the show, and you'll know I'm telling the truth, and I'll ask you to sign my program, and—"

"Stop, stop," Emilie said, laughing and waving her hand to make Arden stop mimicking her.

Arden grinned. "My version is much better, and it's more likely to come true. I know you have some mental blocks against playing this part, but once you step onstage, they'll disappear. This is the chance you were looking for. The reason you came to Ashland in the first place."

Emilie's laughter faded. "I know it is. But Gemini used me, Arden. People think she planned to leave when she did because I haven't been doing well at all in rehearsals. If she had left sooner, they'd have recast the role. And since she got such amazing reviews, a bad performance by me will stand out even more."

Arden felt anger wrapping around her lungs, making it difficult to breathe. "I'm not saying I agree with you, but if what you're saying is true, why would she want to hurt you so badly? She couldn't be jealous of you getting the part, because it was already hers."

Emilie kept her face averted, but Arden could see pain sharpening the edges of her expression. "I don't think it's personal. She was mad at the festival director for not letting her out of her contract, and she must have seen this as a way to get back at him."

Although Arden wanted to hunt Gemini down and scream at her for making Emilie hurt like this, she had to admit to herself that Emilie's story might be true. Em had been telling her how badly rehearsals had gone. Maybe she hadn't been exaggerating like Arden had originally thought, and maybe Gemini had come up with this sick plan to embarrass the festival and Emilie. But none of that changed the fact of Emilie's talent—Arden had no doubt about the truth of her ability not just to act, but to become a character.

"Em, I'm certainly not saying these rumors are based on fact, because this whole thing seems like a bad conspiracy theory, but even if it were true, you can't let this define you. You were picked to be in this company, and you were given some really great roles. You know how competitive the auditions for this festival are. So don't accept being anyone's consolation prize or anyone's tool to use to get revenge."

Emilie hooked her arm around Arden's neck and pulled her close, giving her a kiss on the cheek. "Thank you, Arden."

They sat in silence for several minutes, leaning in to each other. Arden wished she could inject her faith in Em's potential directly into her veins, giving her the confidence she needed to play this role, and her desire to help Em almost eclipsed the familiar arousal she felt every time she touched Emilie. Almost. Not all the way.

When Emilie sat up straight again, sifting her fingers through Arden's hair as she pulled away, Arden could see the same flush she felt on her own neck and cheeks coloring Emilie's skin. But now wasn't the time to ask for more.

"Do you want to run some lines?" she asked. "Or talk about tonight some more?"

Emilie shook her head. "No, but thank you. I'd much rather see the new stage you mentioned. And hear everything Gwen said while she was here. I had a feeling the two of you would have a lot to talk about."

Arden took Emilie to the Japanese garden, where Em got on the stage and initiated it with a Lady Anne speech. They strolled through the park for an hour after, talking about Gwen's visit and the weather and nothing in particular until Emilie had to leave for her play.

Arden hugged her tightly, glad to see Emilie looking less pale and more relaxed than she had earlier. As soon as Em was out of sight, Arden ran to the maintenance shed and changed into some un-paint-spattered clothes. Getting a ticket to tonight's performance was a long shot, but she had to try.

Everything about this play guaranteed it would be sold out. The theater was tiny, the premiere had been a hit, the book was a bestseller...

"You're lucky," said the woman in the ticket booth. "We've had a few cancellations today, and I can get you a seat in the third row. Have you been to the Thomas Theatre before?"

Arden answered the woman's friendly questions, but she had a sinking feeling inside. She ran through a list of excuses as she waited to go inside the theater—anything to keep from believing Emilie's dire theory. It was early in the season, and the plays were rarely as crowded now as they'd be in the height of summer. The forecast had called for rain, so people had opted to stay inside instead of venturing out and risking getting wet.

She sat in her seat and twisted the playbill in her hands, mangling it beyond recognition before the lights dimmed and the show started. She tried to watch objectively, as if she hadn't seen Gemini's opening night brilliance, but even without the comparison, Emilie's performance was lackluster. She didn't miss a beat with her lines, but she was detached from the part like she was having an out-of-body experience and leaving a shell of herself onstage to act.

Arden understood what Em had meant about choreographing the scenes. She hadn't noticed it during the first performance, because the actors had shifted around smoothly, presenting a moving tableau so every audience member had the best seat in the house. Emilie was awkward with her movements, sometimes forgetting and standing with her back to entire sections of the theater for much too long.

The applause for the actors was polite, but brief. Emilie was a fine enough actor to bow and smile with a pleasant expression on her face, although it wavered a little when she faced Arden's row and saw her there. Arden grinned and clapped loudly, giving her a thumbs-up sign that felt as lame as it must have looked.

Afterward, she waited outside the theater, even though she suspected Emilie wasn't going to show. As soon as the time display on her phone showed she had waited exactly fifteen minutes, she left and walked back to her car. She hated the feeling of relief washing over her because she didn't have to face Emilie tonight. She couldn't lie to her—even though she wanted to, Em would see right through it. She'd at least have the night, and maybe longer, to come up with a decent way to phrase her reaction to the play.

CHAPTER FOURTEEN

Emilie leaned against the stucco wall of the festival offices, tucked out of sight between two large rhododendrons. They were almost ready to bloom, and she ran her fingers over one of the buds. It was still tightly closed at the bottom, where it attached to the plant, but a few millimeters of lacy red flower showed at the top. Arden had told her about the riot of color these bushes would bring to the park in the early spring, and Emilie had loved listening to her talk about the potential simmering just under the surface of the bare late-winter trees and shrubs. Arden saw layers everywhere she looked—all stages of a plant's life seemed to be superimposed, letting her know exactly what she needed to do in order to shape the future.

Emilie sighed and squeezed the bud, hoping to show more of the flower. She loved listening to Arden talk about anything. She just loved being around her. Too much, possibly, since she was all Emilie could think of right now, on what could possibly be one of the most miserable days of her short career.

She had been expecting the call from the office this morning, letting her know that Jay and Lendon wanted to meet with her. She was well aware of how last night's performance had gone, not needing the feedback from the audience to let her know she had failed. Arden had been enthusiastic as she clapped and hooted after the show—Emilie really needed to talk to her about overacting—but the rest of the audience had been as bland as Emilie had been in the role of Cassella.

She had felt distant from the start of the play, like she was watching a car skidding out of control, but she couldn't look away because she was *in* the car. Sitting behind the wheel and causing the wheels to lose traction. Arden and Geoffrey had tried to help yesterday, and Emilie had seen the logic in their statements. She hadn't been able to get out of her head, though, and act. She had been too aware of herself speaking words she didn't feel were hers and wearing clothes that felt like they belonged to someone else—although her costumes were designed specifically for her as understudy, and weren't Gemini's castoffs. She had forgotten the movements she had rehearsed so often, catching herself standing motionless for too many minutes on end and not moving to include the entire audience in the experience.

Part of her was glad Arden had been there. Now she knew Emilie wasn't exaggerating about her ability to play this part. But most of her wished she had lived up to Arden's expectations for her, like the plants she carefully tended. Arden hadn't been able to predict the future for this particular bloom.

Emilie unconsciously closed her fist and the rhododendron bud snapped off the plant. She opened her hand again and looked at the crushed bud, lying on her palm. She had spent the night tossing on her bed, unable to sleep, but she hadn't cried once. Now she was tearing up because of a damned flower. She stuffed it in her pocket and checked her watch. Great. Time for her meeting. She rubbed her fingers under her eyes, wiping away the moisture she felt there, and emerged from the shadows.

She hurried through the office doors and checked in before being sent directly to Jay's office. She had been overwhelmed last time she was here, on her first day in Ashland. She had worried about failing, and her predictions had come true. Her own nerves and fears had gotten in her way, but understanding the concept of a self-fulfilling prophecy was one thing. Keeping it from happening was another thing altogether.

Emilie paused before she rounded the last corner, and straightened her shoulders. She touched her jeans, where she had tucked the broken flower bud, and felt like she had Arden here with her in some small way. She had come to another crossroads in a year too full of them, another time when she could either take action or run away.

She wasn't running away.

She tapped on the open door to Jay's office and walked inside. Lendon got up and shut the door behind her while she went over to an empty chair and sat.

"Emilie. We need to talk about last night," Jay said.

So, no small talk or segues into the conversation. Jay had his hands clasped together, resting on the desk in front of him, and he watched her with an unnerving and intense focus. When she had been here to get her scripts, his attention had seemed scattered in several directions. She preferred that to his current scrutiny, but she would follow the conversational lead and get directly to the point.

"I performed poorly," she said. "I was overthinking and I forgot my placements. I didn't do justice to the play or the character. But you believed I could do better than this when you hired me, and I *know* I can do better. I'm sure you're already looking for a replacement, but I'd like one more chance at the role."

Jay tapped a stack of photographs on the desk, lining them up neatly with the edge of the green leather blotter, while he seemed to give her words some thought. They were probably head shots of all the actors who were drooling over Cassella, praying for the opportunity to play the role.

"It's okay not to be ready for this part, Emilie. It's a difficult play, one that has never been performed before, and the stage is unique. You can't hide behind a sparkly costume on a beautiful set and get away with a mediocre delivery. You have to stand a yard away from the audience, look them in the eye, and convince them you are Cassella. Do you really think you can do this? And do you want to put your reputation—and the festival's—on the line just to prove something that doesn't need proof right now?"

Emilie cringed inside, but she kept her features as relaxed and neutral as possible. Did he mean all her performances, including Titania, had been as weak as last night's, and they were only acceptable because the costumes and set design hid her flaws?

She wasn't pulling on that frightening thread right now. He hadn't mentioned firing her from the company, just this one role, so she would concentrate on it alone. She felt sick to her stomach because she had been holding her breath for too many seconds, and she tried to inhale without making a gasping sound.

"The Saturday matinee. That's all I want. If I'm good enough in the role, I'd like to continue with it. If not, I'll understudy whomever you hire to replace me."

Jay glanced at Lendon, who shrugged. It must have been a shrug for her side, though, because Jay nodded.

"You have Saturday. If we see significant improvement, we'll reconsider keeping you as Cassella, and hopefully you'll grow into the part more and more as the season progresses."

He didn't give an *if not...* to the comment, but he didn't have to. They all knew exactly what would happen if she failed again.

Jay leaned toward her. "Make the most of this chance, Emilie. Not many actors would have one shot at a part like this, let alone two. Do what you need to do to be ready for Saturday. Rehearse more, rehearse less. Think more, think less. Just make a change, and prove us wrong."

"I will. I won't let you down." Emilie swallowed the *again* she was about to add to her sentence and walked out of the office, thanking them at least three times during her short trip to the hallway.

She managed to get outside and back to her rhododendron hiding place before she sank back against the building and forced herself to take deep breaths until the nausea passed. She had won a small battle, but the war was coming for her on Saturday. She had to be prepared.

As much as she wanted to remain in the shadows or run back to her house, she made herself stay in town for the rest of the afternoon. She had to figure out the magic formula for improving her performance, and she only had two days to do it. She couldn't talk to Arden about it just yet, since the memory of her being in the theater last night was still too fresh. And Emilie wasn't sure if Arden was a significant piece of the puzzle she was facing.

Arden was different from anyone Emilie had known before. Arden supported and encouraged her, listening when she needed to talk, and sharing her opinions with an authenticity Emilie knew she could trust.

But Arden also gave her an out. A place to fall when she failed, and a person to turn to when she wanted to run away. Emilie had done it before, and she wouldn't again, no matter how tempting the thought.

Emilie paused by a jewelry store window and stared at the display. Miniature comedy and tragedy masks adorned everything from anklets to earrings, in silvers and golds. Emilie wanted to be part of this world, where theater was a way of life and not a weekend diversion. Would she give up her friendship if it meant success as an actor? No.

She started walking again. She had to change her answer from *no* to *not exactly*, if she was going to be as honest with herself as Arden would be. Emilie valued Arden's friendship, but she wanted more. She wouldn't be satisfied long-term as Arden's buddy, especially if it meant watching Arden hook up with someone else. Emilie had considered exploring the possibility of a more physical—and more deeply emotional—relationship with Arden, but she couldn't let it happen until she was on stable footing here at the festival and could trust herself not to abandon her dreams again.

Emilie stopped again, staring in a shop without registering what was on display. She couldn't let herself date Arden right now, and she couldn't be just friends with her without wanting more. A lot more.

Where did that leave her?

A tap on the windowpane startled Emilie out of her twisting thoughts. She saw Marty, waving for her to come inside.

She stepped through the door and realized she was in an art studio. Marty had told her she was a glassblower when they met at the pub, and Emilie had been meaning to stop by. She hadn't had time to do anything besides work, eat, and sleep, so she hadn't been here yet. She stared at the shelves surrounding her, with hundreds of glass objects reflecting a rainbow of colors in the meager sunlight.

"Wow. This place is gorgeous. Did you make all of this?" Emilie picked up a heavy goblet with beads of a deep red color dripping down the sides, like spilled wine.

"Not all of it. There are two other artists who work here, but the goblet you're holding is one of my pieces. Take it."

"Oh, no, I couldn't," Emilie said. "But I'll buy it from you."

"Nonsense." Marty took it from her and wrapped it in several layers of blue tissue paper. "Consider it a welcome-to-Ashland present. A few weeks late."

"Thank you." Emilie took the package, touched by the generous offer, but not surprised, given that Marty was one of Arden's friends. Of course she'd be kind. Emilie should leave now. Work with her script, concentrate on her job. Not linger here, hoping to hear Arden's name mentioned or to learn more about her. The smart move would be to walk out right now. "I've never been in a glassblowing studio before. Do you have time to show me around?"

So much for smart.

"Sure. The hot shop is back here."

Emilie followed Marty past a curtain and into the industrial-looking space behind the elegant storefront. She recognized some of the equipment from books and movies, but she had never seen the process occurring before her eyes. She was entranced by the colors as they walked through the workspace.

"Ben, the Thor look-alike with the blowpipe, is the owner. Amy is the other artist, over there with the beginner class."

Emilie smiled at the burly blond man standing near the furnace and twisting a steel pipe with a delicate touch, seemingly out of place with his size. He nodded at her before turning his attention back to the impossibly thin blue vase he was creating. Even without any knowledge of the process, Emilie was able to see what a high-quality product he was making. She was even more impressed by the group of beginners, though.

"You teach classes here?" she asked, looking at the interesting shapes the students were making. Nothing as fine as the artisan pieces for sale out front, but beautiful nonetheless. "Could I really learn to do this?"

"You definitely could. Most of our classes are for complete beginners, but we have some locals and some regular visitors who take more advanced sessions. We have a special class coming up for Easter, to make baskets, and you don't need any prior experience to make one."

"Oh, I'd love that," Emilie said, even as she realized she wouldn't be able to take a class. She couldn't put more obligations on her schedule than she already had. She had let herself spend time at the park with Arden, and if anything, she needed to reduce outside distractions and not find more.

Marty had turned away and didn't notice Emilie's shift in mood. By the time she returned from the back of the workshop, carrying a square box, Emilie had her expression under control again.

"Hey, will you be seeing Arden today?"

Emilie felt a curious and happy twist inside because Marty seemed to assume she and Arden were close enough to be together regularly, but the sensation dropped as soon as she thought about why she needed to see Arden right away.

"Yes. I should talk to her today. I mean, I'm going back to the park once I leave here." Marty was looking at her with a strange expression, and Emilie made herself smile. "Is that for her?"

"Yes. It's the medallions for one of her stages." She put the box on a workbench and opened it.

"They're beautiful," Emilie breathed, reaching out to touch one of the flat discs of colored glass. There were three of them—a sun, a starry sky with a crescent moon, and the ever-present comedy and tragedy masks.

"Thank you, but she's the one who designed them. I just blew the glass."

Emilie laughed. "Is that all?"

Marty shrugged, but she looked pleased by Emilie's words. "Easy-peasy."

"I'll be happy to deliver them." Emilie paused, then continued. "She's very talented. Was she always artistic?"

Marty tilted her head to one side while she considered the question. "She was always Arden. Yes, artistic, but also athletic and academic. She was one of those kids who was friends with everyone, involved in things like student council, and always doing some sort of volunteer work. Always involved, but never shining like she could have." Marty leaned her elbow on the workbench and lowered her voice, as if sharing something private with Emilie. "Has she told you anything about her parents?"

Emilie nodded. "I know who they are, and that they left her."

"Right. And that one thing defined Arden. She never recognized how much she had to offer or what she could accomplish because she had failed to be enough to keep her parents here. Like nothing else she would ever do would matter, so she never tried to do anything great. Until you."

"Me?" Emilie asked in surprise, pulling her hand off the sun medallion as if it might burn her.

Marty smiled. "Yes, you. You came to town, and suddenly Arden is creating. Putting herself out there." She nudged Emilie with a playful fist. "You're good for her."

Oh, dear. Emilie couldn't manage to be good for herself right now, let alone be responsible for someone else. She hadn't done anything to make Arden rediscover her creative side—that was all due to Arden's talent and her vision. Emilie returned Marty's smile, though, as she said good-bye. She agreed when Marty told her to think seriously about signing up for a class, knowing she probably wouldn't. She had to make the festival her only priority. She had already slipped off the tracks she had laid when she came here. She walked along the busy streets and breathed a sigh of relief when she got to the park. She stopped near Arden's Elizabethan-gnome stage and watched a young girl and boy making up a play while their parents and a few other bystanders watched and clapped. She set the box at her feet and joined in the applause when the two kids bowed to their audience. Arden had made this magic on her own, regardless of what Marty thought.

Emilie picked up the box and went deeper into the park. She had to make her own magic now—on her own, without any help.

Chapter Fifteen

Arden entered the Japanese garden and walked toward her grandfather's fountain. She saw a young man sitting on one of the props on her stage, and she took a circuitous route so she didn't bother him. He wasn't acting, but was rather sitting and staring into the distance. An internal monologue, she decided, and she quietly kept out of his way.

Gwen was waiting for her by the fountain, sitting on the bench and reading a book. She smiled when she looked up and saw Arden approaching her.

"Thanks for meeting me here," she said, closing her book and resting it on her thighs. She patted the seat next to her, and Arden sat down.

"No problem," Arden said. She had been surprised by Gwen's phone call, but she figured she wanted to talk about the park's stages some more. Maybe give Arden more ideas about how to make them successful. "What can I do for you?"

"I'm looking for an intern for next season. Most of the work is physical—fixing broken set pieces and doing the changes between performances. But the initial work is very creative. We'll be working with directors and designing sets for more than twenty different plays. The pay isn't great, but the experience makes it worthwhile. You'd be given one or two shows of your own, for the second half of the season, and you'd be billed as the head set designer for them."

You'd be billed. What the heck?

Gwen seemed about to continue with her description of the job, but Arden held up her hand to stop her. After Gwen's first sentence, she had been busily thinking about someone she might be able to recommend, and she hadn't realized Gwen was referring to *her*.

"Wait, are you offering *me* the job?"

Gwen looked at Arden with her brows pulled together, making small lines appear on her forehead. "Of course. Did you think I was coming to you as a headhunter?"

Arden laughed. "No. I just have never thought about changing careers."

Not exactly true. Ever since Emilie had taken her on the backstage tour, introducing her to Gwen and giving her a sense of the interplay between sets and actors, she had been fascinated by the idea of stage design. She had even bought some books on the subject at the local bookstore. But give up her job at the park to become an intern? Wasn't she a little old to become an apprentice?

"You have to start at the bottom, but the festival will give you an intensive introduction to the craft. There are few places in the world where you'd have as many opportunities in your first job as you will here. Arden, if your talent lives up to my expectations, you will be able to make a name for yourself. You'd be able to travel, to go anywhere you'd like."

Arden felt herself physically pull back when her mind recoiled from Gwen's words. Arden's world had been shaken time and again by people leaving her to pursue their theater dreams. Was she going to become one of them? Just pack up and leave whenever the whim struck or the next play called?

She took a deep breath and tried to calm her frantically scattered thoughts. Like Emilie had said, she wouldn't be leaving anyone. She didn't have ties to this town anymore, except for the sentimental and habitual ones that kept her in this park. And Gwen had never said she'd have to go—maybe there would be a place for her here, with her beloved festival.

Arden felt herself reaching toward the possibilities Gwen was offering, but tentatively, like a vine slowly twining toward sunlight. A tendril here, a brief touch there, as she imagined working with sets the way Gwen did. Learning a new craft. She had loved the process of working on her miniature stages, but now she was being given a chance to expand and work on a grander scale.

Gwen had been watching her silently, giving her time to process the information, but she seemed to see something shift in Arden's expression and she smiled.

"Let me know by the end of the week," she said, with the smug look of someone who knew they'd won. "It's only a year commitment, Arden. If you like it, you can stay on or move to a different theater. If you don't, I'm sure your supervisor here would welcome you back."

Arden nodded. Jacob would gladly rehire her if necessary. And he'd be jumping up and down in frustration right now if he could hear their conversation, yelling at her not to be a fool and give up this opportunity.

"I'll let you know. And thank you for the offer. I never expected…"

"You're welcome, Arden. You deserve this chance, and I have no doubt you'll make the most of it. If you say yes, of course."

She picked up her book and walked away, leaving Arden alone on the bench. She had always felt connected to the festival, but as a spectator. Or as a cohost to all the tourists, making them feel welcome in the park and the town. She pulled out her phone and did a quick search for the recently announced list of next year's plays. *Macbeth. Twelfth Night.* She scrolled through the list, trying to imagine herself designing sets and painting scenery. It didn't take much effort to see herself on the stages, behind the scenes.

Would Emilie be back in Ashland next year? Would she be acting on sets Arden had designed? Arden sighed. She should be happy she was single and unfettered. She could make a decision about this opportunity without needing to consult anyone else.

She wanted someone else to consult, though. She wanted someone to be part of her decision-making and her future-planning. She wanted someone to care about her fledgling dreams of designing sets, and she wanted to offer the same concern to a partner's goals.

Not just any partner. Emilie. Arden wanted Emilie in her life, standing beside her as they made choices for the future. For their future.

She shook her head. She, of all people, should know better than to expect a lasting relationship with an actor. And now she was considering a job in the theater. She had always been the one left behind, but now she would be on the other side, possibly getting job offers that would give her the urge to move on. Just like her parents.

Arden grew still as she thought about them. They had left, yes, but they had stayed together. Two successful careers, and one life together. She thought about the last few articles she had read about them. Her mom had been in a play in New York until five months ago, when the play closed and they went to California, where her dad was the director of a musical. They had been married over thirty years. Arden leaned her head back against the stone bench. Could she and Emilie ever have a life with each other, with give and take in careers and locations, like her parents had?

She laughed at herself. Suddenly she was holding them up as the ideal relationship. Something to emulate. Crazy.

She saw Emilie's blond hair through the trees and recognized her familiar walk before Em rounded the corner and waved at her. She felt a momentary flicker of pleasure at the idea that her thoughts of Emilie had somehow conjured her up, but she was being foolish. Emilie often came here between rehearsals or before her performances, so her presence wasn't unexpected. And Arden was almost always thinking of her, so there was no real coincidence to be found.

But something had changed for Arden. From the moment she had stumbled upon Emilie, acting in the clearing, Arden's reality had shifted. Toward a new career and toward an uncertain future.

And toward love.

Arden closed her eyes and composed herself before Emilie reached her bench. She didn't want to let these confusing emotions show on her face before she had a chance to figure them out. And she couldn't look at Emilie with an expression of love since she knew Emilie didn't feel the same way about her.

"Package delivery," Emilie said, handing Arden a heavy box. "I was in town and stopped by Marty's shop."

"Ah, the medallions." Arden opened the box and looked at the beautiful glass discs. She would set them in a trifold backdrop of plywood for one of the stages, creating an outdoor setting with a sun and moon. The disc with the masks would go in the center. "Thank you. Did you like her store?"

"It's beautiful. She gave me a wine goblet."

Arden smiled. "She's very talented."

"Speaking of...I ran into Gwen near the entrance to the park, and she told me you were back here. Did she have anything interesting to say today? Anything special to ask you?"

Arden tipped her head to one side. Had Emilie put Gwen up to this? She looked as smug as Gwen had earlier. "She offered me an internship with the company next year. Set design."

Emilie grinned. "And you said yes, right?"

"I said I'd think about it. Did you tell her to ask me?"

"Of course not. I'd heard about the internship, and when I saw a chance to introduce the two of you, I took it. This is all you, Arden, and you deserve it."

Arden draped her arm over the back of the bench and let her hand rest on Emilie's shoulder, giving her a light squeeze. "Well, thank you. For introducing me, and for giving me the inspiration for the stages in the first place."

"You're welcome." Emilie looked at some point ahead of her, showing only her profile to Arden. "So. You saw the play."

Arden exhaled softly. "Yes. I know you asked me not to go, and I'm sorry, but—"

Emilie shook her head. "I don't mind, Arden. I'm embarrassed because you saw it, but in a way, I'm glad you did. You'll be able to understand how much work I need to do if I'm going to improve enough to keep the part."

"Why wouldn't they keep you? You're their new star."

Emilie turned to face her, raising one eyebrow in a *Come on. Really?* kind of expression.

"You are," Arden insisted. "All right, I'll admit it wasn't my favorite role for you, but it's hard to beat Titania."

"Very diplomatic. How long did it take you to think of something true, but not completely insulting to say?"

Two hours. Arden didn't tell Emilie that, though. She just laughed and bumped Em's shoulder as if she thought Emilie was joking.

"I have one matinee to prove myself. Either I do better on Saturday, or they're putting someone else in the role. I wouldn't be surprised if they already have an actor picked out."

Arden was relieved. In all honesty, she had been expecting Emilie to tell her she'd been put back in the understudy role— or worse, taken out of it, too. "Well, you have three days. I'll be happy to run lines with you, or to take you out so you can relax and get your mind off the part for an evening. Whatever you need."

Emilie shook her head. "What I need…what I was coming to tell you is that I won't be coming by the park for a while. This role means too much to me to let myself get distracted, and I'll be rehearsing so much I won't have any free time. You understand, don't you, Arden?"

"Not really." Arden crossed her arms over her chest. She felt cold deep inside, where the love she had been feeling for Emilie only moments before had made her feel warm and hopeful. "Are you saying I'm the distraction you need to eliminate? That spending time with me is the reason your role is at risk?"

Emilie put her hand on Arden's forearm, but Arden didn't change positions or make any move to return the touch. "I'm not blaming you. I'm the one who messed up last night. I'm the one who can't connect with Cassella well enough to perform to the festival's standards. But I am also the one who needs to concentrate on the play until I can step inside it. When I'm around you, I think of…other things."

Arden scuffed her foot through the gravel. Emilie was leaving her, just like Arden had always known she would. But leaving for no good reason, without any notice. Arden had never fought to keep someone with her, if they truly wanted to go, but she couldn't just stand aside and let Emilie walk out of her life.

"Are you planning to sit in your room all alone and read your lines over and over again?"

"If that's what it takes, then yes. The director told me to make drastic changes before Saturday. He expects major improvement."

"So you picked me as your drastic change? How flattering."

"Arden, I—"

"You're wrong, Emilie. You're making the wrong choice. You should be spending more time with me. More time in town and with friends. Not less."

"I have to focus. I'm not here to socialize, but to act." Emilie's voice was sharp, but Arden heard the fear underlying her harsh tone. Fear of failure. Fear that she had been away from acting too long and wouldn't ever be able to come back with the same force and potential she once showed.

"Isolating yourself isn't the answer, Em." Arden tried to keep her voice reasonable, but she felt the woman she loved slipping away from her. Emilie wasn't going to become a brand-new actor overnight. Either she would improve enough to keep the part—and then spend the rest of the season sequestered and staring at a script—or she would lose the role and maybe never recover her confidence. "You're trying to control everything. Work alone, without letting anyone else help. But it's okay to be vulnerable sometimes."

"No, it's not. I was weak and vulnerable in Europe, with hardly any income and trailing along after another person's dreams. I won't let myself feel that way ever again."

"Then you'll never play Cassella well." The words came out of Arden's mouth as soon as she thought them, before she could stop herself from saying them. Their echo lingered between Arden and Emilie, saying everything Arden hadn't wanted to say—that Emilie really hadn't been any good last night, and that Arden had doubts about her ability to ever perform the part better than she had. Both were things Arden would rather have kept inside. Given Emilie's shocked expression, she would have preferred for Arden to shut up, too.

But the words had been said. Arden hurried to explain herself. "Cassella is weak, Em. She's hurting, and she is easily manipulated by everyone around her because she can't trust herself to judge people or situations correctly. So she blindly gives up her child and her freedom, and then she can't get them back. She's everything you dislike in yourself, Emilie."

Arden uncrossed her arms and shifted on the bench until she was facing Emilie. She put her hands on Emilie's shoulders, wanting to keep her close. "You can't play a part like that with control, or by practicing more. At some point you need to be as weak as she is."

"Embrace my inner Cassella?" Emilie's voice was laced with dislike.

"Yes," Arden said. "She's awesome in some ways, too. She keeps trying no matter what horrible things happen to her. And the messier she gets, the stronger and more lucid she becomes. She's resilient and brave, just like you."

Emilie frowned and shook her head. "I don't know. I understand what you're telling me, Arden, but I have to do this my own way. Last night I wasn't prepared for the role because I didn't know I'd be playing it until yesterday morning. But I have a few days before Saturday, and I'm going to prepare the hell out of my part."

She stood up. "It's early in the season. I'll eventually either adapt to the company or not. If I do, maybe we can...Maybe I'll have time to come here and see you more often."

Emilie walked away from Arden, leaving her with the ironic consolation of finally knowing how Emilie felt about her. If Arden meant nothing to her, Emilie wouldn't have bothered cutting her out of her life. She would have been able to see her and chat when she had time. Instead, Emilie saw her as a threat to her ability to concentrate and perform. She needed to feel in control, and her feelings for Arden were getting in the way.

Great. If Emilie didn't care about her very much, she wouldn't have left. And knowing she cared about Arden only made her departure more painful.

Arden picked up the box of medallions and took it to the shed where she had the plywood ready to go. She didn't feel like working on the stages, but she had to keep her mind busy. She'd give Emilie the space she was so determined to have and would take the opportunity to hone her own focus. On her career, and on her stages. She'd call Gwen in the morning and accept the internship. And then she'd see where this new life took her.

Chapter Sixteen

Emilie was lying on her bed, reading through her script and all the notes she had made in the margins for the hundredth time. Every line she read made her think of Arden, and she was seeing Cassella emerge in a new light. She still didn't resonate with the character, and she wasn't convinced she needed less control over herself rather than more, but she was beginning to understand Arden's interpretation of the play. And she was continuing to miss her.

She dropped the script on her stomach and stared at the ceiling. She had gone more than a day without going to the park or meeting Arden in town plenty of times before, but this was different. She had actively pushed Arden out of her life, as if she was reliving the moments before she'd left for Europe but trying to change the end of the story this time. But Arden wasn't Leah.

And present-day Emilie wasn't the one who had run away years before. Unfortunately, she was still as stubborn as ever, and she had to follow through with her plan to immerse herself in *Skywriting* until the matinee—or, as she was calling it now, Audition Day. But even if she stuck to the schedule of readings and rehearsals she had written down, she could still let Arden's suggestions simmer in the background.

Emilie heard a soft knock on her door. "Come in," she called.

"You busy?" Olivia asked, stepping into Emilie's room.

"Yes, but I can take a quick break. What's up?" Emilie set

the script on her bedside table and propped herself up on a pile of pillows. Olivia held up her notebook and Emilie groaned. "Another interrogation?"

"Just a few questions. No, don't get up. You might be more inclined to talk if you're lying down." She pulled Emilie's desk chair closer to the bed and sat down, flipping to a blank page in her notebook. "I saw your reviews."

"Oh, God." Emilie grabbed a pillow and held it over her face, but Olivia tugged it out of her grasp and tossed it aside.

"Have you read them?"

"No. And don't you dare tell me what they said. I have to play the part again on Saturday, and I don't need those words stuck in my head."

"How does this make you feel?"

Emilie raised up on one elbow and glared at Olivia. "Seriously?"

Olivia laughed. "No. Well, yes, in a way. I'm wondering if the reviews change the way you feel about your performance."

Emilie flopped back onto the bed. "Not even a little. I know how I did, and I heard the opinions of the director of the festival. Even if the reviews had been glowing, they wouldn't have changed the way the show went."

"I'm sorry." Olivia tapped her pencil on her notebook. "If it helps, you've gotten some really great reviews for the other plays."

Emilie shrugged. "Thanks."

Olivia put her bare feet on the bed and gently kicked Emilie's hip. "What's the first review you ever got for a play? From anyone, not just in a paper."

"My mom," Emilie said without hesitation. "I got the role of Peter Pan in grade school, but Becky Fisher was jealous and she tripped me during one of the scenes. I cut my lip and had to finish the performance with bloodstains on my costume. My mom came over to me after the show and said, *I told you this was a bad idea.*" Emilie could picture every moment from that production, and the memory made her smile, despite her mother's angry words. "Most of the scenery fell over, piece by piece, so the stage was practically flat by the end of the show. Our teacher spent most of the night in tears. Peter Pan was a bloody mess, and Becky refused to say any of her lines in protest. It was the best night of my life."

Olivia laughed, then shook her head. "You aren't kidding, are you?"

"Nope. Compared to my normal life, this was the most fun I could imagine. And pretending to be someone else was a revelation for me."

"I thought actors liked to play make-believe before they were out of diapers."

Emilie held up her hand, palm facing Olivia. "If you start asking questions about toilet training again, this interview is over."

"Fine," Olivia said with an exaggerated sigh.

Emilie laughed at her aggrieved tone. She thought back, trying to remember games she had played and books she had read when she was small. "My older sister read to me, and she used to do funny voices for all the characters. But she went to college the year I turned four, and both my parents worked long hours, so they didn't have a lot of time for games."

"You were the youngest of five, weren't you?" Olivia made a note on her paper, and Emilie rolled her eyes.

"Yes. I'm sure you already have that information in my file. Anyway, I was in day care most of the time, which isn't necessarily bad, but mine wasn't exactly a stimulating environment. We watched a lot of videos."

"So"—Olivia drew out the word while she flipped through notes from previous talks—"back to your mom's comment about the play…"

"My parents thought acting would get in the way of schoolwork, which would keep me from graduating and getting a job. They didn't consider the theater a legitimate workplace.

Whenever I got a low grade on a test or anything like that, I'd hear the same *I told you so.*"

Almost as if they were happy she had failed in an endeavor they didn't understand or appreciate. Emilie kept that comment to herself, and she also wasn't about to give Olivia details about Europe and Leah. When she had returned to the States, broke and sad, she had gone to her parents' home for solace and a little help getting back on her feet. She had endured an hour-long *I told you so* lecture about the evils of the acting world, and then she had left again, preferring to survive on her own rather than conform to their ideals.

"They wanted what was best for me," she said out loud, defending her family to Olivia and keeping the harsher details to herself. "And in their minds, what was best was getting a job and a husband and having a pack of kids to put in day care."

Olivia gave an unprofessional snort of laughter. "A husband? Didn't they know you at all?"

"A little hint for when you're an actual therapist. Don't laugh at your clients. And no. They thought everything that didn't match what they wanted me to be was just a phase I was going through."

"I'll stop laughing if you stop using your comedy voice." Olivia waved off her protests. "Yes, you do. Especially when we talk about personal topics. Your voice goes all wry and sarcastic. It's funny, but in the biz we'd say you have a classic avoidance complex."

"Maybe it's my way of telling you to mind your own *biz,*" Emilie said.

"Nah. You love it. I'm helping you understand yourself. So you kept acting even though you were discouraged from it."

Emilie sighed and settled back on the bed. Olivia was joking around, since Emilie didn't have some damned avoidance complex. She faced emotions head-on as an actor, putting them on display for the whole audience to see.

As long as they were safe ones. Strength and stubbornness and playfulness—the characters she was comfortable playing were the ones with traits she either liked in herself or wanted more of in her own life. She could play Titania when she was bewitched because it was all in fun, but when it came to Cassella, there were no games involved.

Arden had seen it. She had tried to tell Emilie in the park, but she hadn't wanted to listen. She wanted to power through the role using the very personality traits Cassella didn't have.

She realized she had sprung upright in bed, and Olivia was staring at her with a questioning expression. "Um, acting, yes. I had to keep acting. My life was gray, and acting gave it color. but I learned to hide it from my parents because I knew they wouldn't approve. It was easier to say I was doing homework with a friend than to tell them I was at rehearsals. If I kept my grades up, I was okay."

Until she'd become a professional actor, and then, well, the rest was history. They had been sure she would fail, and when she returned from Europe, heartsick and nearly out of savings, they almost seemed pleased to have been proven correct. They were certain she would finally give up her foolish aspirations and start living a normal life. Instead, she had started off on the journey that had led her here. To Ashland.

And to Arden, who had learned more about her in a matter of weeks than even the people closest to her had ever known. Even more than Emilie knew about herself, apparently.

"Session over for the day?" Olivia asked, as if she understood Emilie's need to be alone and think.

"Please." Emilie swung her legs over the edge of the bed. "Olivia?"

She paused with her hand on Emilie's doorknob. "Yes?"

"Thank you."

Olivia smiled. "For intruding on your personal life?"

Emilie returned her grin. "Exactly."

❖

Emilie joined the *Skywriting* cast onstage Saturday as the audience applauded their performance. She couldn't keep from scanning the seats and searching for Arden, even though she was certain she wouldn't be there. Emilie had been painfully clear that she had thought Arden was part of her acting problems.

She walked backstage to the Thomas Theatre's tiny green room, accepting congratulations from the other cast members with a pleased feeling, and a nod of approval from Lendon with a huge wave of relief. She hadn't been awe-inspiring as Cassella, but she had a feeling she had been good enough to remain in the role. For the time being, at least, and as long as she continued to improve and didn't backslide.

Her hands were shaking as she wiped off the thin layer of makeup. The part had taken as much out of her as she had feared it would, and she was exhausted. But the bone-deep weariness was worth it. She hadn't been as impressive as Gemini in the part, but then again, they each acted it differently. If Emilie could find a way to lose herself in the character during the entire play—not just for moments at a time like she had today—then she might turn this into her part. She might always *be* Cassella, no matter how many others played the part after her.

Emilie changed out of her costume and into jeans and a thick sweater. She still didn't like the character. At all. The past two days had been hell as she prepped endlessly for today. Arden wouldn't have approved of Emilie's intense focus, but she might have forgiven it because of Emilie's methods. She had delved into the past, into her time with Leah and the poor choices she had so willingly made. She had let herself feel all the negativity and doubt she had been trying to keep stuffed inside.

And somehow, over the course of forty-eight hours, the wave of emotions she had always felt hovering over her, ready to crash down and drown her, had become a well of experience she could tap into when she needed it. She was still afraid of drowning if she went too deep, but she would keep trying.

Emilie walked out to the courtyard and was surprised to see a few people waiting there, asking for her autograph on their programs. She smiled and chatted and signed, trying to look cool and casual even though she wanted to hug each person and tell them how relieved she was that they weren't in line at the ticket booth, demanding a refund. She acted like she signed autographs every day, and soon everyone had dispersed and she was alone, walking home in the chill night air.

Once she was by herself, without the matinee hanging over her, she revisited a part of the emotional baggage she had unpacked over the last couple of days.

Arden.

Emilie had traveled back to their first meeting, back through all the times they spent together in the park and in town. Back to their kiss in the catacombs.

Even back to her disastrous insistence that Arden be cut out of her life because she needed to focus on playing a part. She had faced the decisions she had made about Leah, but this one was even harder to look at. Both choices had been made out of fear—the one in the past because she was afraid of taking a chance on acting and the one now because she was afraid of taking a chance on love.

She hoped she could find a way to have both. The career she had always dreamed of having, and the woman she craved beyond anything else. But if she had to choose just one?

Emilie smiled in the darkness as she turned up the walkway toward her house. This time, she would choose love, and not fear. She would choose Arden.

CHAPTER SEVENTEEN

A rden? Are you okay?"

Arden looked up to see Jacob hovering in the doorway of his small office cubicle. She had been waiting for him to get back from lunch, sitting with her elbows on her knees and her head resting in her palms. She must look as bad as she felt if he was using her given name and not his usual nickname for her.

"I'm fine." If *fine* meant she was wallowing in heart-wrenching pain. She hadn't slept much in the few days since Emilie had decided she needed to devote all her time to her job, leaving none left for Arden. She had suspected that losing Emilie at the end of the season, even if they had nothing more serious than a friendship, would hurt her, but she hadn't accurately predicted the depth of that pain. Maybe it was because the break had happened too suddenly, or because it had come in the middle of the festival year instead of at the end as she had anticipated. Maybe she would get over the heartbreak once she had time to adjust to the shock of Emilie's announcement.

Yeah, right.

She wouldn't get over Emilie anytime soon, but she couldn't claim to be surprised by the turn of events. Emilie had been excruciatingly honest from day one about this season, her career, and her need to rebuild her life on her own terms. Arden understood. That didn't make her feel any better, or help with her sleepless nights, but she would support Emilie's decision. Focusing on her own life just might make the process a little easier.

"I need to talk to you, Jacob."

"All right," he said with a cautious tone, his forehead creased in what looked like a concerned frown. He sat across the desk from her. "What is it? How can I help?"

"I'm giving my notice. I think. Maybe." Arden sighed. Way to be decisive. She was really grabbing this new opportunity with gusto. "I might need to quit."

All the worry permeating Jacob's expression and voice disappeared, and he smiled broadly at her. "Great! I was hoping this would happen. Congratulations, Arden, I'm so happy for both of you."

Arden blinked rapidly, trying to catch up with the meaning of his words. "What? You're glad that I'm leaving the park?"

Jacob reached over the desk and patted her hand. "I'll miss you, of course, but anyone can see how you feel about Emilie. I would never want to hold you back from moving away with her."

"Shit. Jacob, it's nothing like that. Emilie and I are friends. We were friends. We're nothing now." Arden paused, more flustered because he had spoken her secret hope aloud than because he had so terribly misinterpreted her meaning. She took a deep breath and started over. "Emilie is concentrating on her career right now, and I'm making plans for my own. I was offered a job with the festival, designing sets. It's just an internship, so I'll probably have time to help out around here when you need me. Or stay, if you can't find someone else."

Jacob sighed and shook his head, but he quickly shifted his expression into another smile, only slightly less enthusiastic than the first one. "That's wonderful, Little Philips. I hadn't realized how much talent you really have until you started making your stages in the park. Focus on this new job of yours and don't worry about us. We'll muddle through without you. Do you start right away?"

"In the fall. That is, if I decide to accept. I'm pretty sure I will, but..." Arden realized she was rambling again and made herself stop for a moment. Too many changes all at once. How could she be sure she was pursuing something she wanted and not trying to distract herself from Emilie's absence? "If I do this, I might get offers to do plays outside of Ashland. I guess I imagined I would stay here, working in the park, forever. Like Gramps."

Jacob put his hands on the desk and leaned toward her. She expected him to say something comforting or nostalgic, and she wasn't prepared for the sternness in his voice. "Your grandfather stayed because he wanted to build a stable home and life for you. Not a prison. He loved this park and was thrilled when you came to work here, but all of us knew you were destined for more than this."

Arden still wasn't sure she was destined for anything in particular, but when she thought about working with Gwen and designing sets for the three theaters at the festival, she felt a shiver of excitement that had nothing to do with distracting herself from Emilie and everything to do with a passion she had never imagined lay deep inside of her. Unfortunately, the passion would always feel connected to Emilie, because Arden doubted she would have discovered it if she hadn't stumbled across Emilie playing Titania in the forest.

"The main work won't start until the season closes," Arden continued. "We'll have some meetings before then, but I want to stay here as long as I can."

"We'll work around your schedule as long as you want." He stood up and came around the desk to stand next to her, setting his hand on her shoulder. "I'm proud of you, Arden. Your grandparents would be, too."

Arden couldn't speak around the sudden tightness in her throat. Her parents were out there somewhere, but Jacob was the closest she had to real family. She nodded, silently acknowledging his support, and he stepped away.

"Joe broke the trimmer again," he said. She was relieved

to have the conversation move away from emotional topics and back to everyday life. "Can you work your magic and fix it? It's next to the door."

"Sure." Arden got up to leave, but he held up his hand to stop her.

"Don't ever sell yourself short, Arden. Not in this new job, and not in any other part of your life. Don't give up on her just yet."

Arden shook her head. "Nice try, Jacob, but she's got other plans."

He shrugged. "Maybe. Maybe not. Today her plan seems to be to walk through the park until you show up."

Arden hated the beat of hope she felt inside. Emilie was here? Why? She kept the muscles of her face relaxed, trying not to betray any emotions.

"She likes rehearsing in the woods. That's probably why she came."

Jacob laughed. "I'm sure you're right. Now go outside and fix that trimmer. And please, let her find you because she's wearing down our paths looking for you."

Arden picked up the trimmer and her toolbox on her way out of the maintenance shed. She sat on a wooden picnic bench next to the river, tucked away in a curve of rhododendrons whose buds were just beginning to burst into pink and red flowers. From her hidden vantage point, she saw Emilie before she herself was spotted. She pretended to be deeply involved in the process of tightening screws on the ancient machine.

After a few minutes, she felt Emilie's presence behind her and smelled a hint of jasmine, but even so she was startled when she felt Em's hands softly cover her eyes. They hadn't touched often, but Arden would have recognized the warmth and texture of Emilie's skin even if she had a thousand hands from which to choose.

"Guess who?" Emilie said. Arden felt the resonance of her rich voice move through their connection and inside her.

"Um, Ally? Karen? No, it must be Leslie."

Emilie removed her hands and slapped Arden lightly on the shoulder. "I guess I deserved that. Do you mind if I sit down?"

Arden shrugged and gestured toward the bench. Emilie sat close beside her, so that her thigh was pressed along Arden's.

"So, how have you been?" Arden asked, relieved that her voice sounded somewhat normal.

"Okay," Emilie said. "Rehearsals for *Richard* are going well. Geoffrey exaggerates every note the director gives him. It's driving her crazy, but he makes the rest of us laugh. And I get to keep the part in *Skywriting*. I wasn't spectacular in this last performance, but I did well enough to convince Lendon to let me stay in the role. For now." She sounded casual, as if everything was fine between them, but Arden knew her well enough to recognize the tension in her quick speech.

"Most of all," Emilie continued softly, "I've been missing you."

Arden closed her eyes and took a deep breath. She opened them again and looked at Emilie, who was staring at the table and tracing the grain of the wood with her thumbnail. "I missed you, too."

"I'd like to go back in time," Emilie continued. A brief flicker of a smile was the only indication that she had heard Arden's barely audible words.

"How far back? Before Europe?"

Emilie looked up toward the tops of the fir trees surrounding them. "That's tempting. But no. If I did that, I'd save myself some heartache, but I'd lose something, too. Maturity, maybe. The chance to come here and be part of all this. The drive to fight for my chance in roles like Cassella. You."

Arden reached out and gently twisted one of Emilie's curls around her finger. Something bright and happy was filling the empty place she had felt inside. "So how far back in time would you go?"

Emilie looked at her then, with eyes full of the same tentative hope that Arden was feeling. "Back to the day I thought I needed to choose between you and the festival. I was wrong, Arden. Whether I succeed or fail on the stage, it's because of who I am and what I bring to the part. I thought you were distracting me, but my problem was that I was running away from the way I felt. Onstage, and with you."

Arden realized she had been holding her breath, and she exhaled with a long sigh. She had seen Emilie doing exactly what she described when she was playing Titania and Cassella. Holding herself apart from the strong emotions that the roles demanded she embrace. And now she was putting Arden in the same category—as someone who made her feel something powerful enough to frighten her.

"If you could go back to that day, what would change?" she asked, running her fingers through Emilie's hair in a steady rhythm, moving deeper through her soft curls each time.

"Instead of stupidly saying I couldn't see you anymore, I'd ask to see you more often. To see more of you, every inch of you," Emilie said, her voice dark and intimate. "Instead of pushing you away and walking away, I'd have done this."

Emilie raised her hand and gently touched Arden's lips with her fingers. The barest hint of friction between the sensitive skin of Arden's mouth and Emilie's slightly rougher fingertips turned Arden's nerve endings into a whirling mass of sensations and heat.

"And this," Emilie added. She leaned forward and kissed Arden, her lips cautious and questioning. Arden answered with a gentle tug on the hand still wrapped in Emilie's hair, pulling her closer and increasing the pressure of their mouths against each other. Emilie relaxed into her, running her tongue across Arden's lips and deepening the kiss with a certainty that Arden hadn't felt in her before. She had heard Emilie talk about her goals and her determination to succeed—and Arden knew her desire to act was a sincere dream of hers—but now Arden was feeling the full force of Emilie's power. She kissed Arden like a woman who knew exactly what she wanted. She wanted Arden, and Arden wanted her right back.

Emilie pulled away slightly. Arden wasn't ready to stop, but she let Emilie move back, reminding herself that they were in a public park, only a few yards off the trail.

"Arden, can you forgive me for saying you were getting in the way? You've never been anything but supportive of me, and I am sorry that I didn't understand that before."

"You hurt me when you pushed me away, but I'm not angry." Arden paused and sorted through the emotions Emilie had ignited inside her. "Frustrated, yes. Sad. But you've told me from the start how much this season matters to you, and I know you thought you had to do whatever it took to keep yourself safe from distractions."

Emilie put her hand on Arden's thigh, and every vein, every capillary, seemed to soak up the feeling of her and spread it through Arden's body until it became as necessary to her survival as blood and air. "I'm sorry. I hate that I hurt you because I was thinking of myself." Emilie shifted her hand, rubbing the length of Arden's thigh with an aching slowness. She gazed at Arden and seemed to see the effect her touch was having, because a smile spread across her face. "I finally figured out that I need to be distracted *more*, not less. And I think you're just the woman to do it."

Arden gave a long-suffering sigh. "I suppose I'll have to make a sacrifice for the good of the festival and completely and utterly distract one of its stars."

"Good. Maybe you should start now, because I have a big performance tomorrow night."

Arden straddled the bench and put her hands on Emilie's waist, scooting her closer. She kissed Emilie again, giving most of herself—but not all—to the moment. Because that's all her relationship with Emilie would be, just this one moment, this one season. There were no promises of tomorrow, but only a recognition of what they wanted today. Emilie gave a soft moan against Arden's lips, and Arden knew that she wouldn't refuse anything Emilie had to offer, no matter how fleeting.

Emilie lost herself in the joy of having Arden in her arms, only moving away when she heard people coming toward them on the trail. She moved a few inches away on the bench as a family with three kids noisily walked past them.

Arden winked at her, and then went back to working on the machine in front of her. She looked unmoved by their kiss at first glance, but Emilie saw hints of it when she looked more closely. A swath of red where Arden's low-cut tank top and open flannel shirt left her skin bare. A slight tremble of her fingers as she used a screwdriver to pry off a metal hood. Emilie wished she had even a touch of Arden's serenity. She was filled with so much relief because Arden had forgiven her that she figured her feelings must be visible for anyone to see. She searched for a topic of conversation that was appropriate for a public venue, because anything more personal would make her want to kiss Arden again. And not stop.

"What's wrong with the patient?" Emilie asked, gesturing at the rusted object. "Whatever it is."

Arden rolled her eyes. "It's a trimmer. Haven't you ever done yard work?"

"No, but I appreciate those who do." Emilie moved her leg so her calf was flush against Arden's. "What do you trim with the poor thing? Rocks?"

"Grass and weeds," Arden said with a laugh. She poked at the battered metal and cracked plastic of the trimmer. "Joe tends to swing it around without paying attention to what he's cutting. Every tool he uses has battle scars."

Emilie watched Arden's fingers as they delicately searched for damage and repaired it. Emilie imagined them moving over her body with the same intention and thoroughness Arden showed when she was caring for her plants and machines, and she gave up on the pretense of making small talk.

"I have the night off," she said, spinning a metal washer

across the picnic table. Arden caught it with a quick snap before it sailed off and onto her lap. "Do you want to go on a date with me?"

Arden stared at the trimmer as she put the washer in place and screwed the hood on again, but Emilie saw the curve of a smile on her cheek. "Tonight? That's kind of short notice, isn't it?"

Emilie bumped her knee against Arden's. "Do you have plans with someone else? If so, I'll send Joe and the trimmer after her. That ought to free up your evening."

Arden laughed. "No, I don't have plans, and yes, I'd love to go on a date. What did you have in mind?"

Sex. Emilie paused before she spoke the word out loud, long enough to make a better decision. They had been too many things in relation to each other in too short a time—friends, estranged, and now on the brink of something new. She didn't want to rush and miss the beauty and excitement of what was happening between them.

"How about dinner? My roommate raved to me about a Thai place on Pioneer Street. I'm not sure what it's called."

"It's new," Arden said with a nod. "I haven't been yet, but I've heard it's great. I think it's called the Bard's Thai Restaurant."

"No way," Emilie said, scrutinizing Arden's expression to see if she was joking. She looked completely serious, but then she grinned.

"No way," Arden mimicked. "The real name is even worse, though. It's called Sweet Balm."

Emilie squinted, scanning through scripts in her mind because the phrase sounded familiar. The memory of a high school production came rushing back. "Oh, from *Antony and Cleopatra.*" The satisfaction of deciphering the clue was quickly replaced with a horrified glee. "Ew, she was talking about poison."

Arden joined in her laughter. "I know. How great is that? I think they did a search online for a Shakespeare reference and didn't bother reading beyond the single line."

"Well, it's settled, then. We have to eat there. Did you want to do something else? I have the whole evening off for once and don't want to waste a minute of it without you."

"I have a few ideas," Arden said with a smile that made Emilie's mind leap back to her initial plan. Sex. Skip dinner, and more sex. Arden shook her head as if reading her thoughts and took hold of Emilie's hand, lacing their fingers together. "But maybe we should stick to things we can do in public. For now. Why don't we each plan something, and then have dinner. I'll be finished with work around four thirty."

A night with no plays, no rehearsals, no stress. Just Arden. Emilie smiled. "I'll be here," she promised.

CHAPTER EIGHTEEN

Emilie got back to the park early, but Arden was already waiting for her at the bottom of the stairs, sitting on a stone bench with her long legs crossed and her loose brown hair shining in the soft spring sunshine. She had changed out of her flannel and grass-stained jeans and into black jeans and a long-sleeved green cotton shirt. The work clothes gave her an earthy, confident appeal, but tonight's outfit was just plain jump-her-bones sexy. Emilie paused before approaching her. She had been an eddy of nerves this morning, as bad as her worst case of stage fright, because she hadn't known if Arden would accept her apology and come back into her life, or tell her to go to hell. She had underestimated Arden's kindness, though. Emilie had spent too much time with people like her parents who ignored her dreams, or like her ex who actively crushed them. She had let them fill her mind with doubts about Arden's generous spirit, but they were receding now. All she saw was Arden. Waiting for her.

Arden was fiddling with her phone, but she looked up and spotted Emilie as soon as she reached the bottom of the stairs. She stood and came toward her, with a smile that Emilie knew must mirror her own.

"Hey. You look beautiful," Arden said, giving her a quick kiss on the mouth.

Not enough. Emilie slid her hand around the nape of Arden's

neck and pulled her close for a longer kiss. She felt a little breathless when they moved apart.

"So..." Arden drew out the single syllable as she ran her forefinger down the side of Emilie's face, leaving a trail of heat along her cheekbone. "Ready to get started?"

"It depends on what you have planned."

"Geocaching."

Emilie raised her eyebrows. "What?"

"Geocaching," Arden repeated. "People hide caches all over the world and post coordinates and clues online. There are a bunch in the park and around town, and there's a new one I haven't found yet. I know you like puzzles, so I thought you'd have fun solving this one."

"That's not exactly the activity I had in mind, but I'm intrigued." Emilie smiled, pleased Arden had noticed that if she wasn't reading scripts, she was usually doing a crossword puzzle. "Do I get a prize if I win?"

Arden laughed. "You don't really win. You find. People usually leave little trinkets behind, and you can take one and leave something of yours."

"Okay," Emilie said. This didn't sound like a typical date activity, and she loved the way Arden brought unexpected things into her life. "How do I start?"

"I've programed the coordinates into my GPS. We'll follow them to the general location of the cache, and then use a clue to find it."

Her fingers brushed against Arden's as she took the phone from her, and Emilie wasn't about to let the tingly feeling slip away. She transferred the phone to her right hand and kept hold of Arden's with her left. She frowned at the map, trying to figure out how to follow the arrow that wobbled each time she moved.

"Huh. This way, I think," she said, starting to walk deeper into the park. Arden didn't follow her, and when Emilie got the length of her arm away she snapped back to Arden's side.

"Try again," Arden said with a laugh.

"Okay, how about this way." She walked in the opposite direction and Arden came with her this time. They walked out of the park and turned right on Main Street before Emilie got the hang of using the GPS.

"A few blocks ahead on the left?" she said with a hint of question in her voice.

"Not even close. Remind me never to ask you for directions," Arden said, bumping into Emilie's side. "How do you manage to navigate those confusing catacombs under the theaters?"

"There are signs pointing the way. And I only got lost once. Maybe you heard about the unexpected appearance of a fairy queen in Caesar's forum?"

"As a matter of fact, I did see that in the paper. The reviewer thought she added a sense of whimsy to the tragedy."

Emilie laughed. "Who knows what character will show up in Rome next. Maybe Lady Anne? Hey, we're supposed to turn right, I think."

"Now you've got it." Arden gave her hand a squeeze, and Emilie nearly dropped the phone. She tried to concentrate on following the trembling arrow instead of the way her insides quivered at even the slightest touch from Arden.

She stopped in front of a small coffee shop. "We're here, aren't we?" She looked at the storefront, with its flagstone patio and wrought-iron furniture. Both sides were flanked by large planter boxes full of geraniums and petunias. "So where's the treasure?"

Arden dropped her hand and got a piece of paper out of her pocket. "Ready?"

Emilie nodded. She was ready for Arden to be holding her hand again. But she'd come this far, and now she wanted to find whatever this cache thing was.

"Don't look down; don't look up; look in between. Find a hidden L-shaped spot where shadows make a scene."

Emilie repeated the words silently as she surveyed the patio. "The planter boxes? They'd make good hiding places and they're an in-between height. Oh, the pergola. It makes a sort of stage."

The crosshatched shadows from the pergola covered the back half of the patio. Emilie walked toward the back beams and found a spot where a two-by-four jutted out of the wall and connected to one of the wooden posts, making an L-shape. She glanced back at Arden for confirmation, but Arden only shrugged. She was grinning, though, and Emilie went over to the section for a closer inspection.

"What am I looking for?"

"You'll know when you find it," Arden said from directly behind her. She had crossed the patio and was standing close enough for Emilie to detect the honey-sweetness of her.

"That's helpful," Emilie said with as much sarcasm as she could fit into the phrase. She reached around the post and felt along the two-by-four. "I'd better not touch a bug. Oh, wait, I found something."

She tugged on the square-shaped plastic box, and it came loose from the underside of the beam with the scratchy sound of separating Velcro. She opened the lid and found a notebook with a tiny pencil inside, along with a pile of charms and coins. She grinned, as happy as if she had discovered real treasure. "What do I do now?"

"Sign your name and date to the register, then swap out one of the little prizes for something of yours. I have a magnet from the park if you need something to leave."

Emilie rummaged in her messenger bag for a pin she had bought at the festival's gift shop on her first visit. They had a bunch of them with Shakespearean insults, and she had bought several. She showed Arden the one with *thou art a boil* printed on a blue background. "How's this?"

Arden laughed. "Perfect."

Emilie swapped the pin for a miniature troll doll with purple hair. "And I'll take this, to complete my collection."

"Excellent choice," Arden said. "While you're signing the log, I'm going to go inside and get us something to drink."

Emilie added her name to the notebook and carefully put the plastic box back where she had found it. By the time she had finished, Arden was back with two fizzy lemonades in plastic cups.

"What's next on the agenda?" she asked as they started walking back toward the festival grounds.

Emilie fished a key tied to a red leather lanyard out of her bag and dangled it in front of Arden. "I have a key to a magical world. Just for you."

Arden wrapped both hands around her cup and gazed toward the sky. "Please tell me it's a key to your apartment." She dropped her supplicating tone and added, "Well, unless you weren't kidding about the troll collection."

Emilie laughed. "You'll have to see for yourself. Sometime. Maybe. Okay, anytime. But this is something different."

She led Arden down an alley to the back entrance of the Thomas Theatre and opened the door with the key. She took a staircase leading down to a dimly lit hallway.

"Looks like they spent all their decorating budget on the foyer and stage," Arden said. Unlike the elegant front of house, with its warm and luxurious textiles, everything around them was bare cement. Stenciled signs provided the only splash of color.

Until Emilie got to the double doors at the end of the hall and tried the handle. Gwen had left them open for her, and Arden stopped as soon as she saw what was inside.

The walls were covered with propped-up pieces of stage sets, ranging from outdoor gardens to indoor city apartments. Rows and rows of wooden framework boxes held smaller painted bits of scenery, and furniture and other heavy props were placed in clusters around the room.

"You might be using some parts of these old sets next year," Emilie said, watching Arden set her drink on a ledge near the door and walk slowly around the room. "These are just the ones

Gwen wants to keep at hand in case they're needed, and there's lots more in storage in other places."

Arden had circled back to Emilie, and she cupped her face gently in her hands. She kissed her softly, lingering for a long moment before letting her go and allowing Emilie's heart to beat again. "This is awesome. Thank you. Can I touch them?"

Emilie laughed at the sound of childlike wonder in Arden's voice, in such contrast to her usual poise and her definitely mature kissing ability. "Of course you can. These will be your sets soon."

Arden started another circuit of the large space with Emilie trailing behind. "I remember this from last year's *Tempest*," she said. "Oh, and this was from the first act of *Romeo and Juliet*, when they met at the Capulets' dance."

Emilie listened in amazement as Arden displayed a nearly encyclopedic knowledge of the festival's productions. She might not have realized her passion for stage design before this year, but her mind had apparently been cataloging every detail of every play she saw in anticipation of her eventual moment of self-discovery.

When they finished the impromptu tour, Emilie put her hands on her hips and scanned the room. "They're putting on *Much Ado About Nothing* next season, on the Elizabethan stage. What pieces would you use for the set?"

"Those trees," Arden said without hesitation, pointing to a large arbor scene. "And the castle interior. What would you pick for *Macbeth*, in the Bowmer?"

"I can picture the witches standing in front of that one." Emilie indicated a piece covered with indefinable dark swirls of paint. "And I'd accept the role of Lady Macbeth if I could have this one as my dressing room."

"Very gracious of you," Arden said. She smiled, but Emilie sensed a sudden shift in her mood. A haze of sadness dropped over them, as if a curtain had come down on a play. She knew Arden expected her to leave at the end of the season, and she would have to if she was offered a role that was impossible to turn down. But they were here now. Emilie's contract and her heart wouldn't let her leave before November.

"Here's a tough one," Emilie said, calling on her acting skills to keep her voice happy and steady, with no quavering. She was determined to make the most of their time together, without allowing darkness to creep in. "A director wants you to design a set for his steampunk version of *King Lear*. What do you choose?"

Arden laughed at the odd juxtaposition of genre and play, and Emilie felt a sense of triumph for making her smile. "Steampunk *King Lear*? Hasn't that been done to death? Well, I guess I'd start with the factory piece over there, which is from a stage version of *Great Expectations* I saw a few years ago..."

Emilie moved closer and took Arden's hand, intertwining their fingers as the game continued.

Arden would have liked to stay in the storage room for another several hours, but eventually she started to notice the rumbling of hunger in her empty stomach. Emilie must have been starving, too, although she never once complained or suggested they leave.

"Ready for dinner?" Arden asked, pulling Emilie closer to her. She had loved their game, partly because it had been fun to make up increasingly bizarre play staging requirements for each other, and mostly because she was impressed with Emilie's quick mind and creative way of thinking. She wrapped her arms around Emilie's waist and leaned forward until their foreheads were touching. She had nearly plummeted too far when Emilie mentioned staying for another season to play Lady Macbeth. Luckily, Emilie had managed to pull her back to the present and keep her from running out the door and away from this relationship. It wasn't a stretch to believe that the role might be offered to her and that she might decide to stay for another year, but it still wouldn't be forever. It would only make it harder for Arden to say good-bye.

Emilie sighed and slid her palms around Arden's neck until her hands were clasped behind Arden's head. Emilie's wrists were a welcome weight on Arden's shoulders, and she felt complete. Solid and grounded.

"I'm hungry," Emilie said, her voice soft and close, her breath caressing Arden as she spoke. "But we can stay as long as you want."

"I'll have plenty of chances to come back here next year, I guess," Arden said. "Although it won't be nearly as much fun without you and your crazy ideas."

Emilie laughed, moving her head back and looking Arden in the eyes. "I think *Romeo and Juliet* set at an amusement park is a brilliant concept. The Capulets and Montagues can have competing concession stands, and instead of dueling, they'll compete against each other at that arcade game with the balloons." She closed the small distance between them and kissed Arden. "Really, you should pitch it to one of the directors. And be sure to thank me when you win your Tony."

"I'll pitch it if you promise to play Juliet, the Bearded Lady."

They shifted apart and left the room. Arden kept hold of Emilie's hand and kept walking, even though she was tempted to remain in this wonderful space where they had privacy and where she felt connected to Emilie.

The restaurant was only a few blocks away from the festival campus. The location was prime, with three theaters that were often full of tourists close by, but the décor was uninspired, with red and gold accents barely drawing attention away from the bland beiges and browns of the carpet, the tables, and the walls. The odd assortment of knickknacks somehow stopped short of being kitschy and cute, and instead looked tacky.

They were seated quickly since they had arrived after the night's plays had started. The streets and restaurants were crowded before and after the shows, and strangely quiet during them, and only three other tables were occupied. Emilie sat across from Arden and surveyed the other diners.

"They seem fine," she said, turning her attention to the laminated menu. "I guess it's safe to eat here."

"Unless they use a slow-acting poison." Arden moved her feet so they were in contact with Emilie's under the table.

They ordered their dinner and chatted while they waited for their food. Arden tried to give her full attention to the conversation, but her mind felt detached, as if she was watching the table from a distance. They talked easily, whether it was about serious topics like Em's acting or Arden's new job, or silly ones. Arden knew she was going to have a breaking point with Emilie. A moment when she couldn't let the relationship go further because it would be too hard to let go. She had no idea when it would hit her, but it was always there, on the edge of her thoughts.

"Do you want to try some of mine?" Emilie asked as soon as their meals had been delivered. She held a forkful of cashew chicken toward Arden.

"You haven't even tasted it yet. Are you using me as a guinea pig?" Arden laughed and twisted some pad Thai noodles around her fork.

"Maybe." Emilie ate the bite of food she had tried to give Arden. "Hmm. It seems okay."

Arden wanted to play along, but she suddenly didn't feel like joking. "I can't do this forever, Em."

Emilie frowned at her plate. "I know. It's not great. Not the worst I've ever had, but—"

"Not eating here," Arden said, laughing in spite of herself. "Us."

"Oh."

The single word, spoken quietly, lingered between them for a few moments.

"I hated it when you walked away the other day, Emilie. And then today, you came back and I was so relieved just to be near you again. I just…I don't want to stop being with you, but someday I might have to end things before I lose myself completely."

"But not right now?" Emilie's eyes were red, as if she was fighting not to cry, but there was a hopeful smile on her face.

Arden shook her head. "Not right now."

Emilie nodded and brushed her thumbs under her eyes. Arden wanted to go over and sit next to her, but she stayed where she was and gave them both a little time to pull themselves together.

"I can't tell you what will happen to me tomorrow, let alone next year," Emilie said. "I haven't had a consistent day since I got to Ashland. One day I'm doing all right, and the next I'm giving the worst performance of my life, and then I'm mediocre and barely good enough to keep the part for another week. I don't know whether I'll make something of myself this season or not do well enough to get any offers in the future."

She reached across the table and grasped Arden's hand. "I have to keep trying, though. I owe myself this year. I want you to be part of it, but I understand that the unpredictability is hard on you. If you need to walk away from us, I'll let you go. But until then..."

Until then, Arden could let herself be close to Emilie, knowing they both were walking into this with their eyes open.

She gave Emilie's hand a squeeze, and then let go and started to eat again.

"I have a ticket for tomorrow night's performance," Emilie said. "Do you want to go? Or are you sick of seeing the play?"

"I'd love to," Arden said, relieved at the change in subject. "I like seeing the plays more than once, even though I'd go bankrupt if I did that every season. I was planning to try to get a seat tomorrow, though."

Emilie stabbed at a slice of carrot with an annoyed expression on her face. "Yeah. You probably wouldn't have had any trouble getting in, since people are still canceling. Not as much as the first night, but still...it's bad for the ego."

Arden smiled. "Give it another week or two, and everyone

will have forgotten Scorpio, or Leo, or Gemini, or whatever her name was. You'll be the one they want to see."

Emilie laughed. "Thank you. I'll be sure to tell Capricorn you said that the next time I see her. Now, are you sure you don't want to try my—"

Emilie went through an elaborate gagging and choking scene before slumping forward on the table, while Arden calmly took a drink of her beer and then went back to eating.

"Aren't you going to rescue me?" Emilie asked, her head resting on her arm and her voice muffled.

"I'll give you mouth-to-mouth later," Arden said, reaching across the table and spearing a piece of chicken with her fork.

Emilie sat up and flipped her hair off her face. "I look forward to it," she said, giving Arden a grin and going back to her meal.

Arden made good on her promise an hour later, when she and Emilie said good night near the park entrance. A stream of people were leaving the theaters and heading back to their hotels or into town, and Arden pulled Emilie off the path and behind a huge oak tree. She rested her palms against the trunk on either side of Emilie's head and leaned forward to kiss her.

The voices and laughter coming from the crowds faded into the background as Arden's lips moved over Emilie's, and she moved willingly when Emilie put her hands on Arden's lower back and pulled her closer until their bodies were flush against each other. She softly bit Emilie's lower lip and felt a shiver run through her.

Arden kissed Emilie's cheek and then her forehead before pushing away from the tree and Em's embrace. She felt tired all of a sudden, worn out from the ups and downs of the day. The morning had been hell, but the date with Emilie had been perfect, aside from the uncertainty about their future.

Emilie trailed her fingertips over Arden's face and neck. "I should get home and get some sleep," she said, as if she had been able to read Arden's weariness through her touch and was coming up with an excuse to leave. "Early rehearsal tomorrow."

Arden nodded. "I have an early morning, too. But I'll see you in the evening?"

"Maybe we can get a late dinner after the play." Emilie gave her another kiss and walked toward the stairs. She looked back over her shoulder once, with a happier smile on her face than Arden had seen so far. She was tempted to call her back, to keep kissing her, to make the night last forever, but she wasn't ready. Twenty-four hours ago, she'd thought Emilie was out of her life for good. She needed more time to process the change.

She watched until Emilie was out of sight, and then turned and started for home.

Chapter Nineteen

Emilie woke up the next morning before her alarm went off. She had left her blinds open, and the rising sun eased her gently awake. Much better than the jarring buzz of her clock. She stretched and sat up, feeling a goofy grin spread across her face as she remembered the night before.

She couldn't remember the last time she had felt this relaxed and happy in the morning. No twists of tension in her belly because she had to face the company director, or a distressing rehearsal, or a potentially disastrous performance. They were all still there, of course, lurking in the corners of the room and waiting to pounce, but for the moment Arden had banished them all.

She took a long shower since she was up early enough and didn't have to rush for once. She kept her hair knotted and out of the water. Her skin felt charged today, tingling from the memory of Arden's touch and from the anticipation of even more contact tonight. The thought of massaging shampoo into her hair and feeling her fingers moving along her scalp sounded wonderful to Emilie, but she wouldn't wash it until after tonight's performance. She wasn't going to subject herself to another diatribe from Velda about the ghastly consequences of too-clean hair on a wig-wearing day.

Emilie slipped into a silk robe and sat at the kitchen counter eating instant oatmeal and doing a crossword puzzle. She wanted to go to the park and talk to Arden before her rehearsal, but they each needed to focus on their day before they had a night together. Arden was working and putting up the last of her stages. And Emilie had to refocus on Cassella. She doubted whether her chirpily good mood was the right mind-set for her to have before she played the role of a troubled and depressed woman.

Emilie shrugged to herself, her thoughts wandering back to Arden as the robe's fabric moved across her bare skin with gentle friction. She had played Cassella when she herself was in a bad place, and that hadn't ensured her success in the part. She'd revel in her positive mood today and let the part take care of itself. She couldn't do any worse than she had the first night.

Well, if she really thought about it, she could. She busied herself washing her bowl and getting dressed so she wouldn't have time to think about it, and then she walked to the rehearsal hall near the theaters.

She practically bounced onto the stage for her first entrance before slowing down and letting the words flow out of her. Full rehearsals had stopped once the production began, but some of the cast had continued to meet with the stage manager since she had been thrown into the part at the last minute. They ran through some of the key scenes, but the mood was more low-key than it had been before. She had the part now, and even though everyone's expectations were fairly low, she wasn't the terrifying risk she had been after her first performance.

They'd needed to make some technical changes after *Richard III*'s first night, so she still had rehearsals for the play this week, and she ran to the next stage as soon as the *Skywriting* cast was released. She doubted they'd need more than another day or two before everyone was comfortable with the altered cues, which was good because she was scheduled to start rehearsals for *Toxic* next week.

Emilie collapsed on her back during a short break while she wasn't needed onstage. Geoffrey, as Richard, sidled over to her with the weird way he had of moving when he was in character.

He had hammed it up during rehearsals, to the director's chagrin, but as soon as he was onstage his movements became subtle and stiffly graceful. He acted with his entire body, and Emilie had learned a lot just by watching him.

He sat next to her and dropped Richard off himself like tossing off a piece of clothing.

"You have been smiling all day. It's very becoming offstage, but Lady Anne looked a little too happy while standing next to her husband's casket. Is this the bloom of love upon your cheeks?"

"Love? No." *Yes.* Emilie couldn't deny it was love, but she didn't know what kind yet. More than friendship, more than casual dating. Less than forever? She wasn't sure. "I'm just giddy because I get to play Cassella again." She clasped her hands together and gazed heavenward. "Oh, please let there be hundreds of critics in the audience tonight."

Geoffrey laughed. "You're improving, and that's what matters. Don't read any nasty reviews in the paper. And definitely stay away from those blogs. Just keep focused on your work, and soon enough they'll be praising your talent like they were the ones who discovered you."

"Thank—wait, what blogs?"

"Did I say blogs? I don't think so. What? Yes, I'm coming. Gotta go, Ems."

Emilie hadn't heard anyone call him, but he got up and trotted off. She wasn't about to start searching for online criticisms, especially not today. She put his words firmly out of her mind and returned to thoughts of Arden and what they'd do tonight. Their kiss had been explosive, setting off pings of fireworks inside Emilie's body. She sensed a hesitation in Arden, though. An attempt to protect herself from their uncertain future. Emilie would respect her boundaries, but she'd be waiting eagerly on the other side of the wall whenever Arden invited her over.

❖

She had hoped a full day of rehearsals and a costume fitting would keep her from stressing about the night's performance, but she didn't need the distraction. She felt good, and the play was peripheral to her mood. She prepared carefully, of course, and made sure she had a small, light meal and a quick nap before she had to be at the theater. She arrived on time and moved through the process of hair, makeup, and costume without feeling like she was going to be sick.

She felt the familiar wave of nerves as she stood backstage right before her entrance, but it was bearable. Welcome, even, since it heightened her anticipation and sharpened her focus. The smile she had worn all day faded, but the sensation of powerful emotion didn't go away. It transformed into something different, something Cassella-like. Emilie didn't have time to wonder about the new feeling because she was onstage and in the part before she realized she had taken a step.

Emilie had one or two moments when she drifted outside herself and saw the play as if from outside, but they were brief and she easily slid back into character. She was as deeply embedded in Cassella as she had been in Titania the day she first met Arden. Five minutes into the play, and she knew she had managed to do what she had always hoped—to live up to her potential. And her grasp on the part wasn't tenuous or shaky. She had hold of Cassella and was able to let go during intermission, and then grab her once again for the second half.

The standing ovation was nice, but she could just as easily have stood in front of a silent, disapproving audience as long as she had the celebratory feeling inside her and the vision of obvious pride on Arden's face in front of her.

Backstage was an uproar with the usual chaos of undressing and coming down from the performance high, coupled with the cast's response to her performance. There was a mix of disbelief and elation as they congratulated her, and she thought the stage manager might start crying.

The rush of success followed her out of the theater and

propelled her into Arden's waiting arms. After a long, tight hug, Arden put her hands on Emilie's shoulders and held her at arm's length.

"I don't have words. You were spectacular. Beyond spectacular. I'm so proud of you, Em."

She hugged her again, and then gave her a little push toward the crowd of people that had gathered around them. "Talk to your fans, and sign some autographs. I'll be right over here when you're done."

Emilie looked back at Arden, not wanting to leave her side for even a moment. But a large number of audience members surrounded her, and she made sure she paid attention to each one while still glancing now and then at Arden.

An older gentleman handed her a program and a felt-tipped pen. She started to sign her name, graciously thanking him when he told her how well she had played the part.

"I saw you as Titania last weekend. You were lovely." He tipped his head to one side and stared at her. "Although I think you rushed your entrances."

Emilie wanted to laugh. Way to drag someone down from a high, and she hadn't even been up there for very long. She caught a glimpse of Arden out of the corner of her eye, frantically gesturing to her, and she remembered their conversation in the pub. Arden had predicted this. What had she told Emilie to say?

"Thank you," she said, with as much sincerity as she could manage. "I'll take your advice under consideration."

He beamed at her, as if he was about to send his prodigy into the world. He took one of her hands in both of his and shook it. "You are the most beautiful Titania I've ever seen. Once you get your timing down, you'll be perfect."

Arden came over to her as soon as the crowd had moved on. She seemed barely able to control her laughter. "Oh my God. The look on your face when he said that. I have never seen anything so funny."

Emilie bumped into her, and Arden staggered back a few

steps, still laughing. She walked back to Emilie and draped an arm over her shoulder. "He'll be telling people for years about how he gave acting advice to Ashland's greatest star. You made his night."

Emilie smiled. The man's words had been jarring, but they had brought her back down to earth. She put her arm around Arden's waist and steered them toward town. "I'm glad. Now, how about you make mine?"

❖

Arden felt as if Emilie was a balloon, about to rise off the ground and float away at any moment. She understood the excitement Emilie must be feeling because the performance had lifted Arden to another realm, too, and the sensation must be magnified exponentially for someone who had been onstage. Arden had seen the play twice already—with Gemini as the star, and Emilie's unfortunate opening night. Even though she was familiar with the scenes and lines, Emilie made it seem as if Arden was watching something totally new. She had watched with anticipation, holding her breath during some parts—even though she already knew how the events would unfold—and crying unashamedly during others.

She reached for Emilie's hand as they walked. Not to bring her down to earth since she was happy to see such joy emanating from her, but to keep a connection between them. She needed to feel Emilie close, and given the way Emilie was gripping her hand, she felt the same.

"What do you want to do?" she asked. "Eat? Go to the pub? Go bowling?"

Emilie laughed. "Bowling is tempting, but what I'd really like to do is walk for a while, and burn off some of this adrenaline. I just wish we could be away from crowds."

"This way," Arden said, swinging Emilie around until they were walking away from downtown. The hill they were on grew steeper as it led them deeper into a residential neighborhood. Arden intentionally walked out of step with Emilie because it gave her an excuse to jostle her and make her laugh every few feet.

They hadn't gone far before Arden turned up a driveway and alongside a slate-blue and gray ranch-style house. The front yard was neat and well tended, with a few bright spots of flowering plants and a curved bit of lawn. Arden opened the side gate and gestured for Emilie to go into the backyard.

Emilie hesitated. "Is this your house? Or are we trespassing?"

"It's mine. There's a place back here where you can walk in peace." Arden followed behind Emilie as she went through the gate. This was the first time she had ever brought a date to this part of her property. She had invited women into her home and bed, but they didn't go into her yard. She wanted Emilie to see it.

"Whoa. This is...Did you...?" Emilie halted just inside the fence and stared at the garden. Arden had found a small house with a huge lot and had transformed the backyard into a massive garden. Herbs were the stars of the show, but other shrubs and plants that she chose for either their colorful flowers or their interesting foliage were added here and there. The beds were laid out in an intricate pattern, with pink-hued crushed gravel paths twisting and turning throughout.

A white wire archway marked the opening, and Emilie walked through with Arden close behind. She was planning to remain silent and let Emilie have some space after her emotion-drenched performance as Cassella, but Em pointed to plants here and there and asked Arden what they were. Arden happily described how she had chosen each one and showed Emilie all her favorites. Occasionally, she broke off a stem or leaf for Emilie.

"This is marjoram," she said, crushing some tiny, velvety leaves between her fingers. Emilie took her hand and sniffed, brushing her nose against Arden's sensitive fingertips. The light touch made Arden's heart rate increase to what was probably a code red level.

They circled around several times before arriving in the middle, where Arden had built a small brick patio with room for two chairs. A stone bust of Shakespeare nestled in among some sage plants nearby, and a birdbath with little rock frogs perched on the rim was placed in the exact center of the garden.

Emilie closed her eyes and inhaled deeply through her nose. "I can pick out some different scents, but you've created the most beautiful perfume by putting them together."

Arden moved to her side and brushed a tendril of hair off Emilie's forehead. As soon as she let go, the curl dropped back where it had originally been.

"I love your post-performance hair," Arden said. "It's stubborn, with a mind of its own. Just like you."

"It's just relieved to have been released from bald cap hair jail. It's making the most of its freedom."

Arden smiled. Now that she had started touching Emilie, she didn't want to stop. She traced the lines of Emilie's face and neck, the sexy curve of her collarbones, the edges where the fabric of her clothes gave way to bare skin. Emilie had closed her eyes again, receptive to Arden's wandering hands, but when Arden reached under the collar of her T-shirt and followed the swell of her breasts with restless fingers, Emilie looked at her with widened eyes, and a soft flush of red spread across her neck and chest.

Arden switched positions, putting her hands on the hem of Emilie's shirt and sliding upward, taking the folds of material with her. She lifted the shirt until she had access to Emilie's chest, and she leaned down to kiss along the path her hands had taken. She nipped gently at the fullness just above the line of Emilie's bra, reveling in the way she could feel Em's breathing grow more rapid against her mouth.

She tugged Em's shirt back into place. "Do you want to come inside?" she asked, barely recognizing her own voice. It sounded huskier, as if she had been parched for years, and Emilie was the only one who could quench her thirst.

Emilie shook her head. Arden felt a sharp pang of rejection, but Emilie kissed her and pushed that emotion out of the way.

"I don't want to leave this place," she said. She backed up, bringing Arden along with her, until she reached the grassy area next to the birdbath. She knelt on the ground, and Arden did the same. They paused for a moment, and then Arden took hold of Emilie's shirt and pulled it all the way off this time. She tossed it to one side as Emilie yanked off her shirt as well. Her bra followed seconds later, and then Emilie was kissing her breasts and driving the rest of the world away.

Well, most of it. Arden held on to a thread of sanity, even as Emilie threatened to cut her loose from everything she knew and believed. She would let herself enjoy being with Em, and she was especially enjoying the way Em moved her back until she was lying on the ground, with Em kissing her and enveloping her in a soft wave of wild curls. But Arden couldn't forget what their future held, and she couldn't forget everyone who had loved her and left in the past.

She felt the gentle weight of Emilie's hips resting between her legs, and Emilie's tongue flicking teasingly close to her nipple. Emilie had been irresistible tonight. Her talent and her drive excited Arden. Emilie's passion for her career inspired her. But somehow, in the midst of those flighty and ephemeral emotions, Emilie grounded her.

She was grounding her literally right now, as she kissed Arden's lower belly and made her arch her back, pressing her hips into the grass and dirt. Arden grimaced at the pun.

Stop thinking.

Not all the way, of course. Arden needed to keep hold of rational thought, not let herself be ruled by sensations.

She suddenly realized Emilie had stopped kissing and was watching her.

"Where are you?" Emilie asked, her hand resting on the front of Arden's jeans. She had been about to unbutton them and take them off, hadn't she? Arden didn't want her to stop.

"I'm here," she said. *Mostly,* she added inside her mind.

Emilie shook her head, and the brush of hair against Arden's stomach made her moan. "Are you trying to keep some distance to protect yourself, or are you just not feeling turned on by me?"

Arden lifted herself up on her elbows. "God, Em, don't even think that. I've never wanted someone like I want you. You're attractive in so many ways, I couldn't list them all before sunrise."

"So you're intentionally holding back." Emilie moved as if to climb off Arden, but she grabbed her elbow to stop her.

"You know I've been hurt before, Emilie. Some of those experiences are never far from my mind when we're together because I know the end of the season will be here sooner than we realize."

"Arden." Emilie's voice was stern and determined. "I am careful not to be a diva in the theater, but when it comes to sex, I'm as bad as they come. I won't share the stage with a string of your exes or whoever else is roaming through your mind. Either it's just the two of us here tonight, or it'll be you alone with your memories. You have to choose."

Arden didn't have to stop and think whether she wanted Emilie to stay or not, but the decision to forget about those defining moments in her life was harder to make. She kept herself safe because she didn't let herself forget. But Emilie deserved all her attention if they were going to be together, not what was left over after Arden's past took the bulk of it.

Arden leaned back again and closed her eyes. She inhaled and smelled the heavy, dusty scent of sage and the sweet notes of honeysuckle. She felt the cool blades of grass under her shoulders and the slight, growing ache in her lower back from lying on the hard, chilly ground. Most of all, she felt the softness of Emilie's waist as she rocked slightly between Arden's legs and the point of her chin where she rested it on Arden's stomach and watched her.

The texture of Emilie and the aromas emanating from the garden brought her fully into the present. She was going to say something to Emilie, to assure her that she was here wholeheartedly, but Emilie must have sensed her feelings and thoughts as easily as she had before. She gave a contented sigh and resumed her journey down Arden's body.

Arden lifted her hips and let Emilie pull her jeans down her legs and off her body. Emilie's fingers gripped her knees, spreading them wider apart, and every ounce of Arden's heart and mind was there with Emilie as she lowered her head. Arden gasped at the first touch of Emilie's tongue.

Arden wrapped her lower leg around Emilie's hips, anchoring them together as Emilie brought her closer to the edge with every lick and gentle bite. Emilie was relentless, breaking down Arden's barriers stone by stone until there was nowhere left to hide. Arden came, crying out in the dense garden air, her mind emptied of everything but Emilie.

Emilie had shifted until her head rested on Arden's chest, and the quick staccato of Arden's heartbeat echoed inside her. The aroma of the flowers and Arden combined to make a scent so intoxicating Emilie would pay her entire salary for a single ounce. She wanted to stay in Arden's embrace, in this magical garden, forever. She relaxed for the first time in ages, and felt herself drifting toward sleep.

"Ouch," she said, jarring awake when her thigh muscle started to cramp. She had been trying to hold her knees off the chilled ground.

Arden groaned underneath her when Emilie moved to a new position. "How rude of me," Arden said. "You must be very uncomfortable up there on top of me instead of lying on this cushy, hard-packed dirt. Care to trade places?"

Emilie laughed and rolled off to one side, gingerly coming to a sitting position and rubbing her stiff neck. "No, thank you. Say, you wouldn't happen to have a bed inside, would you?"

"As a matter of fact, I do." Arden put her palms on the ground and walked them forward until she was sitting upright. "If I remember correctly, I was going to take you there a few minutes ago, but you said you wanted to stay out here where it's so delightfully freezing."

Emilie booted at Arden with her foot. "Really? Do I hear complaints coming from you?"

"Not a chance, angel," Arden said, leaning forward and kissing Emilie. The kiss transformed quickly, because now they both had experienced exactly where kisses would lead and Emilie felt eager to move forward again. Arden moved away and grinned at her. "You taste so good, Em. I can't get enough of you."

"I taste like you." Emilie got on her hands and knees before standing up, stretching as warmth and flexibility returned to her body. She held out a hand and pulled Arden up, tugging her close for another soul-deep kiss. "Bed," she whispered. "Now."

Arden kept hold of Emilie's hand, only letting go to grab their hastily discarded clothing and again to fish her key out of her jeans and unlock the back door. Emilie looked around with interest—she wanted to thoroughly explore the space where Arden lived, but the bedroom was the more urgent destination at the moment. She got a series of glimpses now and would look more closely at every detail later.

Her general conclusion was a reinforcement of what she already knew. Arden was a skilled designer, and good at blending color and texture to make a pleasing visual impact. As they walked through the living room and down a hallway, Emilie noticed a few pieces that had probably belonged to her grandparents. A crocheted afghan on the couch, a tall, aged armoire stained a warm chestnut brown, and some framed photos of a little girl with solemn eyes and an expression far more mature than her age would suggest.

"Oh, look at you." Emilie stopped in front of one of the pictures, her finger hovering over young Arden's face, as if she could reach through time and connect with her.

"Yeah, yeah, I was adorable. Come on, Em." Arden pulled her away from the pictures and into a room.

Emilie let impressions from the bedroom wash over her as Arden backed her toward the bed until her knees bumped into it. The colors were earthy and warm, with golds and greens and browns everywhere. Most of the surfaces in the room were bare of knickknacks and other items, but the walls were filled with photographs of Arden and her grandparents, as well as some framed prints from festival plays. The overall look was clean and comfortable, but subdued. Arden had poured herself into her garden more than the interior.

Emilie put her arms around Arden as she lay back, bringing Arden with her without allowing a millimeter of space between them. She traced circles on Arden's back with one hand while the other sifted through Arden's soft, straight hair. The strands tickled her aroused, sensitive skin as they dropped against one side of her neck, and Arden slowly kissed the other side with teasing gentleness.

Arden rolled to one side and propped up on an elbow. She watched Emilie's face without breaking eye contact as her hand explored every inch it could reach, from Emilie's collarbones to the curve of her lower belly. Emilie tried to keep her focus on Arden's face, but her eyelids fluttered closed when Arden reached between her legs. Emilie could feel how thoroughly wet she was, and the sensation of Arden's fingers slipping so easily against her made a soft sound catch in the back of her throat. She struggled to inhale and exhale, to keep the movement of her hips under her own control, but she was failing miserably. Her breathing was out of rhythm, but her body matched the beat set by Arden's hand until Emilie had to give up and let her lead the dance.

She opened her eyes and saw Arden watching her still, an amazed and loving smile on her face. Emilie returned the smile for an instant, before the increasing pressure from Arden's fingers brought her to the point of climax.

Emilie made a pretense of keeping herself under control for a few more seconds before Arden shattered her into a million pieces. As the waves of her orgasm slowly subsided, Arden wrapped herself around Emilie, making her whole again even more powerfully than she had torn her apart.

CHAPTER TWENTY

Arden was reluctantly drawn out of her dreams by a shrill and insistent ringtone. She slapped at her own phone on the bedside table before the memory of the night before cascaded into place.

The sound was coming from Em's messenger bag, where it had been flung near her closet door when they had finally stumbled into Arden's bedroom last night. Still as hungry for each other as they had been hours before.

And the long, drawn out *No* coming from under the pillow next to her was Emilie. An oh-so-familiar shape under the covers, with her untamed curls peeking out from the corner of the sage-green pillowcase. Damn. Even the color of the bedding complemented her, as if the room had been specifically designed for Emilie to be here. Just like Arden's heart had felt last night.

She got up and dug out the phone, bringing it back to the bed and pressing it into the seemingly disembodied hand that was hanging over the edge of the mattress. The fingers closed around the annoying device and disappeared under the covers with it.

She heard a mumbled conversation as she got back in bed and reached out a hand to tentatively rest it on the comforter-covered Emilie. The response was immediate, both in her own body, where a heavy feeling of desire surged low in her belly, and in Emilie, who burrowed against her. Arden sighed, her need to get a little space and process the events of the night before fighting a losing battle against the urge to smash the phone to dust and have her way with Emilie for the third time. Or was it the fourth?

Common sense was on the fringes of her mind this morning, but it had been nowhere in sight last night. They had months ahead of them to let the relationship develop. She had expected to continue at their slow pace, maybe ending the evening with a kiss the way they had the night before, but watching Emilie onstage had affected her in a completely unexpected way. She had seen her act poorly as Cassella, and had seen her do the brilliant, transporting scene as Titania alone in the woods. But last night she had taken her performance to another level, one Arden knew had always been waiting inside her, and Arden had felt prouder than she possibly could have if she had been onstage herself.

Pride wasn't enough to make her push aside her carefully laid boundaries, however. Even though Emilie had seamlessly been Cassella last night, she had strangely been the purest version of herself at the same time. She had given herself wholeheartedly to the role, holding nothing back, and she offered the same fullness and generosity to Arden last night as they lay on the ground enveloped by the bitter-floral scents of rosemary and lavender.

Arden hadn't had a choice but to be with Emilie. Well, she had *had* a choice, but she hadn't wanted one. She had only wanted Emilie.

Emilie's hand reappeared to toss the phone across the room in the general direction of her bag. She reached out and took hold of Arden, pulling her under the covers.

Safely ensconced in the tent made by the comforter, Arden went into Emilie's embrace without resistance. Emilie smiled at her without seeming to have any of the reservations about the speed and direction of their relationship that Arden had.

"You're amazing, Arden. Everything about you, from the way you help things grow and create beautiful spaces like your garden and the park stages, to the way you make me feel when you touch me. Thank you for sharing all of this with me."

Arden was taken aback. She had expected normal morning-after talk, not for Emilie to pull something out of her soul and examine it like a precious object. She wasn't sure what to say in response.

"I've never shown anyone the backyard before. I mean, friends have seen it, so it's not like a secret place. But in a way it is, because I never took anyone I was seeing out there."

Apparently, she had chosen the right words, because Emilie's smile grew wider and she pulled Arden to her for a kiss. A stomach-churning, leg-tangling, hand-wandering kiss. Arden came up for air eventually, lying on top of Emilie now, with Em's thighs holding her tightly in place.

"I have to be in Jay's office in half an hour," Emilie said, her lips tickling the side of Arden's neck as she spoke. "I don't want to leave."

Arden ran her hand up and down the length of Emilie's back. "Neither do I. But I have to be at work, too, so I'll drive you back into town. Do you want to shower here, or at your house?"

Emilie propped her chin on Arden's chest and smiled at her like a cat waiting to pounce on a quivering toy. "I'll shower here. If you'll join me."

Arden was tempted, but they both had places to be and people who were expecting them. She might have given in and let them skip their meetings and work for just one morning, but she was certain that Jay wanted Emilie in his office to talk to her about the performance she gave last night. Emilie had worked hard to get where she was and had faced embarrassment and insecurity at the festival. She deserved every ounce of the praise she was going to get today, and Arden wasn't going to steal a moment of it from her.

Okay, when Emilie got out of bed naked and slowly walked around the room, bending over to pick up her things in an exaggeratedly suggestive way, Arden nearly forgot her sense of reason yet again and followed her into the shower. Em had a gift for expressing state of mind through her body—as Arden had learned so well last night—and she managed to convey sexy and goofy so compellingly that Arden was torn between laughter and soul-melting desire.

This was going to be Emilie's morning to bask in the director's applause instead of his threats to take her part away, and Arden wouldn't let her be late. She chose laughter, throwing a pillow at Emilie before falling back onto the bed and pulling the covers over her. She wouldn't have time for a long shower, but she'd be sure to make it an ice-cold one.

Emilie walked back to the park after her meeting, in enough of a daze that she missed the familiar entrance and followed the set of brick stairs leading to the street instead of the ones that would have taken her into the park proper. She took the long route from the road and past the duck pond, both excited to see Arden and dreading the talk they needed to have.

She had been euphoric this morning, with the lingering elation from her performance weaving in and out of the wonder of sex with Arden. Love and passion—for Arden and for her career—had come together in a glorious way this morning. She had experienced the frantic high of a great performance before, but this had been something else entirely. A homecoming, making her full of peace and a sense of rightness.

She was glad she had been able to have her morning, without the knowledge of how quickly everything was going to change.

She spotted Arden in the distance, near the tennis courts. When she had walked toward Jay's office, still feeling a twinge of nervous anticipation on the walk down the long hallway, even though she knew he would only be pleased with the way the play had gone, she had imagined running into Arden's arms after the meeting. Dragging her to a secluded spot in the woods and continuing what they had started this morning. Instead, she slowly followed the trail, wanting to make the walk last as long as possible.

Arden turned before she had crossed the last yards separating them, as if she sensed Emilie's approach. Her welcoming grin faded slowly as her eyes scanned Emilie's face.

"What's wrong?" she asked, coming quickly to Emilie and taking one of her hands. "He didn't have any complaints about last night, did he? He couldn't possibly."

Emilie shook her head, mute with nervousness.

"Then what is it? You're scaring me." Arden put the fingers of her free hand under Emilie's chin and tipped her head so they were looking directly at each other.

"I'm sorry, Arden. I'm just in shock." Emilie finally found her voice and forced a smile on her face. "He wanted me to meet someone. Her name is Sasha Allston, and she saw the play last night. *Skywriting* is going to Broadway next spring, and she's directing."

"Oh? Oh." Between two blinks of her eyes, Arden's entire demeanor changed as she filled in the gaps in Emilie's story. "Hey, that's great, Emilie. I'm assuming she wants you to play Cassella for her."

Emilie nodded. She grabbed Arden's arm as Arden turned away from her, to keep Arden from walking back to the shrubs she was pruning. "I haven't said yes. I wanted to talk to you first."

"Why, Emilie?" Arden asked, gently disengaging her arm from Emilie's restraining hand. "I'm happy for you, really I am. This is exactly what you wanted. I'm sure this dream was always in your mind when you took this job."

Emilie had imagined an offer like this in the dark nights in Medford, when she lay on her lumpy mattress, the reek of burning grease still lingering in her nostrils even after two long, soapy showers. It seemed unattainable, but it kept her going through the lonely days until she came to Ashland. Then her dreams had become much more modest—just do well enough to keep the part. She still couldn't believe the opportunity she'd just been given, but it seemed smaller now, somehow. What meaning would it have without Arden to share it with her?

"You're part of my dreams, too, Arden. A big part. We have time before I'd be expected to go to New York, and we can find a way to—"

"To what?" Arden asked with an angry, crackling energy in her voice. "To pack my bags so I can follow you? To get tired of each other so we don't care anymore?"

Emilie knew Arden wasn't really mad at her but that she was hurting as she faced what she had dreaded all along. Still, Emilie responded in angry tones as well, because she was in pain, too. Torn between this amazing offer and the beauty she had recognized in her relationship with Arden.

"You've always expected me to move away, Arden, and I've never lied about being uncertain where my acting would take me. We're working on the same time frame we had this morning. Until the end of the season. Why does anything have to change right now?"

Arden picked up her hedge trimmers, then tossed them down again. They speared into the ground and remained upright, embedded in the dirt. She ran her hands over her face and through her hair, leaving a few glossy brown strands out of place. "Everything has changed, Emilie."

Emilie shook her head. She remembered their conversation a mere two days ago, when she had agreed to let Arden go without a fight when she had reached her limit, unable to handle the intrusion of the unpredictable life of an actor into her own steady and ordered world any longer. Emilie had made that promise to Arden because she thought she'd have more time. To connect them, to join them so fully that Arden would be forced to make room in her future for Emilie. Two days? Not nearly enough time for Arden to fall in love as deeply as Emilie already had. Only enough for her to become more aware of the pain she'd feel if they separated, and to give up before they had a chance to try.

"I told you I would decide when I'd gone far enough, Emilie," Arden said, as if reading her thoughts. "This is it. My breaking point. You need to go to New York. See where this play can take you, because I know for certain that you'll go far." Her voice softened. "I'm proud of you, Em. I'm sad now, but I'm happy to know you've got what you wanted."

Emilie brushed at the tears dampening her cheeks. "But I want—"

Arden stopped her again. She closed her eyes. "Don't say it, Em. Don't make it worse for me. Just go, please, and blow their minds in New York."

No matter what she had promised, Emilie wouldn't have been able to walk away from Arden, but Arden didn't wait for her to go. She picked up her hedge trimmers and walked away, farther into the woods.

Chapter Twenty-one

Arden used her boot to sink the shovel deep into the earth, scooping up a heap of dirt and flinging it over her shoulder. She heard a yelp and a curse behind her and turned to see Jacob and Joe standing there with clumps of loamy soil on their shirts.

"Sorry," she said with a sigh. Two weeks without seeing Emilie, and she still hadn't regained control of her emotions. She had been taking out her frustration and sadness on the dirt and tools in the park until her garden implements were as dented as Joe's.

"That's okay, sweetheart," Jacob said in his grandfatherly tone. She wished he'd go back to being her friend and boss and stop acting like he felt sorry for her. She was full of enough self-pity as it was, and his kindness made her want to cry on his shoulder. She'd rather he yelled at her about leaving a sloppy mess of dirt on the park trail.

"I think the hole is big enough," Joe commented in his dry way. He was a seasonal hire from the college, all legs and arms and laid-back attitude.

Arden followed his gaze and saw the massive hole she had dug next to the small azalea she was about to plant. She could fit the entire shrub, foliage and all, in the ground.

"I want to give its roots room to spread," she said. She had to smile at her handiwork, and the muscles in her cheeks felt as if they hadn't moved into a grin for days. "But if Master Gardener Joe thinks it's too deep, I'll fill it in a little."

Jacob laughed and patted her on the shoulder, probably relieved to see her wear any expression besides the dark scowl that had seemed permanently glued to her face for days. He and Joe pulled small trowels out of her bucket and helped her scrape some of the soil back where it belonged.

"Woman troubles, huh?" Joe said. When Arden looked at him in surprise, he shrugged. "Jacob told me. He needed advice."

"Really. And what words of wisdom did you have for him?" Arden stood with one hand on her hip and the other on the shovel.

"I want to make you happy again, Arden," Jacob said, eyeing her shovel with a wary expression, as if he was worried she might whack him with it. "I thought a younger person, someone closer to your age, might understand what you're going through and tell me what to say." He glared at Joe. "But he wasn't any help at all."

"I said you should move on," Joe commented, pulling the azalea out of the plastic pot and settling it in the correctly sized hole. He managed to snap off a few small branches and a handful of leaves along the way. "Have you seen the women around this town? Hot, hot, hot. Yours was one of the hottest, I'll give you that, but there are plenty of other options. If you want, you can party with me this weekend. I'll introduce you around."

Arden bent down to pick up the broken twigs and rescue the azalea from Joe's ministrations. "Thanks for the offer, but I'm a little too old to be hunting for a date at a college party. Besides, I'm not looking for someone else."

"See? I told you it was a bad idea," Jacob said. "What Arden needs to do is go with Emilie. You'd like New York, Arden. Central Park, the Statue of Liberty…um, Rockefeller Center."

Arden patted the dirt loosely around the base of the plant and stood up, wiping her palms on her jeans and leaving muddy smears across her thighs. "Thank you, both of you, for meddling in my personal life. I don't know how I'll choose between those options. A frat party, or sightseeing in New York." She pretended to weigh them in her hands before she glared at both of them—her scowl back in full force—and picked up her bucket.

"I'll see you guys tomorrow." She elbowed Jacob on her way past, just to let him know she wasn't truly angry with him, and walked to the maintenance shack. They meant well, but neither of them understood her situation. She couldn't pack up her life and traipse after Emilie, becoming the very person Emilie herself had been in Europe. Em had been miserable there, without her career and a life of her own. And Joe's suggestion was ridiculous. Arden would eventually find another woman to date—but not at a college party, and not anytime soon. Emilie couldn't be wiped out of her head and heart that easily.

She quickly pulled off her dusty T-shirt and replaced it with a clean shirt. She buttoned it and straightened the collar, going through the motions of her day as if she was a programmed machine. She hadn't been able to spend much time at home, choosing instead to spend the evenings with her friends in Lisa's pub. She hadn't been in her garden since her night there with Em, but she'd have to face it soon. The weeds had probably already staged a coup and taken over the delicate beds of herbs.

A pint of beer was waiting for her in front of the bar stool next to where Rebecca and Marty sat. Arden paused in the doorway for a moment, appreciating her friends now more than ever. They went out on occasion, but for the past weeks they had spent every night sitting in the bar, keeping her company and chatting about anything but Emilie.

They were doing their best to take Arden's mind off her pain, and she was grateful for them and for the moments at the pub when she forgot herself for a few seconds and focused on one of their stories or laughed at one of their many arguments. It didn't help that there was a glossy head shot of Emilie hanging over the bar, but Arden had said no when Lisa asked if she should take it down or cover it with a dartboard. She might be a masochist, but she couldn't stand the thought of the photo disappearing. Emilie was gorgeous in it, of course, with her hair softly curling around her face and an impish smile in her eyes. Arden always felt as if Emilie was looking directly at her, just about to say something that would make Arden laugh.

"Hey," Arden said, approaching the bar and giving her friends a hug. "Thanks for the beer."

"You're welcome," Marty said. Her eyes skimmed Arden from head to toe. "Well, at least you changed your shirt this time. That's an improvement."

Arden looked down and saw the dirty handprints on her work jeans. "Damn. I forgot."

Rebecca patted her shoulder—why did everyone think they needed to do that?—and sat down so she and Marty were on either side of her. "Your socks match. We'll count it as a win."

Arden had to laugh at her encouraging tone. "Have I really been such a mess lately? I thought I'd been doing pretty well."

Not inside, of course, but she had hoped to hide her mixed-up feelings from everyone else. It hadn't worked, obviously, and she was tired of trying.

"Of course you have," Rebecca said.

"Not really," Marty said at the same time.

"I'll get better. Time heals all wounds, or whatever." Arden took a drink of her beer, barely registering the flavor. Her taste buds seemed to have vanished along with Emilie, just like her ability to see vibrant colors or recognize that her clothes were too dirty to wear in public.

"It's been more than two weeks," Marty said, fishing some cashews out of a plastic bowl of nuts. "We're here for you as long as you need us, but you're going to have to snap out of this soon. It's not healthy."

"Marty," Rebecca said in a hissing whisper, as if Arden wasn't between them and able to hear every word. "We were going to give her another few days, remember?"

"*You* wanted to give her more time. I wanted to bring her back to her senses last week."

"It's still too soon. Look at her."

"Hey, guys, I'm right here," Arden held up her hands, one palm facing each of them. "I'll be fine. I'm—"

"Shh." Marty pushed her hand away and continued talking to Rebecca. "Once she hears my solution, she and Emilie can work this out and be happy again. That's all she really needs."

She looked at Arden, who was following their conversation like a Ping-Pong match. "Here's what you need to do. You don't want to follow Emilie, and she doesn't want to give up this dream job. So both of you should make a sacrifice. Don't stay here, and don't go to New York."

Arden frowned. "What are we supposed to actually *do*, then? Move to some random place where neither of us has a job?"

Marty nodded. "Exactly. Start over on neutral ground."

Rebecca rolled her eyes. "Geez, there's a brilliant solution. Both of you give up what you want. That's sure to make you happy. So, Arden, do you want my advice?"

"No, thanks." Arden shook her head firmly. She had heard too many unsolicited and unhelpful suggestions already today.

"What you need to do," Rebecca continued, ignoring Arden's response, "is ask her to stay. You deserve your shot at the internship, and if Emilie really cares for you, she'll do what it takes to support you."

"What if she isn't offered another spot with the company for next season?" Lisa asked. She had come over to refill their drinks and caught the tail end of Rebecca's plan.

"She can work behind the scenes. Assistant stage manager, or in the publicity department. Something like that."

"Maybe she could get a job with the college," Lisa added, setting a fresh beer in front of Arden, "teaching acting."

"I've heard there'll be an opening for groundskeeper at the park," Marty said.

Rebecca clinked her mug against Marty's. "There you go. A very poetic solution."

Arden wasn't sure she had ever heard the two of them agree on anything, and this seemed to be a bizarre time for them to start. She picked up her beer and leaned back slightly, moving out of the triangle of scheming that was taking place in front of her. At least the three of them were focused on Emilie now, talking about the training she would need before she took over Arden's old job, and had taken their spotlight off Arden. She decided to let them ramble for a while and enjoy the peace.

Nobody seemed to understand that she simply hurt and needed time before she stopped hurting. Every time she had fallen for an actor in the past, she had gone through this same process. The sadness would fade, and she'd eventually be able to look at another woman without seeing the face of an ex superimposed on her.

Her feelings for Emilie went far beyond what she'd ever experienced with another girlfriend, but the process should be the same. It just might take longer than normal. Desire faded once the object of her attraction was out of her life. Her response to Emilie was deeper than desire, but shouldn't the principle of *out of sight, out of mind* still apply?

Arden set her mug on the bar because her hands were suddenly shaky and she was afraid she'd drop it. She barely registered that her friends were discussing plans to sign Emilie up for a gardening course at a local community college, and she turned her head to look at the head shot of Emilie.

She loved her. Real, lasting, passionate love. The kind she had seen between her grandparents. And—if she was being completely honest with herself—the kind she had always noticed glimmering between her parents on the rare occasions when she was with them. She had been jealous of their love for each other because it excluded her, but it was there nonetheless. If what she felt for Emilie was love, then she would never get over her. She wouldn't be able to move her memory aside and fall for someone else. She would always, always feel this sense of loss.

Arden blinked back a warm rush of tears, relieved that the threesome was still lost in plans for Landscaper Emilie and didn't notice her. She hadn't cried since Emilie had told her the news about Broadway, and she wished she hadn't picked the busy pub as the place to get weepy. But what was left to do but cry when she realized that the love of her life was going away, and all she had left were the unhelpful options offered by her friends?

"Options," Arden said, speaking the word out loud. She sniffed and wiped away a tear that had escaped down her cheek.

"Oh, Arden, don't cry," Rebecca said, wrapping her arm around Arden's waist and leaning her head on her shoulder. Marty patted her hand awkwardly, and Lisa grabbed a bowl of pretzels off the back counter and set it in front of Arden.

She laughed weakly, awed by the rush of compassion from her friends. "I'm good," she said. "Maybe better than good. There are options."

Rebecca sat upright again. "Of course there are. Plenty of them."

Arden shook her head, unable to sort through what she had just realized, let alone explain it. She had never thought in terms of choices before. She'd fall for a woman, then she would leave for another role. Arden would stay behind. The course was set, and she had expected all along that she and Emilie would follow the exact same path that Arden had been on since her parents left.

"She could stay. I could leave. We both could go somewhere new. I could go to a frat party. Options." Arden laughed again at her friends' confused expressions. "Not all of them are good options, but they exist."

Marty grinned at her, and Arden knew she understood at least the gist of what Arden was saying. She lifted her mug.

"To Arden and her options," she said.

Arden clinked her mug against theirs. The road in front of her suddenly had branches she hadn't expected to see. She was overwhelmed by the choices but ready to pick a new route instead of following the worn, rutted one.

"To good friends," she said, raising her mug again.

"Hear, hear," said Marty, bumping against Arden with her shoulder.

Arden felt a sense of release as all the sensations that had been in hiding since Emilie's news returned in full force. Suddenly she heard the sounds of laughter and music from the other patrons and felt the warmth from the crackling fire. The sweet smell of beer-battered fish and chips frying in the kitchen wafted over to her, and she felt hungry again after days of barely being able to eat. She ordered dinner and talked with her friends, with Emilie's blue eyes watching her from the photo on the wall.

Chapter Twenty-two

Emilie sat in the courtyard outside Carpenter Hall. She stared across the Bricks and toward Lithia Park, toward Arden, feeling as if she had left the most important part of her there among the trees and flowers. All she was left with up here, on this cold wooden bench, were the uncomfortable and lonely parts that surrounded the spot where her heart used to be.

She had let herself feel all the messy, horrible pain. She hadn't tried to numb what she felt, but rather had experienced it in all its raw power, just as she had done with the joy that filled her after her night with Arden. The emotions spilled into her acting, somehow taking on the form required by each role she played. Lady Anne had been drenched with grief, and more than one member of the audience had admitted to her that she had made them cry. Titania was more magical and otherworldly, and the younger Anne had filled the stage with an energetic presence even with so few lines to speak. And Cassella? Emilie sensed the power crackling out of her and seeping into every corner of the small theater.

She had tapped into the truth of her acting talent, but she was miserable off the stage. Would she trade her newfound confidence and success to have Arden back? The answer terrified her. She had finally got what she wanted—how could she be willing to give it away again?

She glanced at her watch and stood. Jay had asked to see her this morning, and she had come early to have some time alone, near the park. If she didn't hurry now, though, she'd be late. She opened the glass doors and walked into the building, thinking of the other times she had been inside Jay's office. From her first day here as a frightened and uncertain new hire to the awful time when she had nearly lost the part of Cassella in shame to the glorious moment when she had been offered a chance to reprise the role on Broadway. Too many highs and lows in such a short time here in Ashland.

But Arden had been a steady, glowing light the entire time. She had supported Emilie without question, whether Emilie was walking away from her or toward her. She had filled in the blank spaces in Emilie's life, those voids where friends and love and playfulness had deserted her. She made Emilie feel whole, and the sense of completeness had given her the strength to face her stage fright, to face her emotions both in person and as the characters she played.

Emilie stopped and leaned against the wall, framed by black-and-white prints from an early production of Hamlet. She had started to believe that the emotional turbulence in her life was the spark that fired her performances, but maybe she was wrong. She had always been fiery and a little chaotic. Until Arden came into her life.

Arden helped her channel her passion. Into love, into her career, and into her enjoyment of life. She had been just as good as Cassella when she was happy because she and Arden were together as she had been when wracked with grief because they weren't. Arden didn't try to keep Emilie from acting, and she wasn't the cause of Emilie's success, but she absolutely was the reason for the moments of peace and fulfillment Emilie had felt here in Ashland. Could she act as well without Arden in her life? Emilie knew the answer was yes, but it also wasn't the most important question to ask. Did she want to live without Arden, no matter how successful she was in her career?

No.

She continued toward the office, still lost in thought. At least she didn't have to deal with a case of nerves as she walked down this hallway. She was finally sure of herself onstage and knew he wasn't going to fire her or threaten to replace her.

She knocked on his open door.

"Good morning, Emilie. Come in." He gestured her forward and she sat in the seat across the desk from him. He leaned his elbows on the wooden surface and propped his chin on his hands.

After a long pause, he gave her a grin. "You've only been here a few months, and I've seen you in this office more times than anyone else in the cast."

Emilie laughed. "I never claimed to be boring."

He shook his head. "You're anything but." He tapped his fingers on a slim folder that was on the desk in front of him. "I'm going to be honest with you, here, Emilie. You've been offered an amazing chance to take *Skywriting* to the highest level, and maybe you'd be foolish to pass up the opportunity. But we want to keep you here."

He held up a hand as if she was protesting, even though she hadn't said a word. He continued with his spiel. "I know we're not Broadway, but we have an internationally acclaimed production company with exciting new scripts and opportunities coming in every season. You have come so far in a short time—just think where you'll be after another season or two here, playing a huge variety of roles and working with several directors every year."

He held up the folder. "Before you say no, look at the parts we want you to play next season. This is wonderful stuff, Emilie."

He tossed the folder across the table, and she caught it and set it in front of her, unopened.

He sighed and shook his head. "I had a feeling I wouldn't be able to convince you to stay. You're going to have a brilliant career, Emilie. I wish you nothing but the very best."

She stood. "I'm staying, Jay. It doesn't matter what parts

you've offered. As soon as you have the contract ready, I'll sign it."

She walked out before he had a chance to say anything more and hurried to the bench outside before her knees gave way and dropped her to the ground. She was trembling, but from excitement rather than regret. She had no idea if she had just made the best move for her career or the worst. She loved being part of the ensemble and playing more than one role each week, and she believed Jay when he said she would really grow here. But Broadway? Who would believe that she gave up the chance to be part of the sensation that *Skywriting* surely would be?

She laughed. *She* believed it. The future was as uncertain as it had been when she first auditioned here last year. She didn't know what parts she was going to play, onstage and in Arden's life. Arden might not want her back because Emilie still couldn't promise to stay here forever, but Emilie was going to do whatever it took to convince Arden to give her a chance. She'd be here another year, so she had plenty of time to try.

She wanted to rush to the park and find Arden, but she was still shaking. She walked, instead, heading downtown and wandering aimlessly through the business district surrounding the theaters. The euphoria of making a choice was beginning to dissipate, and she was trying to think back to the time just after she had agreed to go to Europe with Leah. Before everything had fallen apart. Had she felt this same sense of rightness back then? Was she repeating a mistake because she was afraid to push herself to take a chance on Broadway?

She was lost in memories and nearly jumped off the curb when she was startled by a sharp rap against the glass next to her. She looked inside the ice cream shop and saw Rebecca waving at her and gesturing for her to come inside. Emilie wasn't sure she would be good company right now, but Rebecca would probably know how Arden was doing. Emilie went inside and inhaled the heavy scent of vanilla from the homemade waffle cones.

Rebecca met her at the door with a hug. "How have you been?" she asked, with a look of concern on her face. She must know about what had happened between her and Arden if she looked this worried. Emilie wondered if Arden was getting the same mother-hen treatment.

"I'm great," Emilie said with a big grin that felt phony even from the inside. "Well, good. Okay. How are you?"

She had been about to ask about Arden, but it didn't seem polite to jump directly to her and skip over Rebecca.

"Can't complain. This weather has been beautiful, hasn't it? Kind of makes you want to get outside and do some gardening."

"Really? I guess so." Emilie had more interest in watching Arden work in the park than in actually doing it herself. She pictured her there, bent over one of her plants and coaxing it to grow and flourish. Wearing those jeans with the small rip just under the back pocket so Emilie could see—Rebecca's voice registered in her mind even though she had no idea what words she had said. "What? I'm sorry. I was thinking about... gardening."

"I asked if you wanted something to drink or some ice cream. Their lattes are pretty good."

"I'll get something and join you," Emilie said. Something cold that she could drop inside the front of her shirt to cool herself down the next time she started to picture Arden like that.

She ordered a chocolate mint chip milkshake and joined Rebecca in her booth. She looked across the diner at the table where she and Arden had sat together, weeks ago.

"How is Arden?" She finally gave in and let herself ask the question.

"She's great," Rebecca said with a bright smile. "Well, good. Okay."

Emilie laughed as her words were parroted back to her. At least she knew Arden was missing her, too.

"Congratulations, by the way. I heard you were offered a

chance to go to New York. That's amazing." Rebecca toyed with a small wooden stirrer, tapping it against the side of her paper coffee cup. "I mean, it's amazing if you like working indoors all the time. I've heard it's healthier to work outside, though. With plants and things."

Emilie frowned. "Thank you. Are you talking about Arden still?"

"No," Rebecca said with a shrug. "I just read an article about career changes and thought I'd share. If you're interested in staying around here and exploring alternatives."

Emilie opened her mouth to tell Rebecca that she had accepted Jay's offer, but she closed it again. Arden would be the first to know. "Staying here has its advantages," she said instead. "But maybe it's best to follow a career, not emotions. I did that once before, leaving everything of mine to chase after someone else. I was miserable."

Rebecca smiled at her. "Choosing to follow the wrong person is a bad thing. Following the right person is what love is all about. Compromise. Sometimes sacrifices, as long as they work both ways."

Emilie took a drink of her milkshake, and the icy liquid chilled her throat as she swallowed. Leah had never offered to make sacrifices for her. Arden would, as surely as Emilie would make them for her. But would they both be unhappy then? Or would they both feel fulfilled and inspired by the other?

"I would never try to tell you what to do…" Rebecca paused and gave her a guilty grin. "Well, I probably would. But I will say this—if you try to work things out with Arden, I'll be thrilled and will consider you to be like a sister to me. If you don't, then at least you can know that Marty and I will be here for her. You're not leaving her all alone." She paused and shrugged. "I'll have to talk smack about you for Arden's sake, but I won't mean all of the bad things I'll say."

"Just some of them?" Emilie asked with a laugh. She tried to remember if she had ever had a friend like Rebecca, but she couldn't think of many people that she had let get very close. Until Arden. "Thank you for telling me. I'd never want her to be sad or alone."

Rebecca took a drink of her coffee. "Say, I was reading a different article the other day. This one was talking about the classes people can take if they want to work in landscaping. I'll bet you'll find this fascinating."

Emilie listened while Rebecca inexplicably continued to talk about gardening. She zoned out for most of it and let her mind wander back to Arden. It never stayed away from her for long. She had made a sacrifice for Arden by taking the festival job for the following year. Even though it was probably the smart choice for her career and the one she would find most satisfying on a personal level, she still knew without a doubt that she never would have turned down the opportunity to go to New York if Arden hadn't been a factor.

Did she expect Arden to make a sacrifice for her now, or to owe her somehow? No, although there would come a time when Arden would be the one making a choice to come with Emilie or to stay here without her. Emilie let the image of the future, with its give and take, soften in her mind until it took on the qualities of a dance. Moving back and forth, highlighting one then the other. It wouldn't be the easiest life, but it had a sense of promise and hope to it. Togetherness. Working for each other, not for themselves.

As soon as Rebecca paused to take a breath, Emilie spoke up. "You were right, Rebecca, that really is fascinating. Who knew you could mow grass in so many different ways? Well, I've got to go."

Rebecca stood when she did and gave her another hug. "Take care, Emilie. I hope to see you soon. And think about what I said."

"Oh, I will," Emilie promised, bursting out of the door and onto the sidewalk with relief. She tossed her milkshake cup in a garbage can and headed toward her house. She had work to do before she saw Arden again.

CHAPTER TWENTY-THREE

Arden was a few blocks away from the park when her phone vibrated in her back pocket. She pulled it out, not realizing how much she was hoping the text was from Emilie until she saw Emilie's name and a photo Arden had taken of her on the stage in the Japanese garden displayed on the screen. Arden had debated whether to contact Emilie after her epiphany at the pub, but she had always found an excuse to put it off yet again. She wasn't sure what scared her the most—Emilie telling her that she didn't want to be together because it would involve compromise, or Emilie saying yes, she was willing to try. In the latter case, Arden would need to step out of her comfort zone and, sooner or later, leave her home.

Even before she read the text, Arden felt bombarded by emotions. The remembered sensation of Emilie's kisses and caresses shivered across her skin. The loneliness she had felt without Emilie around to make her laugh louder and think deeper and be happier. Sadness and pain were there, too. Arden stopped and leaned against the wood siding of a children's clothing store because she needed physical support while she read Emilie's message.

There was nothing to read, except two lines of numbers. Arden's immediate reaction was disappointment, until she realized she was looking at coordinates. They were recognizable to her as representing a location nearby, probably either in the park or near the theaters. Arden plugged them into her GPS and resumed walking.

She left the street and went into the park. Even in her distracted state, she noticed the sense of peace that she always found as soon as she left the town behind and was swallowed up by trees and brushy ground cover. Normally, she would stop by the pond and listen to the ducks' raucous paddling or pause by one of her stages and make sure the props and scripts were ready for the day's crowd.

Not today, though. She kept going, her steps getting faster as she realized where Emilie was sending her. Her footsteps echoed through the empty park, and she saw three whitetail deer stop to stare in her direction before fading into the thick band of ground fog that blanketed the borders of Ashland Creek. Arden left the more populated section of the park behind and turned onto a narrow path that led up the hill and deeper into the uncultivated forest. She hesitated before entering the clearing where she and Emilie had met.

She exhaled slowly and stepped around the trees. She was alone. She went over to the stump Emilie had used as a stage and had just sat down when her phone buzzed again.

She looked around before answering—Emilie must have either seen her enter the clearing or had accurately guessed how long it would take her to get here—but Arden didn't see any sign of her. She opened the message and smiled when she saw it was a poem. A clue.

"Double, double, you're in trouble if you trip on me. Reach below me if you dare, where I join with the tree." Arden read the clue out loud before scanning the ground around her feet. It was mostly flat and smooth, with tufts of grass here and there, but once she widened her search to the next layer of trees, she saw a large root protruding from the ground. It curved where it connected to a fir tree, leaving a small hollow between its arch and the ground.

Arden went over and reached underneath, brushing aside a layer of dry fir needles and pulling out a small box made of dark cherrywood. A gentle breeze layered the scent of jasmine over the forest smells of sweet sap and damp ferns, and Arden turned to see Emilie standing behind her in the clearing.

Arden walked toward her, holding the still-unopened box in her hands. She stopped a few feet away, not quite sure how to break the silence between them.

"Aren't you going to open it? There might be a treasure inside."

Arden was grateful Emilie spoke first, or Arden might have stood there all day, trying to sort through everything she wanted to say to her.

Emilie was smiling, with what looked like a combination of uncertainty and playfulness. Arden shook the box slightly and heard something clunk inside. She opened it and found a flat piece of wood, cut out in the shape of a daffodil and painted a vibrant yellow.

Arden picked it up and turned it over in her hands. The back side was plain and looked as if it had been glued to something. "Did you make this?" she asked. She frowned at the flower as she tried to place where she had seen something similar before. "Or did you...wait, is this from the *Midsummer Night's Dream* set? You stole it?"

She couldn't stop herself from laughing. Leave it to Emilie to find a way to horrify and amuse her at the same time. And a way to break the barriers time apart and painful words had erected between them, somehow making Arden feel as if they had never been apart.

"I didn't steal it," Emilie said with an indignant tone. "I was reviewing my marks for the scene in Titania's bower, and I accidentally stepped on it. You could barely see where it had fallen off, so I figured no one would miss it."

Arden furrowed her brow, trying to picture how Emilie could have stepped on an upright set piece. "How did you—"

Emilie waved her hand to stop her. "It's probably best if you don't ask too many questions. The less you know, the more innocent you'll sound if questioned by the police." She shrugged. "I thought you might like to have a memento of the set. I know the play is special to you."

Arden laughed and shook her head. "I love it. Thank you. And I guess I can always make a new flower to replace this one if we reuse the set for another play next year."

"Exactly," Emilie said with a satisfied smile. "And kudos to the set production staff. I had to accidentally step on the damned thing three times before it came off."

"I'll be sure to pass along your compliments when I meet them." Arden sighed. She had missed this, but every funny or wonderful or affectionate moment with Emilie seemed to have a good-bye in the background.

Emilie reached out and traced her finger along the shape of the daffodil, stopping just before she touched Arden's hand where she held the painted green stem.

"You took something out of the box," she said softly. "Now you need to give something in return."

Arden swallowed, her throat tightening as Emilie's voice lost its lightheartedness and turned more serious. "Did you have something in mind?"

"Yes." Emilie moved closer and looked directly at Arden. "Trust. I want your trust."

"What do you mean?" Arden could barely get the words out because her body was demanding her attention. Emilie was so close. It wouldn't take more than a step to put Arden close enough to hold her.

"I want you to trust me when I say that we belong together and that we can find a way to make us work. And trust that I love you, more than anything."

Arden wanted nothing more than to say *okay* and jump into Emilie's arms, but she had spent too many years conditioning herself to accept departures. She let herself bridge the gap between them with her hand, though, sliding her fingers into the wild curls that curved along Emilie's cheekbone.

"I've been thinking about possibilities lately," Arden said, watching the gold in Emilie's hair shimmer where the dappled sunlight fell across her. "I used to only see one. I lived here, and always would. Other people were the ones who left."

"What changed?" Emilie's voice sounded breathless, and she tilted her head toward Arden's hand, drawing her deeper and closer.

"My friends. Jacob. Even Joe." Arden shook her head. "I've been focused on the few who left me behind, like my parents and ex-girlfriends, but I have amazing people in my life who always will be there for me, even if we all don't stay in Ashland forever. And they all had different suggestions for us. Some of them were crazy, and some of them would be difficult, but could work. Possibilities."

"My new favorite word." Emilie smiled, but then her face took on a thoughtful expression. "Did Rebecca's plan have something to do with me taking over your job here in the park when you quit?"

"Yeah. That was one of the crazier options." Arden held up her flower. "Especially if you treat real flowers like you did this one."

Emilie lifted her hand and covered Arden's where it was still tangled in her hair. "So you'll trust me? Trust what we have together?"

Arden nodded. She couldn't say no. She had fought against her desire for Emilie with varying degrees of success from the start, but she didn't want to fight anymore. Surrendering to her feelings for Emilie had always seemed inevitable, but now she was slowly starting to realize that she was winning her. Not losing her.

"I love you, Em."

Emilie's smile clearly showed a relief and joy that mirrored what Arden was feeling inside. She moved her hand to the back of Emilie's neck and pulled her into a kiss. She still wasn't sure how they would manage two careers and one life together, but they would work together. Hell, if her parents could do it—with the selfish tendencies they had shown toward her and her grandparents—then she and someone as generous and kind as Emilie surely could.

She pulled back with a laugh. "So I guess I need to tell Gwen I won't be doing the internship after all, because we'll be moving to New York," she said. She waited for a twinge of disappointment or regret, but none came. She had discovered a passion for stage design, but she could pursue it in New York instead of Ashland if necessary.

Emilie shook her head. "Someday, maybe. Probably. But not next year. You do the internship and make sure the sets for next season are the best the world has ever seen because I signed my contract today, and this Lady Macbeth expects nothing less."

Arden had experienced too many emotions already today, from loneliness to wonder, from uncertainty to the complete and utter trust Emilie had demanded from her. She let go of Emilie and sat on the tree stump. "You signed a contract already? Can you get out of it?"

Emilie knelt in front of her and took Arden's hands in her own. "I don't want out of it, Arden. We'll be here next season, maybe longer if we want, and then we can decide together where we'll go." Arden's hands felt cold, and Emilie rubbed them gently. "And if we don't agree, we can flip a coin or battle it out on the dartboard in Lisa's pub. Sometimes it will be right for us to move for your career, and sometimes for mine. You're supposed to trust this, remember?"

Arden shook her head. "Emilie, I can't be the reason you give up a chance to be on Broadway. You'll hate me for it. I don't want to be another trip to Europe for you."

"I'm completely at peace about this decision," Emilie said, and Arden couldn't deny that her expression had seemed relaxed and happy ever since Arden had told her she loved her. "I never felt comfortable with going to Europe. I knew inside that it was the wrong thing to do from the moment I said I'd go, but I was afraid to back out. I'm not scared of acting anymore, and I'm excited about the parts I'll get to play. And you need to be here, to work with Gwen."

Emilie looked convinced, and Arden wanted to believe her, to trust what she was saying. They would have time to be together and learn more about each other before they moved out of the shelter of the festival and started their life of shared compromise. She had to try once more, though, to know that Emilie was sure.

"*Skywriting* probably won't be an option after a year," she said. "Someone else will be cast as Cassella. You're spectacular in the role, and you should have the chance to take it to Broadway."

"Meh," Emilie said with a casual shrug.

Arden felt her eyes widen. "Seriously? *Meh?*"

"There'll be other parts to play. I'm glad I conquered that one, and I'm proud of how much I've improved since the first horrible night, but I want to see what else I can do. What else we both can do. Together. Supporting each other."

Arden cupped Emilie's cheeks in her hands and kissed her again. She meant for it to be a gentle kiss, while they processed what was happening between them and while she worked on more reasons for Emilie to go, but Emilie had something else in mind. She pressed closer to Arden, moving between her thighs and teasing Arden's tongue with her own. Arden felt acceptance click into place. The final step before she fell wholeheartedly into Emilie and their future.

Emilie wrapped her arms around Arden's neck and hugged her tightly.

"You've been waiting behind the scenes for far too long, Arden," she said, with the whisper of her breath tickling Arden's ear. Arden's thighs tightened around Emilie's hips until they were molded together. "It's about time you get to be the star."

Arden shook her head. "Costar," she corrected her.

"Even better." Emilie kissed Arden with an intensity that was overwhelming, but not frightening at all. Arden matched her passion, letting go of the need for dialogue about their future and craving only action as Emilie's hands slipped under the hem of Arden's shirt and moved across her skin.

EPILOGUE

Emilie checked the gilded coronet to make sure it was secure on her head. Of course it was, and Velda would be irate if she knew Emilie had even a moment of doubt about anything she wore on her head when she was onstage. She was doubting everything right now, though she had thought her stage fright would be gone—or at least significantly lessened—after a full season with the festival. But she felt as nauseated now as she ever had.

She smoothed her sweaty palms over the heavy velvet bodice of her simple navy gown, sending a silent apology to the wardrobe staff in case she crushed the nap of the fabric with her nervous gestures. She had been thrilled to be cast as the iconic Lady Macbeth, but eventually the reality of what she was about to attempt had sunk in. A role like this was tricky at best, and disastrous at worst. If she gave a standard, time-honored interpretation of the character, she would be called uninspired and bland. If she pushed past some conventional boundaries and brought something unique to the role, she might be accused of ignoring the great actors who had come before her. What was she supposed to do? Change her approach in every scene so she made everyone happy?

Emilie rested her hand on the plywood backing of the set, drawing strength from the wood Arden had designed, touched, and created. Arden was nervous tonight, as well, but as far as Emilie was concerned, she had absolutely no reason to be. Gwen had given her this production as her special project, and Arden had been the main driving force from the initial conversations with the director to the final touches onstage. The set was stunning. During the dress rehearsal, the movement of the play had flowed through Arden's minimally designed spaces with an ease that framed the characters' scenes and allowed the words of the play to be constantly in the forefront of the production.

Arden had a real gift for spatial design, and Emilie wasn't the only actor who thought so. All of them had been in enough productions where they'd felt as if they were fighting against the scenery or hindered by the set to recognize real collaborative talent when they experienced it. A wave of love rolled through Emilie, washing away most of her nausea just in time for her first cue. She got into place and was about to make her entrance when she saw a flash of yellow near her right foot. She paused when she recognized the tiny daffodil she had appropriated for Arden from the *Midsummer Night's Dream* set. She smiled, and then carefully brought her features under control as she swept into her palace.

❖

Arden had to be on hand during every scene change, but she was able to watch most of Emilie's performance from the wings of the Bowmer Theatre. When the other actors were onstage, she was focused on her set and how it worked for the play. She had a list of minor tweaks she'd take care of before the next performance, since no one could predict how the set would work during a live production, but the changes she would need to make were minimal. When Emilie was onstage, though, Arden couldn't focus on anything but her.

She had seen her share of Lady Macbeths, since this play was in the standard repertoire. She believed in Em's talent with her whole heart, but she had been worried about how she would make this role her own without changing too much of what others had done before her to make it great. After the first scene, her admiration for Emilie was completely untempered by anxiety. Emilie brought a freshness and a unique energy to the role, but she was always recognizable as the classic character. Em walked a fine line, sliding more to the side of modern and new than overly traditional, and Arden knew she was going to be a hit.

After the play was over, Arden discreetly pocketed the little daffodil. She would hide it somewhere for Emilie to find on the set of her next play. She hurried through the evening, chatting with Gwen about the performance and her evaluation of the set design and helping the crew dismantle the scenery because a different production would be held here before the next scheduled showing of *Macbeth*.

As soon as she could get away, Arden ran outside and saw Emilie signing programs on the Bricks. She hovered out of sight, letting Em have her moment, but Emilie lifted her head and looked directly at her. She excused herself from her fans and hurried over to wrap Arden in a tight hug.

"You were amazing."

"Your set was perfect," Emilie said at the same time.

They broke apart, laughing, and headed toward the park. It was technically closed after sunset, but they liked to walk here or in Arden's yard after the plays, centering themselves in the real world again, and with each other. Emilie took Arden's hand and led her along a back trail until they reached their clearing.

They stood facing each other, and Arden put her hands on Emilie's hips, sliding them around her back and into the back pockets of Emilie's jeans. She kissed her gently, her tongue dipping into Emilie's mouth with a soft caress.

Emilie sighed against her, pressing closer, and Arden willingly increased the intensity of her kiss. She pulled back, breathless and smiling, and twisted one of Emilie's wild post-performance curls around her forefinger.

"This play will be the one to make you a star, Em," she said. "Even more than Cassella. You're going to have offers pouring in once all the critics and directors have a chance to see you."

Emilie looked away, biting her lip. "I've already had one offer," she said. "I don't think I can refuse it this time."

"I'm ready to go anywhere you want," Arden said, kissing Emilie's cheek and then moving down her neck, enjoying the shivery response she felt as Emilie's skin moved beneath her lips. She didn't hesitate to promise Emilie she'd leave with her. Before, she had been concerned about being left behind or moving away from Ashland. Now she knew for certain that wherever Emilie went, she would go, too. And Em would do the same for her. They'd sooner leave a limb or organ behind than each other.

"Well, we'd be staying here. Just for another year. Or maybe two, but at least this one."

"You're sure? What's the part?"

"Well, I don't technically have it yet since they just announced next year's schedule, but it's Imogen, in *Cymbeline*. They hardly ever produce this play, and I'd hate to miss a chance to play the role. Would you mind staying and working with Gwen another season? Or two?"

"Of course not," Arden said with a laugh of relief. They'd eventually move, but she had a feeling this would become their home base. Wherever they went, they'd find their way back here at least some of the time, to see their friends or for one or both of them to be part of the festival. Emilie was her home, first and foremost, but Ashland would always be part of her. Of them, now.

"I'd be glad to stay or go. You'd be a wonderful Imogen. That's a part you could really make your own."

Emilie bounced in her arms, full of excited energy as usual after a performance. Arden was the opposite, and the evening after one of the plays where she had worked on the sets always left her with a happy, languid feeling. They managed to combine the two sensations, somehow, and by morning they'd both be evened out. Deliciously satisfied and relaxed.

"I know," Emilie said, still talking about the part while her hands stroked Arden's back. "But I have to focus on this season first. It wouldn't hurt to start pestering Jay in a day or two, though. Or tomorrow."

Arden arched closer to her and gently nibbled on her earlobe. "Tomorrow," she agreed. "But not tonight."

Emilie gave a small gasp when Arden's tongue followed the curve of her ear. "No. Tonight is for you, my love. For us."

About the Author

Karis Walsh is a horseback-riding instructor who lives in Texas. When she isn't teaching or writing, she enjoys spending time outside with her animals, reading, playing the viola, and riding with friends.

Books Available From Bold Strokes Books

Change in Time by Robyn Nyx. Working in the past is hell on your future. The Extractor series: Book Two. (978-162639-880-1)

Love After Hours by Radclyffe. When Gina Antonelli agrees to renovate Carrie Longmire's new house, she doesn't welcome Carrie's overtures at friendship or her own unexpected attraction. A Rivers Community Novel. (978-163555-090-0)

Nantucket Rose by CF Frizzell. Maggie Jordan can't wait to convert a historic Nantucket home into a B&B, but doesn't expect to fall for mariner Ellis Chilton, who has more claim to the house than Maggie realizes. (978-163555-056-6)

Picture Perfect by Lisa Moreau. Falling in love wasn't supposed to be part of the stakes for Olive and Gabby, rival photographers in the competition of a lifetime. (978-162639-975-4)

Set the Stage by Karis Walsh. Actress Emilie Danvers takes the stage again in Ashland, Oregon, little realizing that landscaper Arden Philips is about to offer her a very personal romantic lead role. (978-163555-087-0)

Strike a Match by Fiona Riley. When their attempts at matchmaking fizzle out, firefighter Sasha and reluctant millionairess Abby find themselves turning to each other to strike a perfect match. (978-162639-999-0)

The Price of Cash by Ashley Bartlett. Cash Braddock is doing her best to keep her business afloat, stay out of jail, and avoid Detective Kallen. It's not working. (978-162639-708-8)

Under Her Wing by Ronica Black. At Angel's Wings Rescue, dogs are usually the ones saved, but when quiet Kassandra Haden meets outspoken owner Jayden Beaumont, the two stubborn women just might end up saving each other. (978-163555-077-1)

Underwater Vibes by Mickey Brent. When Hélène, a translator in Brussels, Belgium, meets Sylvie, a young Greek photographer and swim coach, unsettling feelings hijack Hélène's mind and body—even her poems. (978-163555-002-3)

A Date to Die by Anne Laughlin. Someone is killing people close to Detective Kay Adler, who must look to her own troubled past for a suspect. There she finds more than one person seeking revenge against her. (978-163555-023-8)

Captured Soul by Laydin Michaels. Can Kadence Munroe save the woman she loves from a twisted killer, or will she lose her to a collector of souls? (978-162639-915-0)

Dawn's New Day by TJ Thomas. Can Dawn Oliver and Cam Cooper, two women who have loved and lost, open their hearts to love again? (978-163555-072-6)

Definite Possibility by Maggie Cummings. Sam Miller is just out for good times, but Lucy Weston makes her realize happily ever after is a definite possibility. (978-162639-909-9)

Eyes Like Those by Melissa Brayden. Isabel Chase and Taylor Andrews struggle between love and ambition from the writers' room on one of Hollywood's hottest TV shows. (978-163555-012-2)

Heart's Orders by Jaycie Morrison. Helen Tucker and Tee Owens escape hardscrabble lives to careers in the Women's Army Corps, but more than their hearts are at risk as friendship blossoms into love. (978-163555-073-3)

Hiding Out by Kay Bigelow. Treat Dandridge is unaware that her life is in danger from the murderer who is hunting the woman she's falling in love with, Mickey Heiden. (978-162639-983-9)

Omnipotence Enough by Sophia Kell Hagin. Can the tiny tool that abducted war veteran Jamie Gwynmorgan accidentally acquires help her escape an unknown enemy to reclaim her stolen life and the woman she deeply loves? (978-163555-037-5)

Summer's Cove by Aurora Rey. Emerson Lange moved to Provincetown to live in the moment, but when she meets Darcy Belo and her son Liam, her quest for summer romance becomes a family affair. (978-162639-971-6)

The Road to Wings by Julie Tizard. Lieutenant Casey Tompkins, Air Force student pilot, has to fly with the toughest instructor, Captain Kathryn "Hard Ass" Hardesty, fly a supersonic jet, and deal with a growing forbidden attraction. (978-162639-988-4)

Beauty and the Boss by Ali Vali. Ellis Renois is at the top of the fashion world, but she never expects her summer assistant Charlotte Hamner to tear her heart and her business apart like sharp scissors through cheap material. (978-162639-919-8)

Fury's Choice by Brey Willows. When gods walk amongst humans, can two women find a balance between love and faith? (978-162639-869-6)

Lessons in Desire by MJ Williamz. Can a summer love stand a four-month hiatus and still burn hot? (978-163555-019-1)

Lightning Chasers by Cass Sellars. For Sydney and Parker, being a couple was never what they had planned. Now they have to fight corruption, murder, and enemies hiding in plain sight just to hold on to each other. Lightning Series, Book Two. (978-162639-965-5)

Summer Fling by Jean Copeland. Still jaded from a breakup years earlier, Kate struggles to trust falling in love again when a summer fling with sexy young singer Jordan rocks her off her feet. (978-162639-981-5)

Take Me There by Julie Cannon. Adrienne and Sloan know it would be career suicide to mix business with pleasure, however tempting it is. But what's the harm? They're both consenting adults. Who would know? (978-162639-917-4)

Unchained Memories by Dena Blake. Can a woman give herself completely when she's left a piece of herself behind? (978-162639-993-8)